THE
SAFECRACKER'S
SECRET

THE
SAFECRACKER'S
SECRET

SANDRA BRETTING

LEVEL
BEST BOOKS

First published by Level Best Books 2021

This novel is entirely a work of fiction. The names, characters and incidents portrayed in it are the work of the author's imagination. Any resemblance to actual persons, living or dead, events or localities is entirely coincidental.

Sandra Bretting asserts the moral right to be identified as the author of this work.

First edition

ISBN: 978-1-953789-96-9

Cover art by Level Best Designs

This book was professionally typeset on Reedsy.
Find out more at reedsy.com

For Roger, of course.

Chapter One

Gene

An electric shock ran through Gene's middle finger when the "fence" finally dropped in the combo lock's gate. He instinctively checked his watch; a force of habit. Two hours fifteen minutes to crack the first two wheels. *Not bad. But not great, either.*

The young pros would snicker at his time, those skinny twenty-somethings with pale fingers weaned on Super Mario Kart or Donkey Kong, who liked to race each other whenever the Associated Locksmiths of America held a convention. Hell, it was easy to manipulate a lock when you sat in an air-conditioned ballroom in the downtown Houston Marriott and not on the dirty floor of a stash house next to a dried puddle of vomit.

Gene rolled his shoulders and got back to work. Two wheels down. One more to go. Time to dial for dollars and call it a night. When the door to the safe finally popped open, after the fence fell into the last gate with a satisfying click, he glanced away. "You're in."

Sergeant Rios moved behind him. "Thanks. We'll call ya."

The police sergeant offered Gene a hand, but he ignored it. He didn't need anyone's help to get off the floor, dammit, and especially not Rios's. He braced his palms against the tile instead and painfully straightened. He'd been living in the same body for seventy years, but it still surprised him whenever his spine refused to cooperate.

He moved past the sergeant once he straightened, and then he walked stiff-legged to the living room, where a few cops stood around discussing the case.

"Didja get it?" Boudreaux, a chatty Cajun from New Orleans and one of Gene's few friends on the force, glanced at him curiously. Since Gene wasn't one of *them*, since he didn't serve with Houston's finest on the HPD, most cops wouldn't give him the time of day. But not Boudreaux. Boudreaux was different.

"Yeah, I got it. Whaddya doing here?" His friend normally worked homicide, not drugs.

"Neighbor thought she heard a gunshot." Boudreaux shrugged. "I'm an IFR, so I took the call."

Although he tried to downplay it, Boudreaux got off on being an investigative first responder. It meant he could stay with a case from beginning to end; from first tipoff to final report. He kept with the program even after the police chief nixed it for the rest of the city to save money. To hear Boudreaux tell it, IFRs were a dying breed, so he and Gene had *that* in common.

"*Laissez les bon temps rouler.*" Boudreaux's French was as rough as his looks. Deep creases bracketed the man's forehead tonight, and his ruddy cheeks looked even coarser than usual.

Gene glanced around the filthy room. "You sure have a funny idea of 'good times.'" A dozen singed red Solo cups dirtied an expensive fireplace mantle behind the cops' heads, the cups spilling ash on carefully stacked limestones. The hardwood floor underfoot was no better. A smashed Whataburger sack spewed ketchup all over the Brazilian mahogany, and a hard, brown streak of it shot across the floorboard like dried blood. No furniture to speak of, other than a raw-wood picnic table someone had pushed against a far wall. The least they could've done was thrown a fake fern on the table instead of piling on some rubber bands.

The bands were the reason the captain called him out in the first place. Find a rubber band and a safe couldn't be far behind, since dealers used them to cinch their cash. *When will drug dealers learn?* A secret safe could stay that way forever if only they learned how to use a paper clip.

He stepped through the front doorway and landed on a cheesy welcome mat plaited with plastic butterflies. At least the house looked decent enough on the outside. People driving past the two-story Mediterranean probably wouldn't think a drug dealer lived there. The Uber drivers who left their spoiled charges on the doorstep of the pricey private college across the street wouldn't, even though their customers paid the rent for this place. Nor would the landlord, who no doubt charged double for a near-River-Oaks address and happily cashed whatever rent checks came his way, no questions asked. Certainly not the good kids, the college students who stayed away and played chess or lacrosse or whatever the hell it was good kids did nowadays.

He paused under the glow of a midnight moon to catch his breath, and then he shuffled to the Chevy Tahoe. Maybe he should thank his lucky stars the captain still called him out for jobs like this. Cap could've requisitioned an auto-dialer instead and let some computer decipher the combination lock, instead of Gene. That would've saved the department three hundred bucks, which would magically appear tomorrow morning in Gene's B of A account when, or if, he finally got around to checking his computer.

That was how he knew these jobs couldn't be legit. If they were, if everything was on the up and up, and Cap got his bills approved by the police brass first, it'd take weeks for a pale blue check to arrive at Space City Lock Shoppe, instead of a few hours for a new entry to blink at him from the computer screen.

He pulled away from the curb and cruised down the empty road, the Tahoe's headlights joined by a telltale glow that brightened a guard shack across the way.

The shack stood in the Jesuit college's parking lot, like an eerie underwater pod in a sea of black asphalt. What would parents say if they knew their hard-earned tuition was going to pay for a rent-a-cop who'd rather scroll through his cell phone than watch a drug bust going down only thirty feet away?

Served 'em right for paying that kind of tuition. Gene shook his head and swung right onto Westheimer Road, which ran through Houston's midsection like a scar. He traveled east to west, from the Galleria to an arm filled with western suburbs.

The road started out clean enough near the mall, but soon mirrored skyscrapers gave way to one-story strip centers, once-grassy medians turned to indiscernible islands of rubble, and leafy pin oaks became creosote-soaked telephone poles that tipped drunkenly over the street.

He couldn't complain, though, because almost no one drove down Westheimer this late at night, and he cruised through three green lights in a row. The apartment buildings on either side of him had been there *forever*—the Royal Palms, The Bayview, The Moroccan—all beige stucco boxes that didn't look anything like their names.

After a few minutes, Gene arrived at a development of mid-century ranches called The Oaks on Westheimer, where he hooked a right at the first palm tree. The street was fast asleep, the wheeze of AC units a communal snore in the September heat. He drove to the last cul-de-sac in the bunch and ended up at a vinyl-sided ranch house that hadn't been touched in thirty years.

"Honey, I'm home," he said to no one in particular as he swung open the car door and stepped onto the driveway.

He fiddled with his key ring as he trudged across browned crabgrass, the feel of the rotary dial still faint on his fingertips. It was a phantom pressure, born more of memories from the past than tonight's job for the HPD.

When he finally found the right key and opened the screen door, Knox snuffled on the other side.

"Atta, boy." He reached around the screen to scratch his dog's muzzle.

One step inside the ranch and it was plain to see not much had changed inside the house, either. Mexican pavers with chipped corners covered a tiny foyer that led to a sunken living room. Here, vacuum cleaner tracks crisscrossed an avocado-green carpet worn too thin to be useful. A needlepoint sampler—*Home Is Where the Heart Is*—leaned against one of the boulders that faced the fireplace. It was the last sampler she ever made, as it turned out, so he refused to move it.

"Did you miss me?" he asked Knox.

The dog's tail spun around like a propeller that threatened to lift it right off the ground. Not quite a year old, the pit followed Gene home from a drug bust one day, and then it wouldn't leave.

Knox—as in Fort Knox—never should've been a drug dealer's dog in the first place. The breed loved nothing more than to play keep-away with whatever happened to fall on the ground, so Knox probably snatched up crack pipes, hypodermic needles, you name it. Hairless scars still circled the dog's furry neck from where a dealer tried to "train" him with a choke collar.

Now he padded beside Gene, grateful for the company, even at midnight. "C'mere, boy."

The two shuffled into a galley kitchen, where avocado-green carpet segued to earth-toned linoleum laid on the diagonal. First stop was a matching refrigerator, its front panel shiny from a go with the Windex bottle.

Gene yanked open the fridge and peered inside, pretty sure of what he'd find. He'd forgotten to go to the grocery store again, what with a trickle of customers all day at the lock shop and the bust near River Oaks tonight. Maybe a stray six-pack would magically appear on the bottom shelf anyway. He pushed aside a full jar of Vlasics only to find more empty space beyond it.

"Crap." He shut the door and pulled the key ring from his pocket again. When his cell buzzed at the same time, he reached for it and squinted at the seven-one-three area code on the phone's screen.

Uh-oh. He reluctantly accepted the call. "What's up?" Rios never called him twice in one night.

"Gene…good. I'm glad I got you." He sounded relieved, as if they hadn't seen each other only ten minutes before.

"Miss me already?"

"Very funny. Actually…my guys found something else. I need you to get back here."

Damn. A run to the Stop-N-Go for more beer would take a few minutes, but this…this could take some time. Already, he worried about being stupid at the shop tomorrow with so little sleep under his belt.

"Look, I know you're already home," the sergeant continued, which was as close to an apology as he'd ever offered, "but my guys found another room."

5

"With a safe?"

"Bingo. Just past the master closet. And this one's big."

"Sure you don't want to just blast the box?" Lately, the department had been using a drill on some of the newer, cheaper safes. They bored the hell out of the top, or maybe the side, depending on the make, and hoped nothing inside got damaged.

"Nah, I wanna keep this one for evidence, too."

"Let me guess…you're looking for the books."

"Right again."

The first time Gene cracked a safe for the cops, they found an accounting ledger thick as a telephone book inside, back when folks still *had* phone books. That was when he realized why most dealers kept two safes. They hid a fake set of books for the IRS in one, and then they stashed a second set—the real McCoy—in the other.

The sergeant cleared his throat. "Any chance you can get back here?"

"I suppose." Something in the man's voice still sounded funny, though. "What else did you find?"

"I'll tell you when you get here. Just be quick."

With that, the sergeant clicked off the line. Even Knox seemed to know something was up, because the dog pricked its ears forward.

"Sorry, buddy, but I've gotta go. Sarge is acting weird tonight, and that's really saying something."

Chapter Two

Skye

The dream felt so real, she waited for the *splat* she knew was coming. When it didn't happen, when she awoke to the sound of "rippling stream" on the Soothing Sounds Sleep Machine on her nightstand instead, she closed her eyes and willed the scene to continue playing behind her eyelids.

She'd just gotten to the good part. The part where Alexandra fell off the cliff with her hair extensions flying and screams trailing behind her like trail dust from the bottom of her Gucci wedges. But it was no use. No matter how hard she tried to see what came next, Skye couldn't.

Besides, Axl kept kneading the lumpy comforter between his paws, which was probably the reason she woke up in the first place.

"Axl...it's midnight. Your timing sucks." She softly pushed the cat away before rolling off the mattress.

Bleary-eyed, she plodded across the room to the door, swerving around a wooden desk she'd outgrown ages ago, only she didn't have the heart to tell her dad.

Nearby was a North Face backpack she'd tossed beside the chair, the seafoam-green college forms spewing from its top like something it barfed up overnight.

Once she cleared the bag, she moved into the hall, the hungry cat on her heels. Her dad was sitting at the kitchen counter, with his laptop.

7

"What'sa matter?" she asked. "Can't sleep? I thought you took Ambien."

"Nah." Blue light bathed his face. "Thought I'd stop taking it for a while. Gotta stay sharp. What're you doing up?"

"Axl got hungry." She moved to the stainless-steel Frigidaire and yanked open the door.

Dad had restocked the shelves again, and bags of arugula, kale, and baby bok choi filled the space. Just once, she wanted to find a six-pack of Hunts chocolate pudding cups staring back at her, instead of organic vegetables with weird names.

"How were your classes today?" he asked. "First day back, right?"

So, he did remember. He hadn't mentioned it to her that morning when she joined him at the breakfast table. As if she always got up at the crack of dawn to eat with him before he left for the clinic. She just assumed he forgot.

She grabbed a carton of soy milk from the top shelf and poured some into Axl's bowl. "It was okay, I guess. Nothing's changed."

Which wasn't a good thing, but he wouldn't see it that way. She found out a long time ago she couldn't complain about anyone else at The College of the Immaculate Word because that would only bring on a lecture about Getting Along with Others, or Being like Water that Flows Through a Crack, or something equally zen-y that belonged in a fortune cookie.

"Hmmm. You need notebooks or anything?" He peered at her over the top of the screen, his chunky glasses looking a lot like hers. "Need money for books?"

"Nah. I'm good." Sweet of him to ask, since most of his money went toward alimony. She didn't want to tell him she ordered her textbooks three months ago. "But there is something else I could use. Do you think I could have some money for new clothes?"

"Sure. No problem. I'll put some in your account tomorrow. We're good 'til the end of the month."

He refocused on the glowing screen, which meant she could leave the room now. She always felt like a patient who'd been dismissed at the end of an appointment whenever he did that. Like someone who didn't live in the same house with him and share the same sucky food from the same refrigerator.

"Gotcha. G'night, Dad."

By now, Axl had wandered away from his bowl, since even he didn't like soy, apparently. She scooped the dish off the floor and rinsed it in the sink before moving from the room.

Her socks swished over cool floorboards as she walked. Maybe she'd hit up the Galleria this weekend. Even though she'd rather sit through a month of chemistry lectures than walk into a dressing room at The Gap—which always smelled like Herbal Essence and desperation—she could add some stuff to her closet, and then maybe Alexandra and her friends would have one less thing to gossip about.

For some reason, they seemed to think it was a big deal she wore Vans and Nike shorts to class every day, instead of Tory Burch or Michael Kors, although she couldn't understand why. What difference did it make if she'd rather shop at Houston Premium Outlets than the Galleria or if she didn't own a single Louis Vuitton satchel?

She should've said something when Alexandra ambushed her in the social sciences building the day before and faked a compliment: *Ooohhh...skater-girl shoes. How retro!* But it wasn't worth the time, or the effort.

She hoped the snarkiness would end once they got out of high school, but it didn't. If anything, it got worse. Since the clique had fewer people to torment at the private college, they only doubled down on the insults.

She swept Axl off the floor when she reached her room, despite his mewls, and cradled him in her arms. Maybe if she made half an effort to get some new clothes this weekend and she pretended she actually liked going to school, Dad would stop asking her about it. Which meant he might even forget about the symphony auditions tomorrow, which she had no intention of attending.

As long as she practiced her flute every once in a while, he'd think she tried out for the fall performance only she wasn't chosen, and then he'd feel so bad about asking her, he wouldn't bring it up again.

The last place she wanted to be was on stage at Nguyen Auditorium for the Symphony Showcase. At last year's performance, Alexandra and the rest of the student council—the same ones who painted neon posters that read *It's Cool to Be Kind*—sat in the front row and mouthed obscenities the whole time. Who needed that?

She flopped back onto the bed and elbowed Axl into his usual spot. Hopefully she could fall asleep again and dream the same dream. But this time, she'd listen harder for the *splat* when the time came.

Chapter Three

Gene

Gene pulled up to the Mediterranean house for the second time that night and parked alongside the curb. No need to ditch the car at the Stop-N-Go since everyone else was long gone. The only thing left at this late hour was for people like him—the clean-up crew—to move in and finish the job.

By now, the flickering blue light had disappeared from the guard shack, which meant the security guard was passed out in his chair. Gene swung open the Tahoe's door and stepped onto the asphalt, and that was when he noticed a white van sitting in the home's driveway. The unmistakable crest for the Harris County Medical Examiner's Office scrolled along the side-panel like a warning sign.

Damn. No wonder Sarge sounded so weird. Not only did someone find a body at the house, but the corpse had been there at least a day or two. Otherwise, if the victim was "fresh"—the cops' words, not his—he'd see an EMS truck parked out front instead of the ME's van.

He avoided the driveway as he moved to the front door, his fingers automatically reaching for the collar of his polo. Sitting next to a dried puddle of puke on a laundry room floor was one thing, but smelling dead flesh was something altogether different. A day-old corpse always smelled like someone's ass; someone's unwashed ass. Now that cops had found a body, the smell would flow through the house.

The living room was empty this time as he stepped over the cheesy welcome mat. The sergeant stood at the foot of the stairs.

"Glad you're here," he said, as Gene approached.

"Let me guess…an overdose. Male. Probably another dealer."

Sarge shot him a funny look. "Not quite. This one's a girl. About twenty, maybe a little younger." He glanced away before Gene could read more in his voice.

"Huh. That's too bad."

"Anyway." The sergeant was silent for a beat or two. "Another safe is up there with her. Same brand as the last one. Both Sentrys. Dealer probably got 'em at a two-for-one sale."

"Okay. But it's still a dialer, right?" Gene's thoughts leapfrogged ahead. If he got lucky and the dealer happened to buy a Sentry safe with a keypad, Gene could open the thing with a bent piece of wire and a well-placed swipe at the reset button. That'd take ten minutes, tops. Otherwise, he'd have to spend another couple of hours sitting God-knows-where, next to God-knows-what.

"Yep, it's a dialer. Boudreaux's up there with it. Top of the stairs, master bedroom. It's the first room on the right."

They were both too tired to say more, so Gene plodded up the stairs. The stench hit him on the very last step. He hunched his shoulders to raise the polo's collar higher. Maybe he'd charge double this time since it'd take hours for his lungs to forget the smell.

Boudreaux met him at the foot of a king-sized mattress, which forensics had stripped bare.

"You're back." His friend gave him a cursory glance.

"Did you miss me, too?"

"Har-dee-har-har."

Out of all the cops on the force, he liked Boudreaux best. Maybe because they had the most in common. The guy'd been around since the seventies, same as him, but somehow, the Cajun never got off the beat. Maybe Boudreaux didn't want a desk job. Maybe he liked busting down doors and facing drug dealers and smelling day-old corpses.

"So, what've we got here?" Gene asked.

"Someone tried to hide a door in the closet." Boudreaux jerked his stubby thumb over his shoulder. "Thought it was only a bad drywall job at first, so I kicked it in. Sure enough, there's a whole 'nother room back there."

"Huh. So, you're a hero tonight."

"Some hero." Boudreaux shook his head. "The ME wheeled out the body a little while ago. Bloated up like a balloon. *Poo-yee-yi.*"

Boudreaux tried to make light of the smell, but it was no use. You never knew how cops were going to react when the victim was young. Sometimes they acted like blowhards, like it didn't bother them, while other times they clammed up, like they forgot how to talk or something. It could go either way, and Gene learned a long time ago not to take anything personally.

"Okay, then." It sounded like Boudreaux didn't want to talk about it, anyway. "Where's the safe?"

"Over there. You really think I'm a hero?" His friend sounded hopeful now, which seemed a little strange, given the circumstances.

"Sure," Gene lied. "Why not? Now the ME's got a chance to identify the body. Who knows how long it would've stayed there otherwise?"

"Here's the thing." Boudreaux screwed up his face. Whether at the memory or the smell, it was hard to tell. "If I'm such a hero, why do I have to stay behind and babysit you? I should be the one who gets to go home, instead of breathing in this shit."

"Just lucky, I guess." Gene ducked around the cop, ready to get to work. Sure enough, he found a door in the back of the closet, kicked in by Boudreaux's boot. He held his breath and ducked through the maw, and when he emerged, it was into the haze of a single bulb that hung from an extension cord overhead. A shadowy pile of something or other leaned against the far wall of the attic.

A dogpile of empty leather handbags with brass locks and a logo even *he* recognized. The hill of Louis Vuittons climbed up the wall, dusted by a ring of candy-colored computer notebooks and those pointy shoes they called Jimmy Choos.

The loot no doubt all came from the same place: the girls at The College of the Immaculate Word. Given for birthdays or Christmas or high-school graduations and lovingly wrapped by parents who had no idea their little darlings would trade them in for pot, coke, or heroin, even.

He whistled under his breath. At a thousand bucks a pop retail—easy—the Louies alone would net twenty grand. No wonder dealers took them instead of cash. It was nothing to schlep a designer purse to a pawn shop and hand it over to some pimply-faced clerk who didn't care one way or the other. Those guys made it too easy.

"The bozo had his own shopping mall," Boudreaux said behind him.

Gene startled at the voice. He'd forgotten he wasn't alone. He turned.

Boudreaux stood on the other side of the busted doorway.

"Where'd they find the body?"

"Over there." Boudreaux jerked his thumb again. "Under some fancy-schmancy coat in the corner. Couldn't even reach the girl's parents since they're out of town. Safe's on the other side." Boudreaux spoke quickly now, probably because he wanted to get away from the smell too.

Gene followed his friend's gaze to a shiny black box that stood waist-high. The safe mirrored the one downstairs, down to the same blocky dial on its front.

Good thing he remembered to toss some kibble into Knox's bowl before he left the house for the night. No telling how long this would take, even with the stench urging him on.

Chapter Four

Skye

The next morning, Axl tried to wake her up again, only this time it was for real. The cat pawed at her cheek over and over, as if she'd never wake up otherwise.

She thought about hiding under the covers, since it was only the second day of classes and already she wanted to stay home. But then what would Dad say? He even promised to pay for some new clothes this weekend, so maybe she'd make the best of it. She'd do it for his sake, not hers.

She glanced at her cell, which shared the nightstand with the sound machine. At least the college was close by and she could wait until the very last second to throw on some jeans and an Astros T-shirt. Maybe even shove a protein bar in her mouth and take a Gatorade along for the hike.

She did all that—and even remembered to dump some food into Axl's bowl—before she slammed the front door behind her and headed for the sidewalk.

They moved into the rental house only a few months ago. Right at the end of her freshman year at Immaculate Word and right before Dad took yet another job, this one at an urgent care center. The house was nothing special, but it did have a really cool front door made of hammered steel that weighed about a thousand pounds and got all sparkly when the sun hit it just right. Like the owner thought maybe a huge front door would make up for the tiny porch or the pathetic lawn or the lone tree, which leaned sideways whenever the wind blew. It didn't, of course, but the oversized door *did* make it easier for her to describe the place to the delivery guys from Oodles of Noodles, Kashra Persian Palace, or Bellagreen.

She humped the backpack higher and followed the sidewalk until it hit Westheimer Road. She could make it to campus in fifteen minutes flat if she timed it just right. First, she hustled past a tear-down house on the corner whose days were numbered, and then she slid past a couple of storefronts in a tumbledown strip center. The places all had cheesy names like Happy Lucky Nail Salon, Kool Kutz, or Space City Lock Shoppe.

Given the college charged seventy grand a year, which she only raised through a patchwork of academic scholarships, you'd think the neighborhood could look a little nicer. But parents didn't seem to care about the community as long as the college offered security gates and a guard shack in the parking lot.

She quickly slid into the business building. For some reason, the campus seemed unusually quiet today, or maybe it felt that way after the chaos of everyone returning to school yesterday. She humped the backpack higher and headed for Econ 201.

"Yo, Skye. Wait Up." Harper, her best friend, hustled toward her.

Poor Harper was supposed to lose weight over the break, only she smuggled Skittles and Pixy Stix and anything else made with sugar into the ritzy fat camp her parents sent her to every summer. Harper thought she could hide the extra weight under a Gap XL sweatshirt, but that only made her look big *and* sweaty. Of course, Skey would never tell Harper that.

"What's up?"

Harper's breath came in fits and starts when she reached Skye. "Didja hear what happened yesterday?"

"No—"

She was about to say she couldn't hear *anything* yesterday, what with the chaos of people coming back together after three months apart, but Harper didn't wait for her to finish.

"Well, you wouldn't have heard it yesterday. It didn't happen until last night."

"What happened last night?"

"One of the girls' dads got called real late. He works for this big law firm downtown. Norton, Rose, and something."

"Yeah...and?" Skye turned all the way around.

At least her friend didn't seem to notice Skye had traded in the skater shoes for a pair of TOMS today. And it had nothing to do with what Alexandra said yesterday.

"Maybe the name's Fulsome. Or, Fulton," Harper said. "No wait...that's not right."

"Okay. I get it. It's a big law firm." Unfortunately, Harper had the attention span of a gnat. Usually Skye overlooked it, since she and Harper had been friends since high school, but today she wasn't in the mood. She didn't want to have to explain to Dad how she missed her first econ class because Harper couldn't focus. "What happened with the girl's dad?"

"He got this call, see." Harper's gaze fell to the floor. "Nice shoes. Anyway, it was the guy who owns that house across the street from here. You know... the one that looks okay and everything on the outside, but we all know what goes on inside. Hey...are those TOMS?"

"Harper, please focus. And take a breath." She was about to give up on ever finding out what happened at the house across the street. "You said this guy got a phone call."

"Oh, yeah. Sorry."

They rounded the corner before econ, where a senior on the girls' lacrosse team knocked into Harper's shoulder extra hard—just for the fun of it—before she moved inside. Harper pretended not to notice, although it had to hurt.

Skye wanted to say something—she really did—but then she'd definitely get called out by the professor for being late, so she kept her mouth shut and moved into the classroom, too.

"Anyway," Harper spoke behind her. "Someone died at that house across the street, and now the owner has to lawyer up. Guess the cops finally raided it, only they didn't expect to find a dead body there. How cool is that?"

Skye turned around. "Cool?"

"Well, there's more." Harper rolled her shoulder forward, a delayed reaction to the body slam. "You know Libby Sullivan never made it to class yesterday."

Like everyone else on campus, Harper insisted on calling Elizabeth by her nickname, to make it seem like they were friends or something. Even though Libby, Alexandra, and the rest of them made Harper's life a living hell in high school, she always seemed to forget that little detail whenever she talked about the clique now.

Maybe it was the money. Forget about shopping at Saks Fifth or Neiman's. Those girls hopped a G-6 to the Big Apple for back-to-school shopping, where they kept open tabs at Gucci and hired personal shoppers at Armani Emporium. Which wouldn't matter, but then they bullied anyone else who wasn't lucky enough to win the genetic lottery, like they did.

Skye hadn't seen any of them all summer. Not that she looked for them, of course.

"Elizabeth probably stayed over in New York City," Skye said. "Running the poor Gucci guy ragged."

"No, she didn't." Harper couldn't wait to correct her. It wasn't every day Harper knew something she didn't. "It was her body they found last night. Nobody's saying anything, but I'll bet she overdosed. It had to be an overdose, right?"

"Are they sure it was her?"

"Yep. Dead sure. Not to be morbid or anything. Looks like her clique is getting smaller."

"That's crazy. What did her parents say when they found out?"

"They don't know yet." Harper pushed a wayward strand of hair from her eyes. She said she meant to dye it pink, but she forgot to take off the color in time, so it turned out red instead. "I guess her parents are still in Paris. They had to get a housekeeper to come down and identify the body."

"That sucks. They're gonna freak out when they get back."

"I know, right?"

Finally, Mr. Carlson walked into the room, carrying a sweating Diet Coke. "Good morning, class. Settle down, now."

18

Skye headed for a seat in the middle row—the safe zone—away from lacrosse players in back and suck-ups near the front. Harper followed. Her breath warmed Skye's neck when she leaned over to whisper something new.

"Hey, Skye. Are you going to symphony tryouts today?"

Skye shook her head. Thank goodness Mr. Carlson started to write something on the Smartboard so she wouldn't have to turn around and explain why she wouldn't be at the auditions. As first clarinet, Harper lived for that stuff.

How could Skye explain she'd rather die than practice for another concert no one wanted to hear? She'd find a way to tell Dad, of course, but she'd wait until cold and flu season started, when his caseload exploded and he didn't have time to breathe, let alone worry about some dinky college concert. And if he found out early? She'd change the subject and tell him all about how poor Elizabeth Sullivan died in the house across the street from the school.

Compared to that, she'd look like an angel. For now, all she had to do was listen to another econ lecture and hope Harper forgot all about the auditions.

Chapter Five

Gene

By the time Gene woke up the next morning, white light flooded the kitchen. He tried to focus, but it was hard to see straight with the vise-grip on his temples.

Maybe the six-pack he polished off after cracking the second safe wasn't such a good idea. Hell, he probably should've ignored the Open sign at the Stop-N-Go, but it was right on the way home from the stash house and the clerk there worked all night, every night.

He only woke up because something wet touched his knee. Knox had planted his muzzle there, apparently, and moist brown eyes stared back at him when he finally lifted his head from the table.

"Lemme guess…you're hungry." He heaved upright, which was no easy feat, considering the vise-grip on his temples.

The dog led him to the pantry, where Gene grabbed some Kibbles 'N Bits and tossed it into a plastic doggie dish. Got most of it in, too.

As an afterthought, he threw a rawhide chew on top to make up for his absence the night before. The dog sniffed it suspiciously.

"Go on," Gene said. "It'll clean your teeth. FYI…your breath smells like shit."

Knox finally snatched the treat from the bowl before trotting off to the sunken living room, as if Gene might change his mind and take it back from him. The dog had issues, after all.

Gene sludged his gaze back to the clock on the kitchen wall. The numbers stood at nine forty, which meant he had just enough time to shower and change before the shop opened at ten.

He insisted on unlocking the front door himself, since he didn't quite trust anyone else to do it. Especially the new kid, who probably didn't know how to work a light switch, let alone a mortise lock on the front door.

He cautiously picked a few stray kibbles off the floor—careful to straighten nice and easy this time—and then he tossed them in the sink before heading for the shower. His shirt still smelled like someone's ass, so he peeled it off and chucked it in the laundry hamper before pulling a fresh polo from the dresser.

Every black polo he owned had the same yellow-threaded logo on its sleeve: Space City Lock Shoppe. He thought it was a great name for a business, even with the snooty British spelling Marilyn asked him to use.

He couldn't wait to show her the shop's new Yellow Pages ad when it finally came out. He rushed home from work with it, only to realize people would have to flip past Acme Lock & Key, Anderson Unlimited, and on and on, until they finally hit the Ss. That mistake with the S cost him plenty of new business at the beginning, but Marilyn loved the shop's name, so he kept it, for her sake.

And now it was all about the internet anyway, so the name didn't really matter. Now he needed stuff like "shares" and "likes" and "page hits," and all those other strange words he paid some IT consultant to make go away. What would she think if she saw the shop's website now, with its fancy "buy" buttons and links to Facebook?

He chuckled as he swatted the dresser drawer closed and headed for the shower. Once he finished under the nozzle and got dressed again, he headed for the kitchen and grabbed a box of crackers from the pantry. A quick shout to Knox in the living room and then it was time to pile into the Tahoe for the short drive to work.

Maybe he should ask one of his guys to open up the lock shop for once. Ask them to show up to work early and handle some of the details that went into running a small business. What would happen then?

Nothing. That was what would happen. Absolutely nothing.

Ted was a whiz when it came to duping keys, and Albert could schmooze housewives all day long while he jimmied their car doors open. But neither of those guys gave a crap about the showroom. Not like Gene did, anyway.

He even loved the smell of it, and he inhaled loudly as he stepped through the front doorway and caught a whiff of WD-40 and oiled brass. It always smelled like home. He flicked on the overheads, and that was when he noticed the display case hadn't been cleaned yet. He distinctly remembered asking the new hire—Reef—to clean the counter yesterday. Speaking of which…

The kid wandered into the showroom a little bit later. Skinny, with black hair to his shoulders, he looked like he spent most of his time inside, playing video games in someone's basement, which he probably did. Gene wanted to reach over and swat a shock of hair from the guy's eyes, but he didn't trust his balance at the moment.

Instead, he pointed. "Hey, Fabio. See this?" He blew on the counter and dust scattered everywhere.

"Dude." Reef watched the dust swirl with his good eye. "You should clean that."

Gene was about to remind him he'd asked Reef to do that, but what was the point? Reef wouldn't remember, and Gene was too tired to care.

"That's a great idea, Reef. Why don't you grab some cleaner from the back and start in on that?"

The new kid didn't blink.

"The storeroom is behind the bathroom. Remember?" Gene spoke nice and slow this time. "I showed it to you yesterday. The cleaners are in that sack by the toilet paper."

"Oh, yeah." Finally, a spark of light. "But you don't want the toilet paper, right?"

"No, Reef. I don't want the toilet paper. Just find the blue bottle that says Windex. And grab some paper towels."

"You got it, dude."

Reef started to walk away, but he didn't look at all confident about which way to go. At the last second, he hooked a left and disappeared through a back doorway that would take him to the storeroom.

Gene sighed. What was he supposed to do?

He only offered the kid a job to make his dad happy. It all started when he got in a jam with Mr. Abdullah's lawnmower last week. He never should've asked to borrow his neighbor's riding mower in the first place, since he could barely guide an old-fashioned push mower around the massive tree roots in his front yard. But he didn't have a choice. Not unless he wanted another snarky note from the homeowner's association threatening to sue his ass if he didn't cut his front lawn, *pronto*.

So, he'd marched next door to the stucco McMansion and asked his neighbor to loan him his riding mower. The minute the steering wheel locked up on him, though, Gene knew he was in trouble. He went right back to Mr. Abdullah, never imagining his neighbor would invite him in and shove a cup of something brown and milky into his hand.

Long story short, he also got a lecture about how Raynesh—Mr. Abdullah's only son—needed a part-time job to keep him busy after school. Maybe then the boy would learn some discipline. Some *shik-shaw*, his neighbor called it. Apparently, the kid—whom everyone else called Reef—couldn't be counted on to cut the family's own lawn, so the mower languished in the family's garage.

Mr. Abdullah grinned when Gene reluctantly agreed to the plan. Like he thought Gene was doing him some huge favor, when all Gene wanted to do was to hand over the busted steering wheel and the untouched tea and get the hell out of there.

But maybe it wouldn't be so bad if he let the kid work at the shop a few days a week. Then they could call it even on the busted mower. Deal?

By the time Gene turned around again, Reef had disappeared into the hall. If today was anything like yesterday, he'd have to send the new kid back to the storeroom for something else. No telling how long *that* would take or how many times he'd have to tell Reef that, no, he didn't want the toilet paper, too.

Chapter Six

Raynesh (Reef)

His dad was right. Mr. Jacks looked wasted this morning. What little gray hair his new boss had stuck straight out from his head, like Albert Einstein, and he could barely keep his balance when he bent over the display case.

The guy made a big deal out of blowing some dust off it, as if Reef was too stupid to know how to clean it. But that wasn't it. He just had more important things to worry about yesterday than wiping away some dirt that would only come back anyway.

"He's gonna figure out what you're up to, Dad," Reef said, once he heard about his father's plan to help his neighbor. "He's gonna know why you asked him to hire me."

"Nonsense. You will be able to keep an eye on him. To make sure his drinking does not ruin his business. And you need more to do after classes than ride around on a silly piece of wood."

Reef wanted to remind his father that "silly piece of wood" was a handmade, custom Yocaher longboard with polyurethane Pig wheels and black Penny trucks. But his dad wouldn't understand.

In the end, it always came back to skateboarding. And not just because Reef wrapped a brand-new Range Rover around a stop sign last year and his dad refused to buy him another one until he graduated from college.

No, skateboarding was more than a way to get around. Always had been.

It was the only thing that saved him when he first arrived in America seven years ago.

He took one look at the crazy freeway overpasses back then, and the treeless subdivisions that looked nothing like his old neighborhood in Delhi, and he wanted to get right back on the plane. Until he found skateboarding, that was.

"I don't have time for a part-time job now," Reef said. "I've got too much stuff going on."

The last thing he wanted was to sell locks to old guys during his free time, when he should be practicing at the skatepark with his best friend, Kenny.

"You can do both," his father said. "I am not asking you to go to medical school like I did. I am asking you to do something good for a neighbor. To let me know whether he can handle his responsibilities. If he can not, we will help him, of course. But first, we must diagnose the situation. The diagnosis always comes first."

His father didn't pause for breath. "You know, it is important 'to be good and do good.'"

His dad loved Hindi quotes, almost as much as he liked "fixing" other people's problems. His dad considered himself the ultimate fixer. He was born to help people, he'd say. Which explained the psychiatry degree from Yale and private practice nearby. As long as his dad could help people in the way he wanted to help them, everything was cool.

"You need to learn some discipline." The old man didn't stop talking. "Make something of yourself. I did not bring you all the way to America to waste your time with a toy."

In addition to being the ultimate fixer, his father considered himself a true patriot. Never mind the family didn't emigrate until Reef was in middle school, when it was hard enough to make friends without a funny accent and curry in his lunch sack.

"We have it all worked out." His father beamed now, unaware of anything but the sound of his own voice. "He will let you work behind the front counter. That way you can greet customers and convince them everything is on the up and up. They need never know about Mr. Jacks's little problem."

Little problem? An eye roll itched behind Reef's eyes, but he ignored it. Last Saturday morning, when Reef finally woke up after spending the night at the skate park, he spied Mr. Jacks's Tahoe sitting sideways on the guy's lawn. His neighbor couldn't even navigate straight up his own driveway. And that sounded like way more than a "little problem" to Reef, but whatever.

Reef took off on his board the next day and headed for Space City Lock Shoppe. Where he tried to look happy about applying for a job he never asked for and earning money he didn't need.

Who knew there were so many different kinds of locks, though? Row after row of them greeted Reef when he entered the shop for the first time, the displays deep and wide, like the trenches in the old man's yard the day after his bender.

Then again, some of the safes in the back looked kinda cool. But Mr. Jacks warned him to stay away from those because those were for big-time spenders who needed lots of technical information. He really seemed to think Reef was an idiot. Was it the hair? The skateboard?

What would he say if he knew Reef stood to make a hundred grand a year when he finally turned pro? Just because his college GPA hovered at two-point-five didn't mean he was too stupid for school. It only meant he didn't care.

All those tests he took that asked for names and dates and places? They never held his attention. He forgot the information as quickly as he heard it, which was obvious from his grades.

Even back in high school, his teachers made the same comment every year, and every year, his father fixated on it.

Raynesh doesn't apply himself, his teachers would say.

"Where do they want you to apply, Raynesh?" his father would ask, since he obviously didn't get it. "And why don't you?"

It wasn't that Reef couldn't cut it. It didn't make him happy, like being at the Lee & Joe Jamail Skatepark with Kenny and his buds did. Lately, they'd started making YouTube videos of the crazy tricks they pulled off on the half-pipes, quarter pipes and snake runs there. Those videos were Reef's ticket out of Houston and onto the competitive circuit, where companies paid big-time to have their names plastered on a pro's skateboard.

He couldn't figure out why his dad cared about Mr. Jacks anyway. As a psychiatrist, his father treated lots of alcoholics, but he always kept them at arm's length. He gave them a one-hour appointment and maybe some naltrexone—his father loved to dispense meds and prove he was an actual doctor—but that was it. He didn't sic Reef on them to make sure they could run their own business.

"Don't forget, we must be good and do good," his father said, seemingly unaware Reef had already tuned him out. "I think the man will take you under his wing and train you, like a little sparrow."

A sparrow? The words echoed in Reef's ears as he trekked back to the storeroom now, away from Mr. Jacks. One thing was clear. If he wanted to ditch this job and get back to the skatepark, he'd have to figure out a way to find out what was happening with Mr. Jacks's store. Maybe get into the guy's computer or something. Check out his tax returns. Decipher whether the old man needed help to run the business or not.

Then, Reef could report back to his father. Show him once and for all his son could be counted on to be good and do good.

Wait. Where did that come from?

Chapter Seven

Skye

The last class couldn't end soon enough. Skye found a scrap from the school newspaper lying on the floor, which she used to bookmark *Introduction to Literary Theory,* and then she bolted from her chair. She wanted to reach the exit and disappear before Harper could find her and ask about symphony tryouts again.

If she ran into Harper, she was screwed. Harper was the only person on earth who could make her do something she didn't want to do, like try out for the school's quidditch team, even though she hadn't read a single Harry Potter book, or wear matching sweatshirts to homecoming, even with September's sky-high temperatures, or suffer through another Ricky Martin concert, so Harper could ogle the guy from the top row of Toyota Arena.

She *really* didn't want to try out for the Symphony Showcase. She worried about it all day, when she was supposed to be studying the Laffer curve or parsing the difference between *tutoyer* and *vouvoyer,* or reading about post-structural literary theory. The concert would be fine without her. Plenty of people played flute, and maybe they wouldn't mind performing for a few dozen parents who'd rather be anywhere else than sitting in Nguyen Auditorium on a stifling Friday night.

She'd almost made it to the exit when a voice stopped her cold.

"Nice shoes." Alexandra leaned against a nearby wall.

What was better…ignore her, which would only egg Alexandra on, since the girl seemed to love a good challenge, or respond and waste precious time?

Screw the tryouts. "Thanks." Skye fiddled with the zipper on her North Face, which she bought years ago at Houston Premium Outlets. "Maybe you should see a professional about your foot fetish, though. It's kind of embarrassing."

"Ha, ha." Alexandra didn't move, as if she had all the time in the world to waste on Skye's footwear.

"I'm serious." Skye jerked the zipper extra hard. "They say it's the gateway to hardcore porn."

"You're hilarious." Alexandra leaned in, which meant Skye probably should've ignored her in the first place. "As if I cared about you and your feet."

With a final yank, Skye ripped the zipper free. "Look, Alexandra." She shoved the torn zipper into her pocket, "I'd love to stay and chat with you. I really would. But I kinda have stuff to do. You should try it sometime."

"Oh, I have plenty of stuff to do."

"Really?" Skye nodded at a poster behind the girl's head. "Like paint something? Maybe you should read the stuff you write before you hang it up."

When Alexandra turned to see what she was talking about, Skye took the opportunity and hustled away. Thank goodness the rubber-soled TOMS gripped the linoleum as she moved, which made for a quick getaway.

The rustle of students echoed through the hall as she barreled through the exit. The minute she landed outside, she took the stairs two at a time and hopped onto the hot pavement.

Sweat plastered her ponytail to her neck by the time she'd reached the strip center on the corner. She debated whether to text Harper right then and there and explain why she couldn't hang around for symphony auditions, but tryouts would last all afternoon, and Harper wouldn't even have a chance to read the text until later, so what was the point?

Instead, she moved past the frosted window of Happy Lucky Nails and paused at the next store over. The cheesy lock shop with the unnecessary "e" on the end of its name. Inside the display window, she spied several backpacks.

No doubt the store owner wanted to lure college kids into the shop with those. This particular display featured big backpacks, little ones, and everything in-between. One was so tiny, it looked no bigger than a lunch sack.

Skye humped her old backpack higher on her shoulder, which pressed sweat against her skin. Dad *did* say he was going to put some money into her account today, and it wouldn't hurt for her to finally have a new backpack that worked.

She moved into the dark shop, which smelled like motor oil and wet cardboard, and tucked some flyaway hair behind her ear. A line of metal boxes winked at her from the back of the store. They looked like safes of some kind, since they all had flat faces and round dials. She lingered in the doorway until her eyes adjusted to the dim light.

After a few seconds, she moved over to the display window, where she picked through a pile of backpacks. She chose a red one. When she turned, someone appeared behind the counter.

"You want that?" the guy asked her.

"Oh. Yeah."

He seemed to be about her age, and he wore a plaid flannel shirt and black jeans, although it had to be a million degrees outside. He was cute, in a slacker kind of way. The hair was too long, and he'd pulled his jeans low to show off his boxers, which also were plaid, in case anyone cared.

"So, do you want that?" he repeated.

She nodded and crossed the store. He reminded her of the skaters who cruised around her neighborhood on beat-up longboards. The guys—never girls—who didn't care about anything or anyone but their precious skateboards.

"Nothing else?" The guy took the backpack from her.

"Just that." She never understood why people asked her that when she tried to buy stuff. Did they think she forgot something and they needed to remind her she wasn't finished shopping yet? "It's for school."

"Gotcha." His eyelashes were extra-long, and they curved around soft-brown irises, which would drive Harper nuts. He quickly glanced at the cash register. "That'll be...uh...eighteen dollars and ninety-nine cents."

"No, it won't," she replied. "You forgot to add tax."

"Oh, yeah." He squinted at the old-fashioned cash register. "I've gotta be honest with you. Today's only my second day. Haven't learned how to work the cash register yet."

"We're in Harris County," she said, without thinking. "That's eight-and-a-quarter percent. So, it works out to...um...twenty dollars and fifty-five cents."

"Whoa." The guy blinked, or at least she thought he blinked, because the curtain of hair moved in front of his eyelashes. "Not bad. You're good with numbers."

"Thanks." She grinned at the compliment, even though it came from some guy she'd just met. "I like math."

"Seriously. You should go on a game show or something."

"You mean like *Jeopardy?*" She scrunched her nose since she'd never once heard host Alex Trebek ask a question about math. "Ancient History" or "Dead Poets" or "Before & After" maybe, but never something about fractions or percentages.

"That's it." The cute guy nodded, as if he knew exactly what she was talking about, even though he probably didn't have a clue. "That's the show."

"Yeah, that's what I figured. I watch it on Netflix all the time. With my dad, that is."

"Cool."

Someone new wandered into the showroom then. It was an old man in a black polo, with a big Santa Claus belly. He looked groggy, like maybe he just woke up from a long nap, or maybe he needed one. "Everything okay out here?"

"We're cool," plaid-shirt guy said. "Just helpin' a customer."

Santa stared at her, hard. Not in a creepy way, but in a what-are-you-doing-talking-to-this-guy? kind of way.

He took the backpack from the cashier. "You go to Immaculate Word?"

He was talking to her now, and he nudged the cute guy out of the way so he could ring up the purchase.

"Yes, sir." *How does he know that?* Skye glanced over her shoulder. Maybe coming into the store wasn't such a good idea after all. It was kinda dark inside and really, really quiet. Would anyone know if she screamed? The two guys could kidnap her and stuff her into one of those metal safes along the back wall and the nail ladies next door probably wouldn't suspect a thing. "I broke my other one. I'm kinda in a hurry."

"How do you like that college?" the old guy asked.

"It's cool. Can I please pay for the backpack?"

He smiled at her, which split the skin on his cheeks into a million wrinkles. "Sure. I'm not trying to give you a hard time. I could use someone like you around here."

She cut her gaze to the cute guy. "It looks like you already have someone around here."

"I need a good cashier," the old man said. "If you can't tell, we've let a few things slide."

That made sense, since the display counter looked like it could use about a gallon of glass cleaner and the cashier didn't even remember to charge her sales tax.

"I don't know." She felt awkward talking about a job with the other guy standing *right there.* Not that he seemed to be paying attention to them. Instead, the cute guy drummed his fingers on the countertop to a beat only he could hear.

"Have you ever thought about getting a part-time job?" the old guy asked.

"Not really."

"Well, you should think about it. I pay nine bucks an hour. That's more than minimum wage."

Skye's breath stalled. It was twenty percent more, considering most jobs in Harris County paid only seven dollars and twenty-five cents. That worked out to nineteen-point-four-four-four percent more, to be exact.

And come to think of it, she could use the extra spending money. Although she spent the summer helping her dad, filing patient charts and trying not to look bored, Christmas was right around the corner. Already, the toy section at the local Walmart looked like Santa's workshop, and they kept playing ads for holiday gifts over the loudspeaker. In a few weeks, the stationery section would bloom in reds and greens and they'd blare "Jingle Bell Rock" twenty-four seven. Where would she be then? She hadn't saved a thing for Christmas yet, and she wanted to get Dad something really nice this year.

"A job, huh?"

Not to mention, she had grad school to think about. Although she planned to apply for every academic scholarship under the sun, those things usually didn't cover textbooks and stuff.

"You know I go to school every day, right?"

Even though he asked her about Immaculate Word, it wouldn't hurt to remind him. Dad would never let her ditch out of school early for a part-time job.

"I know...college. You wouldn't have to start until after three. It's pretty quiet around here before then, anyway."

She watched the skater dude finish drumming the song on the counter. *Really, how hard can this job be?* The inventory didn't look all that complicated, and she was the only customer there on a Thursday afternoon. Plus, it'd give her a good reason to leave school on time, instead of heading for symphony practice. She couldn't very well practice for the Symphony Showcase and hold down a part-time job, now could she?

And if those reasons didn't work, she had one more up her sleeve: grad-school apps. A part-time job would look great on the ol' resume. Dad would love that one. It was all about the end game, right?

"I've got homework every night," she said. "Which means I'd have to leave at nine."

Santa smirked at her. Not in a mean-Alexandra kind of way, but in a way that let her know he thought she was funny. "You drive a hard bargain, missy. But I think I can work around your schedule. You interested in locks?"

"Sure?" She didn't know what else to say. It was like being asked if she liked air or water or gravity; something she never thought about before. "Looks like you've got a bunch of them in here."

"C'mere and I'll show you."

She didn't move. In fact, the only thing that shifted was her gaze, which shot across the store to the open door and freedom beyond it.

"Forget it." He seemed to read her mind. "Why don't you think it over first? Let me know what you decide. Here."

He reached into the pocket of his polo, where he found a pen and one of those old-fashioned thingys called a business card. She'd seen one of those before: all black ink on one side and shiny white paper on the other.

He jotted something on the card and slid it toward her. "That's my cell number. Let me know what you decide."

She dusted the paper on her jeans before she read it. He'd written a telephone number under "Gene Jacks, Owner." Now she knew his name, Mr. Jacks didn't seem all that bad. To be honest, he was probably someone's grandpa and he needed a cashier he could count on to charge people sales tax.

The guy in the plaid shirt finally stopped drumming on the counter. "Does that mean she'd work with me?"

"Yes, Reef." Mr. Jacks spoke slowly, like maybe the cute guy was deaf or had special needs or something. "But you're going to have to work in the stockroom now. Why don't you go check it out, while I finish talking to the girl?"

Skye held her breath. After what seemed like forever, the cute guy finally grinned. A crooked, lopsided grin that began and ended with a pair of dimples. Dimples! Harper would go absolutely nuts.

"Cool!" He ducked behind the counter and scrounged around for something on the floor. When he shot up again, he held a tricked-out longboard against his chest. Just like she thought.

He headed for the stockroom with the board, while Mr. Jacks sighed.

"He took that really hard," he said. "Look kid...the cashier job's all yours. If you want it, that is."

Skye nodded. Little did Mr. Jacks know, but she'd already made up her mind. It was a no-brainer, really. If taking a job like this meant she could skip symphony practice *and* sock away some cash for Christmas, the answer was yes. The trick was to get Dad on board. Make him think she could hold down a part-time job and still make the dean's list. Maybe she'd tell him she wanted to be like water that flowed through a crack. That would show she'd been listening to his lectures all this time. How could he say no?

Chapter Eight

Gene

When Reef sailed through the back entrance, he looked like Knox bearing down on a tennis ball. Like an overgrown puppy, all flying legs and paws, as if freed from a leash for the very first time.

He sure hoped the kid in front of him would take the cashier's job. For one thing, she looked him dead in the eyes when they spoke…and he could see both her eyes. She didn't slouch, either, even with a beat-up backpack strapped to her shoulders.

Not that he cared, but she was *this close* to being pretty. She had clear skin and strawberry-blonde hair, which she pulled into a ponytail with a rubber band. No clip, just the band. She missed the mark with the glasses, though. They looked like something a math teacher would wear instead of a cheerleader, which used to be the goal for girls back when he was in college. *But what the hell do I know?* Maybe everything had flip-flopped since then and the geeky look was what got dates nowadays. In that case, this girl was a shoo-in.

He barely noticed her looks when she spoke to him, anyway. That was when he realized he'd made the right decision.

"I owe you twenty bucks and fifty-five cents," she said, the minute Reef sailed around the corner. "That's with tax."

She dropped her backpack to the ground and rummaged around for change. She kept her nails nice and short...another good sign. She wouldn't be wasting his time shopping for beauty products on the internet when she was supposed to be working.

After a second, she pulled out two bills—a twenty and a one—and handed them across the counter. He turned his back on her to ring up the sale.

"You owe me forty-five cents," she said before he could even start.

Yep, she was gonna work out just fine. He swung around again. "So, give me a call when you make up your mind, okay?"

"I'll do that." She thrust out her hand to give him a firm handshake. "By the way, my name's Skye. I'm a sophomore at Immaculate Word. Want me to get you a transcript or something?"

"Nah, that's okay." He withdrew his hand to fish her change from the till. "I trust you. And here's your forty-five cents. Want the receipt?"

"Sure."

He curled the edge between his thumb and forefinger as he passed it across the counter. "I'll be waiting for your call. You can start Monday if you want. After three."

The minute she started to leave, though, he had his answer. If she didn't trust him, if she never wanted to see him or the shop again, she would've backed away from the counter nice and slow. At least that was what he'd come to expect after working with cops for so long. *Never take your eyes off someone you don't trust.* Hadn't he learned that lesson from Boudreaux, Rios, and the rest?

But not this girl. She turned all the way around and marched down the aisle.

Gene smiled as he shut the till, and that was when his cell phone vibrated in his pocket. He whipped it out and accepted the call.

"Jacks here." What with everything else on his mind, he forgot to check the number on the screen first, so he had no idea who was calling him.

"Hey, it's Boudreaux. I'm at the station."

Gene jimmied the phone between his chin and shoulder. "What's up?"

"Remember that safe from last night?"

"Of course." He absentmindedly wiped Reef's fingerprints from the counter. "There were two safes. Which one are you talking about?"

"The second one. The one behind the closet."

"What about it?"

"We found something interesting there. Ya happen to look inside?"

Gene shook his head, although Boudreaux couldn't see him. He learned a long time ago not to peer into a safe once he opened it. Every safecracker knew that. Otherwise, you might end up seeing something you'd rather not see. Stuff like cash, drugs, or diamonds, even. No, nothing good could come of it.

"You know me better than that," Gene said. "When have I ever looked into one of those things?"

"Good point. But I want to pick your brain about something."

"That'll be slim pickings." He might as well make the joke himself, before Boudreaux could beat him to it. "There's not a whole lot rattling around up there. But what do you need?"

"Information. Turns out the drug dealer we got wasn't very original. He kept his books back there. The real stuff. Not some fake crap for the IRS. Anyway, he wrote a name on the first page, and I wanted to run it by you."

"Me? Why would you run it by me?"

"Because your shop's down there by the college. Figured you might have heard something about this character."

"I don't know," Gene said. "We don't get many students in here." In fact, before today, he hadn't gotten a single one all week. "They don't usually hang around a lock shop. Usually, they go to Starbucks or the Galleria. But I'll give it a shot."

"Okay, that's more like it." Boudreaux inhaled deeply. Leave it to his friend to milk the moment for all it was worth. "He wrote down the name 'fireplug.' You ever heard of a character called that?"

"I don't know. I've heard of a 'plug' before, if that's what you mean. Isn't that what they call a drug dealer? And, by the way, that's a noun, not a nickname. That could mean anything."

"Look, I didn't say this was easy." Boudreaux sounded wounded now, as if Gene had hurt his feelings by telling the truth. "But it could mean something.

The dealer gave this guy a lot of credit in his books. Had entries going back a coupla years. Figured the guy was working for the dealer or something."

Gene thought it over. "Doesn't ring a bell. But I'll tell you what. I'll keep my eyes and ears open. By the way, how's the sergeant doing?"

Nothing but silence on the other end.

"You know...Rios?" Gene prompted. "He sounded pretty broken up about the dead girl last night. He doin' okay?"

After another beat, Boudreaux finally replied. "Guess so. It was kind of rough on him when our guys couldn't find the parents. They had to break the news to a maid. Most times he talks to the family first. You know, father to father."

Gene wiped away the last fingerprint. Hopefully, the new girl would know how to clean the counter, since Reef obviously didn't. "I get that. You got any suspects yet? Other than the dealer?"

"Nah. It's too soon. We're starting with him. Trying to see what this guy was into. And who was helping him. ME said they'll have an autopsy report tomorrow. But I'm not holding my breath. Things like that usually take a coupla days, and only if there's nothing else going on."

"I hear you. Keep me posted, okay?" Gene brought his finger to the light. Dust coated the tip like aluminum powder at a crime scene. One of the silver powders they used on plastic or glass, not the dark kind for wood or metal. That was something else he learned after spending so much time around cops. "If you run into the captain, tell him I'm available if they come across any more safes. You know...ones they don't want to blast open."

This time the silence felt awkward. He'd touched a sore spot between them, and now he couldn't take it back. Both he and Boudreaux knew his days of helping the police force were numbered. Before long, every police department would have one of those fancy computerized lockpicking programs, which meant people like him would go the way of the dinosaurs.

"Sure, I'll tell him," Boudreaux said, even though they both knew he wouldn't. "It's been kinda slow around here, though, so I wouldn't wait by the phone. Hey, how's your business doing?"

He'd picked a clunky way to change the subject, but Gene couldn't fault him for that.

"Not bad. I'm running a sale on gun safes now that hunting season's here." He had too many American Securitys sitting around, and it wouldn't hurt to clear out his inventory. "You should check 'em out sometime."

"I'll do that. Look, I've got to go. Let me know if you hear anything about a guy called the 'fireplug,' okay?"

"I told you I would. But you shouldn't wait by the phone, either. Most of my customers don't even know what a plug is."

Once the line went dead, Gene slid the cell in his back pocket. He tried to smooth the pocket down afterward, but his thumb shook a little too much to make that happen.

He'd first noticed the tremor in his finger about a week ago. For some reason, his thumb developed a twitch, as if it had a life of its own.

It barely registered the first time around. But nowadays, he couldn't stop staring at his hands. They reminded him of an old person's hands. Something he didn't recognize.

Now, every time he bent to tie a shoelace, his finger slipped off the cord. Made him go back and try again. And when he bent to scratch Knox's muzzle? His thumb glanced off the side of the dog's nose and landed on the dog's collar instead. Maybe it was the booze talking. Telling him to cut back. Either that or old age come to rest on his doorstop and remind him he wasn't a kid anymore.

At least that was what he told himself as he watched his thumb tremble like a floating dust speck.

Chapter Nine

Skye

S kye ripped open a bag of Brad's Raw Leaf Kale and tossed the dark leaves into a bowl. Tonight was the night to ask him about the job. If she didn't do it now, she never would.

She added a handful of gummy low-fat cheese and some water cashews to the mix, and then she tossed the salad with metal tongs. Making dinner used to be a whole lot more fun when she had normal stuff to work with, before Dad got all healthy on her.

At least tonight was pizza, his favorite. Maybe that would get him to say yes.

She turned around to grab some frozen dough from the fridge. The directions said to leave it on the counter for thirty minutes to defrost, which sounded like a lot of work for a stupid pizza, so she set her phone for twenty minutes instead and pulled out a can of pineapple chunks and some baked-chicken tofu. Apparently, no one ever told Dad the Whole Foods/whole paycheck joke, because this pizza would end up costing them three times as much as one they could order from Domino's.

At least he wanted to make sure she ate healthy. To show he cared, since he wasn't around on the weekends, and he didn't even know she skipped out on symphony auditions. But, by God, he could care about what she put in her mouth. To be fair, it was more than she could say for a lot of parents she knew.

"Hey, muffin." He strolled into the kitchen with his computer under his arm, *natch*.

She glanced at a clock built into the microwave out of habit. A little before eight. Not bad, considering some nights he didn't get home until almost ten.

"Good. You're home early tonight."

"Barely. A sprained wrist walked in right before closing. I asked Jeffries to take it. Told him I was having pizza with my best gal tonight."

"Dad." She held back the eye roll, since he was being serious.

"Hey. Is there any pilsner in there?" Dad pointed at the fridge.

"I think so. Split one?"

She grabbed a Gaffel from the bottom shelf when Dad nodded, along with two mugs from a cabinet overhead. Other parents might question why her dad let her drink beer with him—always imported, never domestic—but they'd been doing it for so long, she didn't even think twice now.

It all started five years ago, back when she was only fifteen. The year Mom left for a Walmart run and never returned. The very next day, Dad took her shopping at Whole Foods, where he marched her past the frozen-food aisle and sat her down at a bar by the deli. He ordered a Guinness Extra Stout for him and a chai tea for her, but halfway through their talk, he passed the Pilsner to her under the bartender's sightline. Considering she didn't even have her driver's license yet, his parenting style was unorthodox, to say the least.

"Here you go." She poured out the beer and pretended to study her glass. She'd have to hurry if she wanted to say something before Dad fired up the Dell and got lost in his case notes.

"Something happened today." She tilted the mug and studied the amber liquid inside. "After my classes."

"That right?"

"Um, hum." She slurped some foam and tried not to blanch. Pilsner always reminded her of cough syrup, but she couldn't tell Dad that. "This guy offered me a job."

"A job?" His own mug stilled in the air. "What kind of job? We've never talked about you getting a job. You've got school to think about."

"Well, you never said I *couldn't* get a job. I got to thinking that maybe it's time I did something more than babysitting. You know, sock away money for grad school and stuff."

"But that's what scholarships are for, honey. I don't know. What kind of job are we talking about?"

"It's no big deal." She set her mug down, where little beads of sweat pooled on the counter's surface. "I don't even have to get there until three. He said I could go home around nine."

"He? Who's he?" Dad sounded brusque now, which was never a good sign. But at least he took a big gulp of beer.

"The owner of the store. He's really old and really nice. He's got that shop around the corner from here. The one where they sell locks and stuff. It's called Space City Lock Shoppe. You know, on account of us living in Houston." She stopped talking when she realized she was beginning to sound like Harper. Like a giant gnat buzzing around the room. "Anyway…I stopped there after school today. I broke the zipper on my backpack and he sold me a new one. The guy said he needs a cashier and he's willing to pay me nine bucks an hour."

Finally, the frown softened. Which meant Dad wasn't ready to give her a hard no. At least, not yet.

"A cashier, huh? Well, you do like math. In a lock shop. But what do you know about locks?"

"Nothing. Not yet, anyway." If he was going to put it like that, it *did* sound silly. But she never meant to get offered a job…it just kind of happened. "I don't think it'll be that tough. There's another guy who already works there, and he doesn't seem all that smart." Cute, yes, but he didn't have a clue about the cash register. "I'm pretty sure he didn't want to be a cashier to begin with, so he wants me to work there, too."

She blustered on when he didn't speak. "I guess I'd be ringing up customers, putting stuff on shelves, maybe cleaning up a little. The place looks like it hasn't seen Lysol in forever. But everything's safe. I promise. There's nothing weird going on."

"But what do you know about this guy? I mean, c'mon. People don't usually offer someone a job on the spot."

She hesitated, since there was no way she could tell her dad the whole story in a few seconds. If he wanted a play-by-play, he should've been there.

"Like I said, I needed a new backpack, so I ditched into the store." She deliberately took a long pull from her beer. Maybe Dad would follow suit and let the Pilsner work its magic. "So, I'm standing there, and I'm helping this other kid figure out how much tax to charge me, and Mr. Jacks—he's the owner—was listening. He came over and we started talking. The next thing you know...bam! He offers me a job." She smiled, as if it was the most natural thing in the world. "But he wants me to think about it first. He was real serious about that."

Time to go in for the kill. "I promise it won't interfere with my classes. Scouts honor. If my grades slip, you can make me quit. Only, they won't."

"What about your extra-curriculars? Weren't you going to try out for that symphony thing?"

She blanched. He wasn't supposed to ask about that yet. He was supposed to ask about that later, after they agreed she could take the job.

"Maybe." She casually flicked some water from the counter to buy time. "But I thought I might take a break this year. A lot of other flutes will try out. I'm not even first chair, you know."

The silence thickened. He was either going to call her bluff or he'd fall for it. She continued to flick imaginary drops of water as she waited.

"Hmmm," he finally said. "Well, it sounds like you've given it a lot of thought. And you're sure the conductor isn't counting on you to try out this year?"

"Positive." Since tryouts ended a couple of hours ago and she hadn't heard a peep from the professor, odds were good he didn't need her for the show. "I'll explain it to him first thing tomorrow morning."

"And there's no chance it'll interfere with your schoolwork?"

"None." Another thought flashed through her mind, just in time. "I really want to do this for my grad-school apps. You're always telling me admissions counselors want to see 'real world' experience. I could use it in my essays. You know, write about being responsible, working with other people. Cheesy stuff like that."

"Guess the answer's yes, then." Dad threw up his hands. "Don't let me stand in your way."

"Cool!" She rushed around the counter to hug his neck. He smelled like rubbing alcohol and dried sweat. "You won't even notice. And you can visit me anytime you want." Which was a safe thing to say, since he'd never take time off from work to drop in on her at the shop.

"Really. I mean it. I'll go call Mr. Jacks. We can't eat for a while, anyway. The pizza dough has to rise."

Suddenly, twenty minutes didn't seem like such a big deal, and she grabbed her phone as she skirted around the counter. She'd call Mr. Jacks first and tell him the good news, and then she'd call Harper.

Her best friend would be happy for her—wouldn't she?—especially if she thought it meant Skye could finally shop at a real mall, instead of Houston Premium Outlets.

She had yet to serve one customer at Space City Lock Shoppe, and already she loved the place.

* * *

Mr. Jacks sounded pleased when she told him the news. He told her about a form she'd have to fill out Monday for the IRS, and then they both hung up at the same time.

Things weren't quite as simple with Harper. Her best friend wanted to know why Skye walked into Space City Lock Shoppe in the first place. No one ever went into that store. What if the guy who offered her a job had a sketchy white van and a criminal record?

Skye defended him as best she could, until Harper moved on to the skater dude behind the counter. What'd he look like? What was he wearing? Tats... piercings...anything?

To be honest, Skye had forgotten all about him. But leave it to Harper to zero in on something that had nothing to do with the job.

"Kind of tall, I guess," she said. "And he has a nice smile." Crooked, wasn't it? With dimples that sliced his cheeks.

"Was his hair really long or just kind of long?"

"Long enough to fall in his eyes. Which were brown, by the way."

"Brown? Just like Ricky's." Harper sighed, lost in her love for the Latin singer.

"You know he's gay, right?"

They'd had this conversation a million times before. Harper simply refused to believe Ricky Martin was gay, even though he had a husband and everything.

"Rumors. All rumors." Harper sighed once more. "Tell me more about this guy's hair. What kind of styling products?"

"Um, none? Not that I noticed, anyway. Look, can we talk about the job? I start Monday, after class."

"I can't believe your dad said yes. You're always telling me he won't let you do anything fun."

"I know, right? Maybe it was the beer talking, but he got all interested when I told him I could put the job on my grad-school apps."

"Grad-school apps?" Harper squealed. "You said that? That's brilliant! Absolutely brilliant."

"Thanks. Since school just started, I figured I had a good shot. Hey, did you hear the latest about Elizabeth Sullivan?"

She didn't exactly want to change the subject, but then maybe Harper wouldn't regress to the skater dude behind the counter again.

"You mean Libby? No. What's up?"

"The school newspaper did a story about it." She found the column when she pulled the scrap of newsprint from *Introduction to Literary Theory*. "They said she overdosed on prescription drugs. Cops don't have proof yet, of course, but that's what they're saying."

"Yeah, but our school's paper isn't exactly the *New York Times*. I bet the writers make stuff up like that all the time."

"Maybe. But it's kind of interesting, don't you think? And it makes sense. Those girls can definitely afford anything they want. I never pictured them doing the hard stuff, though."

"Guess so. Hey, my mom's calling me to pick up the dishes. She made meatloaf for dinner tonight. *Gggrrrroooosss.* Anyway...I missed you at tryouts today."

"Yeah. About that—"

"It's okay. Hardly anyone came. The place was deserted. Oh, well...their loss. *Ciao!*"

Harper barely let her say goodbye before the line went dead. It took Skye a moment to run through their conversation. She always needed a second to replay their talks in her head. Time to sift through the information and figure out what was important and what wasn't.

Harper said something about meatloaf, right? Skye yelped and wiggled out of the kid-sized chair in her room. She'd forgotten all about dinner, and she needed to get the pizza in the oven. Especially since it cost them three times as much as one they could buy down the street. Maybe she'd even explain the Whole Foods/whole paycheck joke to her dad while they ate it.

Chapter Ten

Reef

Something about the new girl stayed with him, even after she left the lock shop and headed back to wherever she came from.

He liked the chunky glasses and the reddish hair and the way she didn't apologize for knowing how to figure out the sales tax.

She was definitely different from most of the girls he knew. He thought about her as he cruised home after work and then again when he stashed his longboard in the family's four-car garage. Since his sociology classes didn't start until next week, he could work a full eight-hour shift and still be home in time for dinner.

Thursday night was chicken curry—one of his favorites—so he hurried into the formal dining room as his father bowed his head to pray.

As usual, Reef faked it after the very first *Om*, and then he kicked his little sister's feet until Dad's eyes popped open again.

"You look happy, Raynesh." His father passed him a heaping plate of chapatis.

"Guess so." He hungrily stabbed his fork into the flatbread. "I met someone new at work today. A girl from my college."

Uh-oh. The minute he mentioned it, he wanted to take it back. He knew better than to mention a chick to his parents, no matter how much or how little time he spent with her.

"Reef's in love," his little sister, Sammy, already chimed in.

"Do not tease your brother, Samaira." Dad scowled at her. "We want to hear what he has to say about this girl. Go ahead."

Reef took his time answering. The last time he mentioned a girl to his parents, they had him married off by dessert. Even if it was only some chick he tutored in basic algebra and saw maybe five times. That didn't stop his parents from picking out a wedding date and asking about the girl's family tree.

He couldn't mention a female anytime, anywhere, without getting a full-on lecture about how important it was to choose a good wife. His parents' way, of course.

"Well, Raynesh?" His mother looked as hopeful.

Their fondest wish was for him to date one of their friends' daughters. Girls with names like Aadhira. Pallavini. Kaashi. Names that *meant* something. Even if those girls wouldn't look at him when they spoke or they giggled compulsively when he tried to teach them what "annulus" meant in algebra.

Not like Skye. Skye was different. She looked him straight in the eyes when they talked. He even liked the sound of her voice, so he pretended to drum a song on the counter while she spoke to Mr. Jacks. He didn't want them to think he was eavesdropping on their conversation. Which he was, of course.

"Raynesh?" His father's tone brought him back to the present. "We want to hear about this girl you met. Where is your mind tonight?"

Reef kicked Sammy's ankle extra hard—just in case—to prevent another wisecrack. "It's no one. Just some girl I met at the store."

"It doesn't sound like no one. Coconut?" His mother held out the plate like a bribe.

"Okay, fine. Her name's Skye and she's gonna start working there next week."

"Skye? What kind of a name is Skye?" The plate of coconut stalled in the air as his mother considered it.

"You'd have to meet her," he said. "The name fits."

"We would like to meet her," his father said. "Very much. Where is she from?"

That was the question he'd been dreading. It was code for whether the girl was from India or not. Odds were good she wasn't with a name like Skye, but his dad always hoped for the best.

"Texas, I think." He took some coconut so his mother could finally lower the plate. "I don't know yet. We didn't get to talk that much."

"Texas?" His father frowned. "Those Texas girls are very bold. They speak their minds."

Which was exactly what Reef liked about her, but he couldn't tell his dad that. "Not everyone in America is the same, Dad. That's just being racist."

"Do not speak to your father like that, Raynesh." His mother finally lowered the plate. "We did not raise you to talk back to your elders."

This conversation was going downhill fast. He couldn't say anything, anytime, when it came to his friends, or even some new chick he'd just met. It always ended up in a fight. It played out the same way every time, and every time he swore he wouldn't get sucked into the drama again.

"Whatever, Mom." He shoved some chicken into his mouth and rose from the table. "Kenny's waiting for me. I gotta go. He's driving us to the skate park."

When she started to protest, his father silenced her with a wave. "Let the boy go. At least we know where he is."

Reef jammed out of the dining room and grabbed his longboard before Dad could change his mind. His parents had found a way to ruin his favorite meal: pounce on the first thing he said about a chick and then drive it into the ground until there was nothing left to say. It happened all the time, and every time he swore he wouldn't fall for it again.

Only, this time was different. This time, he actually cared.

Chapter Eleven

Skye

S pace City Lock Shoppe was empty on Monday when she walked through the doorway for her very first shift.

A brass bell clanged in the background as the panel shut, which she hadn't noticed the week before. She waited, but no one came from the back to greet her, so she pretended to study a display of fake rocks called Hide-a-Key.

This is awkward. Maybe she should walk over to the safes so she had something else to look at until they finally noticed her.

The first safe she came to was the size of a textbook, probably made to fit in a dresser drawer. The next one up was more like a microwave, followed by one that reminded her of a mini-fridge the other day. She moved closer to that one—about as tall as her hip—and read the label. Factory fire rating: one hour. Heat rating: three-hundred-and-fifty degrees. Above the label was a bright pink sticker that screamed, "Hot Deal!"

When someone finally came into the showroom, she turned. It wasn't Mr. Jacks, though. He was about the same age, but he was skinny, and he stared at her as if she was an alien.

"Can I help you?" He sounded pissed, like maybe she shouldn't be there.

"I'm looking for Mr. Jacks. He told me to come to work today. I was supposed to be here at three." She nodded at a bald-faced clock over the counter, where the hands pointed at twelve and three.

The skinny old guy didn't say anything. But he eyeballed her, as if trying to make up his mind about something.

"Today's my first day," she offered.

"That so? Funny, but the boss didn't say anything about you."

"Oh. He was supposed to. He told me I'd be helping customers, doing the cash register, that kind of thing."

Come to think of it, Mr. Jacks never told her exactly what she'd be doing. She just assumed that was the kind of stuff a cashier would do.

"We already have a kid who works here." The guy nodded at the clock, too. "Only he's late again. We sure as hell don't need someone else hanging around and getting in the way."

She dropped her new backpack to the ground. "Look. I don't know what to tell you, mister…" Her voice faltered when the stranger didn't supply his name. "Mister whatever-your-name-is. He told me to be here at three. If you don't believe me, give him a call."

"That won't be necessary." Mr. Jacks walked into the room, thank God. He must've slipped through a side doorway.

"Girl says she works here." The grumpy guy with a bad attitude nodded at Skye.

"Back off, Ted." Mr. Jacks smiled at her warmly. "What are you gonna do? Old Ted here is kind of possessive when it comes to this place. He doesn't like outsiders, if you couldn't tell."

She faked a smile for Mr. Jacks's benefit. "Really? I thought it was just me."

"You're funny, kid." He pushed past the creepy guy named Ted and motioned for her to follow him. "Now, don't just stand there. You can put your backpack under the counter. I've got cameras everywhere, so you don't have to worry about anyone ripping off your stuff."

Skye did as he asked, and then she skirted around the counter without coming anywhere near the old guy named Ted.

"Let's go to my office." Mr. Jacks waved her over as he stepped through a doorway she hadn't noticed before. Maybe because it was painted the same color as the walls: a flat, taupe-y gray that reminded her of the gym at Immaculate Word.

Once she stepped into the guy's office, which was only a little bigger than the pantry back at her house, Mr. Jacks pulled some papers from a filing cabinet and tossed them at her. She sank into a cloth chair with duct-taped arms and waited for him to hand over a pen, too.

She filled out the forms as best she could before she handed them back. "Here you go. All done."

He didn't look so hot today. Sure, he seemed tired when he offered her the job Friday, but now his eyes were bloodshot, too. And his fingers! She was surprised he could hold the papers at all, what with the shaking. *Maybe he's sick or something.*

"Are you okay, Mr. Jacks?" She kept aspirin in her backpack, and what if he needed one?

He shot her a funny look. "Why would you ask that?"

"I don't know. My dad's a doctor, so I keep medicine in my bag."

"Interesting." He didn't look interested, though, to be honest. "What kind?"

"General practitioner. He's at the urgent care center by the freeway. Just started a few months ago." She stopped herself. She'd already said too much.

"No, I meant what kind of medicine do you keep in your bag?"

"Oh. Aspirin. Two kinds. And some Aleve, I think."

"That's okay. But your dad's a doctor, huh? I go to Southwest med center. Geez, I hate that place." He motioned for her to pass him the pen and his left hand shook as much as his right. "I have to go there today, as a matter of fact."

"You could, uh, have some aspirin, if you want." Skye blindly reached for the backpack, ready to offer him a Bayer, when she realized it wasn't with her. "I forgot. My backpack's under the counter. Want me to get you one?"

"Nah, that's okay. I'm seeing my doc at four. Listen. I need you to do something for me."

"Sure." Thank goodness they'd moved past the topic of her dad. That was a big botch on her part. What if he wanted to know why Dad wasn't working at the med center anymore?

"Watch out for my other new hire, will ya?" Mr. Jacks asked. "I'm doing his dad a favor, but I don't really want him anywhere near my office. Especially not when I'm gone."

Skye tilted her head. "Okay. I guess so." It was a weird thing to ask, since she was supposed to be helping people out front. "But what if he comes back here when I'm helping a customer in the front of the store?"

"Do your best. Usually, I'd just lock the place up. But I busted my doorknob a few weeks ago, and I haven't gotten around to fixing it."

"Seriously? Don't you have, like, a billion different locks in the store?"

"I know, I know. Anyway, make sure the other kid doesn't touch anything. He's supposed to help out Ted and work in the stockroom. That's it."

"Got it." *Better him than me.* After what she'd seen of Ted, she wanted nothing to do with him, and he seemed to feel the same way about her. "What should I do when you're gone? I don't know how to work the cash register yet. I could YouTube it, though."

Finally, she got another smile out of him. "You kids and your computers. If you get in a pickle, just holler for Ted or Albert. They'll know what to do."

He gave her a look like maybe they were done for now, so she slowly rose from the duct-taped chair. He looked even worse from this perspective. The overheads highlighted the bruised skin around his eyes and turned his skin blue-black.

"Okay. Don't worry about anything. I've got this." She backed out of the office.

By the time she got to the counter, Reef was standing there. She almost ran into him and his longboard, which he held against his leg. He'd changed out of the flannel shirt and now wore a white T-shirt, just like her.

"Hey!" She glanced up in time to see the crooked grin.

"Hey, yourself. I saw your backpack, so I knew you were here. My name's Reef."

He stuck out his hand. The skin was smooth and dark, and it felt warm when their palms touched. Harper would have a field day when she told her about it.

"I know who you are." Skye quickly released his hand. "I heard Mr. Jacks use your name the other day." She awkwardly shoved some hair behind her ear. She'd come straight to the shop after class, and she probably looked wretched. For once, she wished she would've tucked a mirror into her backpack instead of a laminated copy of the periodic table of elements.

"Hope he didn't tell you anything else about me. That guy thinks I'm a real dolt."

"No, he doesn't," she lied. "He just said you'd be working in the back and I'd be out front." And that little part about how Reef wasn't supposed to go anywhere near Mr. Jacks's office. But she didn't have to mention that.

"So, your name's Skye?"

"Yeah." She didn't remember telling him that. "You already know where I go to school. What about you?"

"I'm a sociology major. I go to Immaculate Word, too."

That made sense, given the custom skateboard, bougie jeans, and expensive dental work. He definitely didn't look like a candidate for Houston Community College.

"I knew it," she said. "You fit the type."

"Type? What type?"

"You know...preppy. Lots of money. Probably travel around the world."

He grinned. "You go to the same school I do."

"Yeah, but I'm on scholarship."

That seemed to make him pause. "Well, I should probably get going. I need to get back to the stockroom before I get busted."

"Ok. See you around."

He casually sauntered away, trailed by the awesome scent of Paco Rabanne. Maybe keeping an eye on this Reef guy wouldn't be such a bad deal, after all. Maybe Mr. Jacks did her a favor and he didn't even know it.

Chapter Twelve

Reef

Did the new chick just sniff me?

Reef grinned as he cruised to the stockroom. He liked the strawberry-blonde hair. And the Bruno Mars glasses. She wore Vans with her jeans today, which was a definite plus.

Too bad he couldn't see her tits. That was the thing about these granola chicks. They all wore their T-shirts two sizes too big. Like maybe they were trying to hide something, or whoever bought the shirt was.

The rest of her looked good, anyway. Not too skinny. And the Vans looked lived in. Girls like her usually wore name brands that cost about as much as a new longboard. But not this one. *Definitely some possibilities there.*

He couldn't help but smile as he dropped the Yocaher to the ground and yanked on a chain in the stockroom. Yellow light spilled across the concrete and lapped at a box of Hammermill paper. It looked like someone tried to clean up the place at one point, because the shelf's first row looked reasonably straight. A line-up of locks and lock parts, with a few old owners manuals thrown in.

The vision of Skye faded as he worked his way through the shelf nearest the ground.

He spent an hour dumping out boxes and putting crap back where it belonged before he finally checked his cell. It was close to five, and last week Mr. Jacks took a smoke break right about then.

Reef got off the floor and moved into the hall. He passed Mr. Jacks's door, which was closed, before he stepped into the showroom. Skye sat hunched over a MacBook Pro at the end of the counter.

"Hey. Whatcha watchin'?"

She jumped about a foot in the air. "Oh, my gosh! Don't scare me like that!"

"Sorry."

She swatted his arm, but she seemed more surprised than mad. Like she didn't expect to see anyone in the showroom, especially not him.

"Didn't mean to scare you. Is the boss man smoking a cigarette out back?"

She clicked off the video and closed the notebook. "No, he's not. He had a doctor's appointment at four. Said he'll be back in an hour."

"Okay." He glanced at the computer. "You weren't watching porn on that thing, were you?"

"What? No!" She looked mortified, which was kind of cute. "I wanted to find some videos on how to work the cash register. It's called a Royal Five-Eight-Seven, apparently."

"Find any?" It never occurred to him to do that Friday, which would've made the day go by a whole lot faster.

"Yeah. I was right in the middle of watching one on YouTube. It's super easy."

"Don't let me interrupt." Reef threw up his hands and stepped away from the counter. It seemed like everyone else was busy around the shop, so maybe now he could finally check out the computer in the old man's office.

"I gotta go back to work," he said. "The stockroom's a mess. You wouldn't believe all the crap in there."

He purposely grinned to show her his dimples. They were his secret weapon in the war with women. Thanks be to God, or Krishna, or whoever else happened to stamp folds into his cheeks before he was born, he had dimples like Adam Levine.

"See ya." He turned around and walked away, pretty sure she'd check out his ass when he did that.

He took his time strolling to Mr. Jacks's office. Another guy who worked there—Albert—had already left on a house call and that weirdo named Ted sat in his usual place, cutting a key, so he wouldn't be a problem. He tried the doorknob when he reached Mr. Jacks's office and the panel swung wide open. Considering the guy owned a lock shop, he didn't seem too concerned with security.

Reef ditched around the door and headed for the desk. His boss worked on a big Compaq, circa nineteen-eighty. Made of so much molded plastic, it was hard to know where to look first. A thick band of it framed the monitor, a triangle of plastic popped out the back, and the keyboard stretched on and on. Oh...and the computer came with an actual CPU. A CPU! The guy needed a serious upgrade.

He felt like a Marine in the video game Halo as he reached for the keyboard. Like dust might explode from the spacebar if he so much as touched it.

Where to start? He studied the desk for a clue as to the guy's password, but it didn't offer much help. On it were a Houston Texans' stress ball, a small desk calendar from last year, and an ashtray filled with quarters, since the guy smoked outside. No personal pictures. Most people had at least one picture on their desk, didn't they? His dad kept five on his desk in his study, with six more on the walls.

Reef gazed at the desktop again, which was shiny-clean under the clutter. Even though his boss's personal life was a mess, his stuff sure wasn't.

Looked like he'd have to go with the Texans connection to figure out the password. So, Reef carefully typed player J.J. Watt's name onto the screen and immediately got an error message. The same thing happened with Reliant Stadium and Toro, the team's rank mascot. *Nothing.* On a whim, he tried Space City, H-Town and genejacks01. Blocked every time. His boss was more creative than he thought.

Just when he was about to give up, he glanced sideways, at the door where an old filing cabinet, the same gray as the underside of his Yocaher, stood. Someone had yanked open the second drawer and forgot to close it. Maybe the guy kept hardcopies in there, since Reef couldn't figure out the Compaq's password. It wouldn't hurt to check, and Mr. Jacks wasn't due back for a while, according to Skye.

He quickly shifted over to the cabinet. If his dad wanted to know about the shop's finances, it seemed like as good a place as any to start.

First up was a thick wad of papers from State Farm Insurance, including a fancy certificate edged in gold. He rifled past the insurance policy to the next folder, which had "FICA" scrawled across the top. Apparently, Mr. Jacks wasn't a fan of the alphabet, since everything was out of order.

He wouldn't learn anything from the employee withholding forms, so he moved on. Just past the FICA information hung another folder labeled IRS. *Score.* He carefully pulled out the forest-green folder, as if it might detonate in his hand.

He brought the papers to the desk and placed them on the keyboard. Nothing sounded in the narrow shop but the low-pitched whine of the key-cutter, so he flicked the folder open and pulled out the first sheet in the line-up.

It was the guy's Form 1040. Right there. Right in front of him, plain as day. He'd seen enough of his dad's tax forms to know what he was looking at.

Every March, without fail, his dad shoved a boxful of receipts into his arms and begged Reef to do his income taxes. Not because he couldn't do them himself, but because he thought it would be good for Reef to do them. Teach him something he called *"shik-shit,"* or something that sounded like that.

It was a pain in the ass, but Reef knew he could turn those wadded-up receipts into a brand-new longboard if he finished his dad's taxes on time. He never complained, and he never thought he'd be able to use the information again.

Now, here he was, staring at someone else's 1040. With a practiced eye, his gaze fell on a line halfway down the page. The line that recorded a business's income or loss. His finger jogged right, until it reached the end column. Apparently, the store earned Mr. Jacks more than two-and-a-half-million bucks the year before.

"What are you doing in here?"

Skye's voice cracked like a whip. She stood just inside the doorway with a huge frown.

"Uh...I'm not doing anything."

"Really? It doesn't look like nothing. You're not supposed to be in here."

"I, uh, had to find a form. An order form. Mr. Jacks asked me to get a part. So, you know, I need a form."

She shot him a funny look, like she couldn't decide whether to believe him or not. "Well, you should get out of here anyway. Mr. Jacks will be back soon. He'll kill me if he knows you were in his office."

"Sure. No problem. I was just leaving." He grabbed the folder from the keyboard and rose. "I couldn't find what I was looking for, anyway."

He felt her eyes on his back as he moved across the room, toward the filing cabinet. She sounded much too angry to check out his ass now, and he didn't even bother with the dimples.

What was the point? She busted him, fair and square. Hopefully, she had no idea why he was in the guy's office to begin with. And why he wanted to check out the guy's tax form.

A tax form with five zeroes, by the way. All on account of a dinky lock shop in a rundown strip center. The line of zeroes danced before his eyes as he returned the folder to its rightful place.

For somewhere so small, Space City Lock Shoppe held a lot of secrets.

* * *

By the time Reef got back to the stockroom, he could barely breathe.

Skye probably thought he was mental. The way she frowned at him, like she'd caught him checking out the *Sports Illustrated* swimsuit edition or reading his cousin's Victoria's Secret catalog, took his breath away. Like she was the boss and not some chick who started working at the shop about the same time he did.

On Friday, he thought maybe she was into him. Maybe she dug the dimples and hair and retro Yocaher with the flaming grip tape. But what if he was wrong?

At least she didn't notice the breathing. The way his breath turned quick and shallow the minute she caught him with the folder. For some reason, he couldn't suck enough oxygen into his lungs after that. Like his body forgot what to do, and then his heart beat twice as fast to make up for it.

He knew the signs by now. He'd experienced enough anxiety attacks in middle school to know what one felt like.

It all began when his family came to America. They shipped him off to a private prep school, where he slumped behind a desk and ignored the pale faces all around him. Maybe if he pretended not to notice his new classmates, they'd do the same.

Later, when he opened a makeshift container of curry in the lunchroom, a fat kid sitting next to him took one whiff and pretended to faint. That set off the whole table. Kids everywhere plugged their noses and gagged, as if Reef had opened a stink bomb in the middle of the cafeteria, instead of his mom's special *murgh kari* with parsley sprinkles.

He threw his lunch away, and every lunch after that for at least a month, until his dad finally noticed something was wrong.

"What has happened to you, Raynesh?" his father asked as they ate breakfast one Saturday morning. "You've dropped two kilograms since the start of school. And now you eat like a Preta. Like you will never be full again."

"I don't know." Reef slurped his fourth bowl of Coco Pops. "Maybe I just like cereal."

"Maybe. But I think it is something else. The move, perhaps? I know this has been hard on you. It has been hard on everyone. You just have to be brave."

Brave? Reef was the only one who had to watch a dozen schoolkids thrash on the ground as if they were dying in the cafeteria, and nothing could be worse than that.

But then again, Dad didn't seem too happy, either. Not because he didn't like America, but because Reef didn't. And whenever his father felt guilty about something, he always offered Reef a gift to make up for it.

"Now that I think about it, this reminds me of when you were a little boy," his father said. "You probably don't remember, but you had these terrible anxiety attacks whenever you had to go somewhere new. Your mother wouldn't let me give you medicine, of course. She was afraid it would stunt your growth."

He cast a wary glance at Reef. "But how tall are you now? Five-foot five? Six?"

"Seven," Reef said, proudly.

"Now, you are not too small for medicine." His father rose from the table. "Follow me. Why not? It's what they do in America."

"Are you talking about giving me aspirin or something?"

His father smiled. "Not quite. Let me show you."

Dad motioned for Reef to join him in the hall. Reef expected to be stopped short once they reached the master bedroom, since he'd never been invited inside before. But, no, his dad walked right into the room and motioned for Reef to follow, until they stood in the master bath, where his father opened one of the medicine cabinets.

With a smile, his dad pulled out a gallon-size Ziploc bag full of colorful packages.

"So many salesmen visit me. All with their rolling suitcases and fancy suits. It would be a shame to throw away their gifts." He churned through the bag of pharmaceutical samples; a sea of different colors and names.

Reef read the packages as they slipped through his father's fingers: Percocet. Oxycontin. Xanax. Things he'd never heard of before.

"Hmmm. Now, where is it?" His father finally stopped churning when he reached a certain package. "Aha! You are clearly suffering from anxiety attacks again. It is nothing to be ashamed about. Many people get them." He pulled a white box from the mix, slid his finger under the wrapper, and then he popped one of the pills through the tinfoil backing. An oblong pill gashed down the center appeared.

"Loss of appetite is a classic symptom. So, we will start you at point-twenty-five milligrams. You need to take it three times a day. I can always get more." His dad looked so serious Reef didn't dare question him. "It might take a few weeks for the medicine to work. Do not become discouraged. After a while, it *will* work."

Reef obediently took the pill and cupped it in his hand. He didn't want to disobey his dad. Like his father said, he needed to make a change.

By the next month, he didn't even notice when the fat kid next to him pretended to gag on his curry. In fact, they became best friends. After that, Reef gained back all the weight he'd lost, and then he discovered the skatepark and an even cooler crowd.

Before long, he leapfrogged three steps higher on the social ladder and became known for staying cool under pressure. He owed it all to a nondescript pill he took three times a day. And when he got tired of schlepping the pills to school, his father upped the dose so he only had to take one at night, which made it so much more convenient.

At some point, he stopped taking the medicine altogether. Instead of making a big deal out of it, though, he simply kept the unused stock under his bed, where no one would notice it. Just to be safe. What if the anxiety came back and he had to start all over again?

Only it didn't, and the pile of pill bottles grew and grew until they threatened to spill over onto the rug next to his bed.

Before long, he had a drugstore's worth of pharmaceutical samples stashed there. No one knew he was hoarding it. Not his dad, who would've taken the pills away. Or his mom, who hired someone else to clean their house, so she wouldn't have any reason to be in his bedroom in the first place.

It wasn't hurting anything, so what was the problem?

Chapter Thirteen

Gene

The fifth-floor waiting room at the medical center was crowded by the time Gene got there at four. Chilly and crowded. It looked like Dr. Fischer had bussed an entire wing of the local old folks' home to his office and propped them up in the lobby. Almost everyone had a walker, scooter, or one of those funny-looking things called a HurryCane close at hand.

The people in the chairs looked like soft piles of faded plaid with sensible shoes and matching Coke-bottle-bottom glasses. Most of the women hid behind dogeared copies of *Good Housekeeping* or *Southern Living*, while their spouses stared slack-jawed at a television set mounted to the ceiling.

He shuffled to a laminate counter with a leaded-glass window above it. A sheet of paper on a clipboard asked for his name and appointment time. If they'd just slide the window open, for gripe's sakes, they could ask him face to face. Then he wouldn't have to sign his name with a giant plastic sunflower taped to the end of a pen, which made him feel like a clown with the Ringling Bros. and Barnum & Bailey Circus.

Once he signed his John Hancock, he noticed the person ahead of him had arrived almost an hour early for his appointment. At least Gene had somewhere else to be. At least Gene had a job, and he didn't need to kill time in an over-air-conditioned office on the fifth floor of Medical Plaza One.

Hope that early bird likes what's on TV.

Gene dropped the pen with a clatter, and the window magically creaked open. A girl in maroon scrubs thrust another clipboard at him.

"Here. Take these." Her voice was flat. "And leave your driver's license and insurance card. We'll call you."

With that, the window slammed shut again and the face became a blurry outline behind leaded glass. He slowly turned and found the only chair left in the waiting room sat right beneath the television set. Did he really want people staring at him when they got tired of watching the screen? He didn't need that kind of attention today. Hell, he wasn't even sure he needed to come to the doctor's office at all.

The tremor, which began in his thumbs and gradually worked its way out, had been around for a while now. He tried to wish it away, but sometimes he couldn't avoid it. Like today, when the new kid stared at his fingers as he passed her a payroll withholding form. She looked like she wanted to say something, only she was too scared to speak up to the boss, which was just as well, because he didn't know what to say anyway. One day his thumbs felt normal, and the next day they didn't.

He reluctantly sat in the chair under the television screen. Maybe if he propped his ankle on the opposite leg, he could settle the forms in-between and get a little privacy that way. It seemed to work until he got to the Patient Consent Form and someone tapped his shoulder.

A lady next to him in a plaid shirtdress pointed to the floor. "You dropped something." Her soft voice reminded him of Marilyn's.

Sure enough, one of the forms had slipped between his legs and floated to the floor. He carefully bent over, mindful of the six-pack he'd polished off the night before.

"Thanks." He slowly straightened. "Thanks a lot."

He returned his attention to the patient privacy crap until a new girl—this one also in maroon scrubs— stuck her arm through the window.

"Mr. Jacks!" She waved his license and Cigna card in the air, as if he'd forgotten all about them.

That was the problem with places like this: it was *us* versus *them*. Workers hidden behind glass and patients forced to watch their shadows come and go. Orders barked and commands given, without so much as a please or thank you. No wonder people got crabby by the time they finally entered the inner sanctum.

Marilyn would hate this.

If there was anything good to say about her passing—anything at all—it was that she went quickly. She never had to endure a round of doctors' visits. Never had to shiver in a freezing-cold lobby in the middle of September, watching shadows come and go behind a leaded glass window. By the time they got her to the hospital, it was all over. Nothing to be done. One day she was there and the next day she wasn't, and they were all very sorry for his loss.

Although, she might've liked the pen.

He was coming up on twenty years without her, and still, it felt like yesterday. Gene folded his arms and dropped his chin to his chest, hoping sleep would take him away. The drone of the television grew soft as his eyelids fluttered closed. The next thing he knew, he was swimming in a giant pool of Louis Vuitton handbags. The purses floated by his head, swirled around his arms, and brushed across his feet. The rich smell of new leather filled his nose. Just when he wondered how much lower he could sink before he ran out of oxygen, someone called his name. He tried to answer—tried to speak up—but he couldn't find a breathing spot amid the leather. A hand reached through the darkness to help him, but instead of yanking anything away, it jostled his shoulder.

"Hello?" The voice sounded like Marilyn's again, but that couldn't be right. "Wake up, dear."

He opened his eyes to see his next-door neighbor smiling at him.

"It's your turn." She glanced sideways. "They're waiting for you."

He shook his head to clear the fog before he stumbled from the chair. The gal in maroon scrubs tapped her foot impatiently until he made it to the door. She motioned for him to enter the hall, and then she pointed to a fancy-schmancy scale bolted to the wall.

Too bad the scale was broken, because it showed he weighed ten pounds less than last time, and that couldn't be right. His blood pressure was normal, though, the gal told him, as she took off the Velcro strap. After that, there was nothing to do but sit in an exam room and stare at clouds that scuttled past a mirrored bank building across the way. At some point, he must've nodded off again, but he awoke when he heard a man's voice.

"Mr. Jacks?" Dr. Fischer bustled into the exam room, all business, as if he wanted to be on time for their appointment—he really did—only he couldn't get away from the pesky patients who stood in his way.

"Hi, Doc." Gene threw him a sleepy grin and gamely stuck out his hand. Say what you would about Dr. Fischer being late, but the guy had the world's firmest grip. Gene braced himself for the squeeze he knew was coming.

After shaking his hand, Dr. Fischer grew serious again. "What brings you in today?"

"Got a little problem." Strange, but the doctor's grip didn't feel nearly as firm that time. Maybe the doctor wasn't feeling well, either. "I know it sounds crazy, but I've got a little shake going on in my hands. And it's not from booze."

There. I said it. Now the doctor wouldn't blame Gene's problem on too much Miller Lite. Although he might lecture Gene about the drinking later, it wouldn't dominate the conversation right from the start.

"What do you mean, 'a little shake'?" The doctor looked dubious.

"My hands kinda have a mind of their own these days." It sounded crazy when he put it that way. "I mean, I can still do stuff, but it happens all the time now. To my feet, too."

Dr. Fischer frowned. He probably thought Gene had nothing better to do than waste his time with phony medical problems. As if Gene wanted to hang out in a chilly waiting room with soft piles of plaid.

"I see." At least the doctor didn't roll his eyes. "How long has this been going on?"

Gene shrugged. "A couple weeks?" It sounded like a question, not an answer. All he knew was that one day his fingers didn't shake, and the next day they did.

"Look, I want to run some tests." The doctor slowly unfurled a stethoscope from around his neck. "We'll start with a urine sample and blood panel."

He leaned forward and placed the cool stethoscope against Gene's chest. "There's another test I want to run, too. Can you stay for a while?"

"I guess?" He had to stop sounding so wishy-washy. If the doctor didn't think he was bonkers before, he would now. "Yes. I can stay. That's not a problem."

"Good. I'm going to test you with something called an electromyogram. It might sting a little, since we have to use needles, but I know you can handle it. Don't go anywhere."

Gene didn't want to be a smartass, but he couldn't help it. It had become painfully obvious who was calling the shots. "Guess I'll have to miss the flight to Tahiti, then. Seriously, Doc. Where am I supposed to go? You're the one giving orders."

"Good point." The doctor didn't even smile. He had something else on his mind; that much was clear. "I'll call for the technician. She'll explain the procedure. Once you go to the lab and leave some samples, it shouldn't take more than a half-hour or so."

Gene studied his feet. That sound didn't sound so bad. If he was lucky, he might even get another nap out of the deal.

"Whatever you say, Doc."

* * *

The final electrode hurt the most. It wasn't the sting of the needle that bothered him but the way his skin refused to lay flat afterward. The flesh puckered around the site, all prune-y and withered, as if it forgot how to be skin.

Once the technician applied a bandage, Gene carefully slipped off the exam table. The doctor wasn't kidding when he said it would hurt. Which was worse…the way the technician sewed needles through his soft flesh, just like Marilyn with a canvas and needlepoint thread, or the way the lady frowned at her screen afterward?

By the time it was all over, he didn't really care. He just wanted to leave the office building with its over-conditioned air and feel the sun on his shoulders again.

He climbed behind the wheel of the Tahoe and carefully took the steering wheel with crab claws. He couldn't work the blinker, so he hugged the right-hand lane all the way down the 610 Loop, while humidity thawed the chill from his bones. By the time he arrived at the lock shop, the parking lot had emptied and his hands no longer felt numb.

No telling where the new kid was, since he didn't see her car, bike, or anything else she might've used to get there. Unless she walked, that was. He cruised into the first available parking space, and then he gingerly stepped into the shop. The bell on the door jangled as he passed over the transom.

"Hello?"

The new girl sat the counter, all right, where she belonged. She jerked her head up at the sound. "You're back."

She quickly turned off a computer she'd been studying.

"Yeah. I'm back." He took his time walking over to her. He didn't expect to find her goofing off. "You're not watching porn on that thing, are you?"

"What? No. Of course not!"

"I'm just kidding." He picked up the pace, since she obviously didn't get the joke. "Just teasing you a little."

"Yeah, but you're the second person who's asked me that today." She frowned. "It must be a guy thing."

"Ted, huh?" Leave it to Ted to cause a sexual harassment lawsuit on the girl's very first day on the job. Maybe it was time to discuss workplace etiquette with him. "Sorry about Ted. He's not very good with people, if you haven't noticed."

"It wasn't him. It was Reef."

Even worse. "Anyway…what's been going on around here?" He started to motion with his hand, until he remembered the bandages.

"Oh, my God," she said. "What happened to your hand?"

"Nothing much. Some kind of test. I wasn't really paying attention. How did things go around here?"

"Pretty quiet. But you got a bunch of mail." She hopped from the stool and disappeared behind the counter. When she reappeared, she held some glossy flyers and a stack of number-ten envelopes.

She stared at his hand as she passed over the pile. "Did it hurt?"

"Nah." Then again, there was no reason to lie to her. "Okay, maybe a little. I'll get over it. Did you ever figure out how to work the cash register?"

"Um-hum. It wasn't that hard." She slid back onto the seat. "I didn't even mess up on my first customer."

"Good. That's good." He threw her a smile because he wanted to encourage her. Especially after that crack about the porn. "It's pretty easy once you get the hang of it. I'll show you how to do a return tomorrow."

"You were gone a lot longer than I thought you'd be. I tried to stay busy."

He glanced at the display counter between them. *No dust.* And the packages on the pegboard wall behind her head looked oddly symmetrical now.

"Did you color-code the luggage locks?"

"It seemed like a good idea." She spoke quickly, as if he really *had* caught her doing something wrong. "Should I change it back to the way it was? I don't mind. I should've asked you first."

"What? No. Of course not. They look great. So, what're you watching?"

She opened the laptop again and fired up the screen, which made him feel better. If she wanted to hide something, she wouldn't have done that.

"I found this video about locks and stuff," she said. "I was kinda messing with the safes back there. I hope you don't mind."

He glanced at the Amsecs along the wall. For the first time, he noticed how much they looked like a display of black GE refrigerators with the handles all turned the same way. "Really?"

"Yeah. I thought I'd dust them off, but then I started to play with them. Look, I even found a video on how to open a safe in ten minutes or less."

He groaned. *Of course.* Given a drill and a punch rod, any idiot could bore a hole in a safe to get at the contents. The trick was to crack a dial with your bare hands. And that took time. Sometimes, a lot of time.

"You actually watched a whole video about safecracking?" He studied her face to see if maybe she was lying. "Most teenagers couldn't care less, you know."

"I think safes are cool."

She didn't blink, and she didn't glance away, which meant she was telling the truth, after all. He'd never once heard someone her age express an interest in safes. Hell, even the HPD cops who worked with him didn't seem all that interested. Like it was no big deal he could open a lock without a key. That he could conjure the exact string of numbers to pop open a door, as if by magic. Rios didn't care. Boudreaux, either. Even Ted acted like it happened every day. Like any idiot could figure out how to crack a combination lock, which wasn't true.

He glanced at her laptop again. Sure enough, a time stamp on the video showed she'd been watching the thing for thirty minutes already.

"You're really interested in safes, huh?" He expected to see a music video or a candy-colored videogame, or whatever the hell kids watched nowadays on their computers.

"Of course. Who wouldn't be interested? I found a couple of videos when I was doing my homework." She clamped her hand over her mouth, as if she'd made a mistake.

"That's okay. I don't mind if you do your homework here. As long as you take care of the customers."

She dropped her hand. "Of course. And I even cleaned the bathroom, so I thought you wouldn't mind."

"Kid, if you cleaned that bathroom, I'll let you do anything else you want."

"I was hoping you'd say that. Anyway, I found another video when I was doing my homework. It's about a guy named Richard Feynman."

"Feynman? Didn't he have something to do with science?" Locks and safes Gene knew. Science...not so much.

"He did theoretical physics." Skye's voice was halting, as if she felt funny knowing something he didn't. "We had to study him last year. Anyway, he worked at Los Alamos during the war. The poor guy's wife died and he had a lot of time on his hands. That's when he taught himself how to crack a safe. He freaked everyone out by opening their file cabinets at night. Isn't that cool?"

She wasn't kidding; she really liked this stuff.

"Did you give it a whirl?" He jerked his head toward the closed Amsecs.

"Yeah. It's harder than it looks."

"That's an understatement." She might know all about Richard Feynman, but he knew everything there was to know about manipulating a dial. "Maybe I'll give you a lesson tomorrow. You can even read this tonight."

He tossed her a brochure from the mail pile. He'd noticed it right away when she forked over the stack.

"What is it?"

"It's from a group I belong to, called the Associated Locksmiths of America. You might want to check out some stuff in there."

"Thanks. I'll read it when I get home. Anything else you want me to do? We still have an hour to go before closing."

"Nah, you're good." He glanced around the store again. "I think you've done enough for one day. And it sounds like you still have some homework to do."

She threw him a grateful smile and hopped off the barstool. Once she shut the computer down and stuffed it in her backpack, she headed for the door. "See you tomorrow," she called over her shoulder.

"Hey, Skye?"

"Yeah?" When she turned, the backpack slipped from her shoulder and thumped her in the chest. It was a miracle the thing didn't knock her right off her feet.

"Feel free to invite your parents to visit sometime," he said. "I'd like to meet 'em."

"Of course. I'll ask them. No problem." She swung open the door and disappeared into the night.

He watched her leave, still impressed by her interest in safes. Skye really was different from any other college kid he knew. And *that* was a good thing.

Chapter Fourteen

Skye

She flopped against the cinderblock wall outside the shop the minute she made it through the plate-glass doorway. *Why does he care so much about my parents?* The backpack dug into her spine, but she barely noticed. She wanted him to forget all about her mom and dad.

What did he expect her to say? The last time she tried to contact her mom was five years ago? It was the truth. It happened right after her grandmother slipped up and mentioned her mother was living in a place called the Star of Hope Mission on Reed Road. That was before the alimony kicked in, apparently, and her mom was desperate to get away.

Skye decided right then and there to write her mother a letter. She carefully tore a piece of paper from her Guns N' Roses notebook, and then she calligraphed the words in her best handwriting. She even doodled some hearts and stars on the front of the envelope when she was done.

She did all that work, only to have a mailman scribble through the doodles and send it back: *Moved. No known forwarding address.*

She couldn't ask Dad about it, not with the way he shut down after Mom left. He told Skye in no uncertain terms she should never, ever, try to contact her mother. No phone calls, no letters, and certainly no babysitting money stuffed into a calligraphed envelope. He wouldn't even let her send Mom a little something for the woman's fortieth birthday. Now, *that* was harsh.

He called her mother "crazy." As in, "Your mother's gone totally crazy. I should cut the alimony and be done with it." That was what he said. He could've told her that her mom needed to "find herself," or she had to take a break from being a parent for a while, or maybe she ran off and joined the circus. Anything. He should've lied, instead of telling her the truth.

What fifteen-year-old wanted to hear the truth? It only confirmed what Skye already knew: her mother left because of her.

Mom was supposed to join the Navy and see the world. At least, that was what she always said whenever she faced a sink full of dirty dishes and a farsighted kid at the dinner table.

Never mind her mother couldn't swim, let alone dog-paddle, and she freaked out the one and only time they rented a paddleboat at Hermann Park. It happened only a few minutes into the ride when her mom's anxiety kicked into high gear. She yelled at Skye to get them back to shore. *Now.* Her face matched the boat's whitewashed hull by the time they got back to land. In fact, her mother could barely hold her hands steady to drive them home.

In other words, her mother traded a shiny future for a mother-daughter outing with a farsighted kid she didn't necessarily like.

Once her mom mentioned the Navy, there was no taking it back. Skye fell asleep at night and dreamt she was a giant, rusty anchor tied around her mother's neck. An anchor wearing chunky black glasses, something her mom desperately wanted to jettison over the side and be done with.

How could Skye begin to explain all that to Mr. Jacks? He'd think *she* was mental. Or worse, he'd feel sorry for her. It was bad enough when the counselor at her high school found out about it. The day word got out about Skye's mom, Mrs. Tinsdale—the one everyone else called Mrs. *Titsdale*—stared at her as they passed in the hall. The look she gave Skye was pure pity, complete with pursed lips and slanted brows. Which the counselor probably thought telegraphed her concern. Only it didn't. It only made her look constipated.

Maybe it wouldn't have been so bad if Dad had been the one to leave. *I mean, come on...who spends every single day with two people and then just takes off without saying goodbye?* No note. No phone call. No forwarding address.

Nothing. The only reason Skye found out about the Star of Hope Mission on Reed Road was because of her grandmother.

Skye humped the backpack higher and set off down the sidewalk. She'd just have to lie again. Tell Mr. Jacks her parents had demanding careers that didn't leave room for anything else. It was true of her dad, at least.

Other than that, everything was cool at the store today. She didn't even mind taking a scrubber full of Clorox to the toilet bowl and wiping away brown stains from the lid. Or scraping mold from the bolts that anchored it to the ground.

It helped that someone went into the bathroom ahead of her and stuck a Glade Plug-in onto the wall. Whoever did it chose red honeysuckle, which smelled way better than guy piss.

She finally rounded the corner before her house and spotted Dad's silver Volvo bathed in moonlight on the driveway. She heaved open the front door and scuttled through it before the thing could crush her in its maw.

"That you, muffin?" Dad's voice pinballed down the hall.

"Sure is." She dropped her stuff by the door and kicked off the Vans. "What're you doing home early?"

"Thought I'd catch up on my notes. How was your day?" He sat at the counter again, the top of his glasses barely visible above the Dell.

"Good. Really good. Did you eat all the pizza?"

The glasses seesawed back and forth. "Nah. There's still some in the fridge. So, sit down and tell me all about your first shift." He shut the notebook with a *click* and glanced at her expectantly.

Whoa. So, this was what it felt like to have his undivided attention. Whenever he glanced away from his notes—even for a moment—she felt like a patient again. But this time, it felt good. Surprisingly good. She knew she had his full and undivided attention. It might last only for a moment, but, for that moment, he was all hers.

"Well, I sold a few things at the shop." She quickly moved to the counter, since the clock was ticking. "Nothing big. Just a remote control and a Quickset. And I got to check out the safes. The store has a bunch of 'em."

"Safes?" For some reason, Dad looked surprised, as if a lock shop shouldn't carry those.

"Yeah. You know…really fancy safes. You would've loved it."

"That so." He nodded at the fridge. "How about you grab us some Pilsners?"

"Sure thing." She pried open the refrigerator and reached for two Gaffels on the bottom shelf, plus a leftover piece of pizza.

"Here you go." She pulled out the bottles first. Next came an opener and the food, which looked stone-cold but still edible. "I saw this really cool video about safes and stuff when I was doing my homework. Did you know Richard Feynman learned how to crack a safe back when he worked at Los Alamos?"

Unlike Mr. Jacks, she didn't have to wonder if her father knew who she was talking about. She inherited her math skills from his side of the family, while the musical stuff came from her mom's.

"Wasn't Feynman too busy building nukes?" Her dad popped the top off his Gaffel and took a swig.

"He had a lot of time on his hands. His wife died when he was out there. So, he figured out the math. That's what's so amazing. He knew there were a million possible combos on a standard lock, but he brought that number down to a hundred and eighty-seven. You know…because every dial has a plus or minus tolerance of two numbers."

Dad looked amused. "Well, that makes sense. You sound pretty excited about this."

"I mean, who wouldn't be? It's all about math. I love this stuff."

"Do I have to worry about you breaking into my safe now?"

"*You* have a safe?"

"Of course I do." He sounded so blasé about something he had never mentioned before.

"Can I see it?"

"Tell me about Feynman first."

"Well, he used to break into other people's file cabinets." She spoke quickly, in case he changed his mind about the safe. "He snuck into their offices. He just wanted to see if he could do it."

"And I'm guessing he could."

"Oh, yeah. He asked other guys for their birthdays, their anniversaries, anything they could use for a three-digit combo. He knew people were too lazy to memorize three random numbers if they didn't have to."

"I thought safes came with a preprogrammed code." Her dad took another long, slow pull from the beer. "I thought new ones have a number already built-in."

"Some do, but some ask you to program in three random numbers. And people usually pick ones that mean something to them."

"Did you learn anything else today?"

She finished a mouthful of pizza before answering. It wasn't half bad, given it was three days old and made with sucky ingredients. "Just that the default combination is usually twenty-five, fifty, twenty-five. That's what a lot of people use, since it's so easy to remember."

Her dad smiled again. "No, I didn't mean that. I wanted to know if you learned anything else new at the shop today."

"Oh." Come to think of it, she'd been so busy talking about safes, she couldn't remember anything else. "No, I don't think so. I think I thrilled my boss when I cleaned the bathroom. Don't think that happens very often."

"You cleaned a bathroom? I'd be thrilled, too."

"Subtle, Dad. I didn't forget. But I've still got homework to do. And Mr. Jacks gave me a brochure to read. He belongs to some group called the Associated Something-Something. He thought I'd be interested in it."

"You know I'm only kidding about my safe, right?" he said. "I don't mind if you try to break into it sometime. Knock yourself out."

"Seriously?"

"Of course. It's on the floor of my bedroom closet. Have at it."

"Thanks, Dad." She waited for him to take another gulp of beer. He tossed off that last sentence as if it meant nothing to him. "Can I try it now?"

"Sure. I just started working, so I won't need my room anytime soon."

She gobbled the rest of her food, soggy cheese and all, before she dumped the plate in the trash. Axl trailed behind her as she hurried down the hall. As soon as they reached the master bedroom, she flicked on the light and skirted around the unmade bed.

Dad was a slob, too. He washed his clothes often enough, but he never got around to folding them, so clean shirts puddled at the foot of his bed like mismatched sheets.

She opened the closet door and peered inside. Sure enough, an ancient beige Sentry sat on the ground. She scooted over to it and dropped to her knees. An old gym bag blocked the way, so she shoved it aside. Whatever was inside the bag rattled like crazy, but she was too interested in the safe to care.

"Hey, Axl. Watch this." She blew on the safe's dial and dust billowed up like a thundercloud.

The cat rewarded her with a yawn, clearly unimpressed. She moved closer to the safe to get a better look. It seemed solid, impenetrable. It was one thing to fiddle around with a brand-new safe at work, when she knew it was empty. But this was different. This one could hold anything. *Anything*. Maybe her dad kept a secret wad of cash or a fake passport or a life insurance policy he didn't want her to know about.

Then again, he never would've mentioned it if he had something to hide.

Either way, she was up to the challenge. It was like finding a Christmas present perfectly wrapped in shiny silver paper. Dying to know what was inside but tickled to keep it a secret, too.

She took a deep breath and stared at the safe. That was what Feynman did, as if he had X-ray vision that could burn through three layers of tempered steel.

All that stuff about putting her ear against the safe's door? Pure Hollywood. It might've looked cool on a movie screen, but there was no way a person could hear anything through tempered steel, no matter what a screenwriter thought. Especially not a faint *plink* when the right number triggered a lever.

She reverently touched the dial. The safe seemed ancient. So old, she had to force it around to clear the numbers. Unlike the new safes at work, this one jerked from number to number. On the fourth time around, she slowed her hand and let the numbers crawl by.

Two seconds later, it happened. A tiny movement, almost imperceptible, yet impossible to ignore. She yelped and turned to Axl. "Oh, my God! I felt it."

It was like finding the right note on her flute. Like placing her fingers on the Bundy just so, until the right key made the right sound at just the right moment.

Maybe all those flute lessons weren't such a waste of time, after all. Those hours she spent in the practice room at Woodridge Elementary, playing scales over and over, moving her fingers higher and higher up the register, when all she wanted to do was shove the Bundy back in its case and go outside to play.

It was all in the fingers. She couldn't exactly stomp on the flute's keys and expect it to do what she wanted. So, she learned to quiet her hands and make them listen to her brain. Anticipate the next move in her subconscious. It took her forever to learn how to do that. But once she did, she forgot all about the monkey bars, the jungle gym, and the freedom outside the walls of the practice studio. Too absorbed in learning how to conjure something beautiful out of nothing to care about anything else.

"Hey, Skye!"

She jumped at the sound. The noise surprised even Axl, who stiffened.

"Yeah, Dad?" She knew her father hated to yell—probably because it reminded him of all those fights with Mom—but she was right in the middle of something important.

"Harper's on the phone," he hollered.

She sat back with a sigh. She hadn't spoken to Harper all day. No doubt Harper wanted to hear about her first day at work. "Coming."

She shooed Axl from the closet, and then she followed him into the hall. By the time she reached the kitchen, her dad had placed the phone sideways on the counter.

"What gives?" He must've pulled the phone from her backpack.

"Your cell rang, so I answered it. Sorry."

He didn't look sorry, but she grabbed the phone anyway and turned around. "Hi, Harper."

"Skye...I'm so glad you're home!"

"Yeah, my boss let me go early." She moved down the hall again, but this

79

time Axl didn't follow her.

"So, how was it? Your first day at work, I mean."

"It was fine. No problem. I could do that job in my sleep." When she reached her bedroom, she flopped onto the unmade bed and wiggled a pillow under her head. "I figured out how to work the cash register, so I totally know what to do."

"And?"

"And I did some other stuff when Mr. Jacks had to leave for a while. By the way, you're wrong about him. He's not a creeper. Even though he did ask me if I was watching porn on my computer."

"He asked that? I thought you couldn't say stuff like that anymore."

She could picture Harper grimacing. "He was only kidding. The cute guy said the same thing. I think they were trying to be funny."

"That's why I'm calling." Harper's voice quickened. "Tell me all about the cute guy. What's he like? Don't leave anything out."

"There's not much to tell. Turns out he goes to the same college. Only he's studying sociology."

"Huh. Whaddya know. I've met some people with that major. It just means the guy's nice *and* cute."

"Whatever. All I know is, he smells good. He was wearing Paco today."

"Paco, huh?" Harper fell silent for a moment. As if she had to process the guy's brand of cologne or something.

"Harper?"

"Sorry. I was just thinking about something else." Harper cleared her throat. "So, what else happened at work?"

"Not a whole lot." Skye squinted at the phone.

It wasn't like Harper to change a subject so quickly. Usually, she dissected every word in a conversation. She held them up to the light and picked them apart, syllable by syllable, like a fermented frog in bio class.

"Like I said, I got to work the cash register. There's nothing to it."

"Huh. Good for you. Anyway, I have news, too."

"Really?" This wasn't like Harper. The way she stopped asking questions about Reef. Something was definitely up. "What's your news?"

"I ran into one of Alex's friends in the quad."

Again, with the shortening of names. Why couldn't Harper just call the girl Alexandra?

"You'll never believe what she said," Harper continued.

"I'm all ears." For Harper to talk to one of those girls was one thing, but for her to wait this long to tell Skye about it was something else.

"Maybe I shouldn't tell you, though. At least, not until I figure out what to do."

"Figure out what to do about *what*?" As usual, the girl was being vague.

"About the party she invited me to. It's next Saturday."

Skye blinked. "Party?"

"Yeah. There's a party at her place, and she asked me if I wanted to go. Guess they're looking for someone new to hang out with since they don't have Libby around anymore. Looks like they want me."

"You are *not* serious." The words sounded a lot colder than she intended. But no matter what kind of spin Harper put on this, it was *not* good news.

"Of course, I'm serious," Harper said. "I wouldn't make up something like that. Geez, do you think I'd make that up?"

"Think about it. Why do they want to hang out with you now?" Again, she didn't mean to sound cold, but Harper couldn't be that dense. It was the same girls who ignored Harper all through high school and their freshman year of college. Why would they warm up to her now?

"Because they like me? Is that so hard to believe? Oh my god...you're jealous."

"I'm not jealous." Skye spoke quickly, unable to stop herself. "Listen to what you're saying. They don't like us, Harper. They never have. What makes you think anything's changed?"

"Because we're in college now. People grow up, Skye. Geeze, way to judge them."

"You're not listening."

"Yes, I am. And that's the problem. I should've known you'd be like this."

"What do you want me to say? That I'm happy for you? I just don't see it happening."

"Maybe that's because you don't want it to happen. Goodbye, Skye."

With that, Harper ended the call. It was the first time she'd hung up on Skye and it made the whole situation seem even more surreal.

Chapter Fifteen

Gene

The phone call came a few days later. Gene knew it was going to be a crappy Thursday when he couldn't find any milk in the fridge worth drinking. Here he had a big bowl of Kellogg's Corn Flakes and nothing to pour on 'em.

He was about to funnel the flakes back into the box when his cell phone jangled. "Y'lo."

"Hello, Gene."

It sounded like Dr. Fischer, but that couldn't be right. What doctor called at this time of day? He glanced at a clock built into the microwave. Sure enough, it was only eight.

"That you, Doc?"

The caller cleared his throat. "Yes, it is. I, uh, wanted to talk to you about your test results."

Test? What test? It took Gene a moment to realize what the doctor was talking about. Then the memory came rushing back. The trip to Medical Plaza One on Monday afternoon. The chill of over-conditioned air on his arms. A waiting room full of people who looked like they had no time left to be waiting for anything, let alone a doctor's appointment. A kind stranger with a voice like Marilyn's. "You mean that thing I did in your office Monday? By the way, it hurt like hell."

"Yes, that's the test. Can you come in this morning?"

Gene picked up a withered flake. The last place he wanted to be was back in the doctor's office. "I guess so. What's up?"

"I want to go over the results. Try not to worry about anything until you get here."

"Can't you at least give me a hint? C'mon, Doc. You're killin' me here."

"I think it's best if we wait until you come over. We can talk about everything then. I'll see you soon. Goodbye."

The phone went dead before Gene could protest and he returned the cell to his pocket. It was just like Dr. Fischer to leave him hanging. Why didn't he just say whatever he had to say and get it over with? Why the melodrama?

Gene left the cereal bowl on the counter and grumbled all the way to his bedroom. Once he pulled out a clean polo and yesterday's blue jeans, he quickly dressed and returned to the kitchen to find Knox standing by an empty dog dish.

"I didn't forget about you." Gene quickly scooped some kibble into the bowl. "So, you can stop giving me the stink-eye."

When the dog bent to eat his grub, Gene left the house and locked the front door behind him. Most people had already left for work, so he traveled to the medical center on empty roads, all the way to Medical Plaza One.

Humidity greeted him the minute he threw open the Tahoe's door. The weather guy promised the heat would break one of these days. Just not today.

Unlike the last time, the waiting room was empty when he walked into the internist's office. He expected to see at least a few old folks camped under the television set. Even though the office didn't officially open until nine, he thought maybe an early bird or two would fly in ahead of time because they had nowhere else to go.

"Hello?" Gene stepped up to the leaded glass window. As soon as he slid it aside, he exposed a pile of medical charts.

"Just a second." A voice sounded from behind the stack and someone's head popped up. It was the girl who held the door open for him earlier in the week. "Hi, Mr. Jacks. Come on back."

It felt surreal to walk through the empty lobby. Much too quiet without the drone of a TV set or the murmur of voices. What this place needed was a joke. Something to lighten the mood.

"So…what do you call a medical practice with only two doctors?" Gene loped along next to the girl.

"I don't know." She didn't look the slightest bit interested. "Doctor's waiting for you in his office."

"It's a joke. A medical practice with only two docs is a pair-a-docs. Get it? A paradox." He waited for her to laugh or grin or something, but she just stood there with a puzzled look.

"Never mind."

She continued to walk, as if he hadn't spoken. As if he hadn't tried to lighten the damn mood.

"He's back here," she said when they arrived at a certain door.

The room belonged to Eugene Fischer, MD, FACP, according to a metal plaque on the wall.

"Here we are," she repeated, unnecessarily.

He stuck his head around the doorframe and spied the physician sitting behind a large mahogany desk. "Uh, hello?"

Dr. Fischer glanced up, but he didn't smile. "Good…you're here. Come in, Mr. Jacks. Come in."

Gene bumbled into the office, his arms and legs like jelly now. "For chrissakes, Doc. I've been coming to this office for ten years. Call me Gene."

"Of course. Have a seat, Gene."

The doctor motioned to an upholstered chair by the desk. Unlike Gene's armchair back at work, this one was covered in fancy fabric. Plaid fabric, of course.

"You've got some snazzy digs here, Doc."

"Thanks. You've never been in my office before?"

"I've never had a reason before." Gene perched on the edge of a chair as if poised for flight. He wanted to relax—he really did—but every muscle in his body strained against the thought.

"How are you?"

"Is that a trick question?" He chuckled dryly. He really had to stop it with the jokes, since no one seemed to appreciate them this morning.

"Yes, well." The doctor's voice fell even more. "I wanted to speak to you before the day got away from me. I was going over your test results again." He nodded to a computer at the desk's edge. Brusquely, as if he didn't like whatever it was he had to say. "I was looking for something, anything, I might've missed."

Gene didn't move. Barely breathed, as a matter of fact. Why the drama? It wasn't as if Gene suddenly detected a suspicious mass on his stomach. He didn't exactly spy blood in the toilet bowl. Nothing important like that. Hell, it was only a tiny shake that started with his thumbs and then moved on to his pinkie fingers.

"There's no easy way to say this." The doctor turned the computer screen out, as if it would explain everything. "The results are consistent with amyotrophic lateral sclerosis. We call it ALS. We also call it Lou Gehrig's disease."

The words floated over to Gene, end over end. As if the doctor had pitched them over the desk, where they stalled in midair. "Excuse me?" *Why are we talking about Lou Gehrig and baseball, for chrissakes?*

The doctor didn't flinch, though. He fixed Gene with his bottomless gaze and tried again. "It looks like you have ALS. It's a neurological disease that affects the cells in the brain and spinal cord. Makes them forget what to do. Researchers are getting closer to a cure for it, but we're not there yet."

"A cure for baseball?" The conversation wasn't making sense. Not only that, but a low drone had invaded Gene's ears, so the doctor's words sounded muffled. Soft. As if filtered through cotton.

"Do you understand me, Gene?" The physician peered at him. "I think you have ALS. Your tests came back positive for Lou Gehrig's disease."

Now Gene *knew* he was hearing things. "Can you repeat that?"

The doctor sighed. "I understand your reaction. I really do. But there's no cure."

"There's gotta be some mistake, Doc. You probably got my test results mixed up with someone else's. Geez, ask people to do one little test right, and they still screw it up."

"There's no mistake. The results show you have ALS. Now, the first thing I want to do is—"

"No." Gene didn't mean to yell, but it was hard to hear anything above the noise in his head. "I don't believe it. Someone made a mistake."

"There was no mistake. The tests came back positive."

"Then run them again." Gene didn't lower his voice. "How difficult can it be to keep some little tests straight? Geez."

"You're not listening to me. You don't have to take the tests again. And I know this is upsetting. But we have to stay calm."

"Calm? You want me to stay calm?" Gene shot out of the chair then, propelled by adrenaline. "That's one tall order, doc. A real tall order."

"Please sit down. We need to discuss this. We need to put you on a medical protocol. The sooner the better."

How could the doctor not understand? Maybe he didn't want to admit someone on his staff had screwed things up. *Of course.*

"Look, I'm not mad at you," Gene said. "People make mistakes. I get that. I'll just take that little needle test over and we'll call it even."

"Gene." Finally, the doctor dropped his gaze.

And in that moment, before the doctor spoke again, Gene glanced at the ceiling above their heads. A loose bulb overhead made everything flicker in shadows of gray and white.

The flicker resembled the static on one of those old-timey television sets they had when he was a kid. The kind with silver rabbit ears that scrambled everything on the screen. He heard the crackle of static as the image wavered. The image of a lanky ballplayer in a number-four jersey, who leaned into an old-fashioned mike and said something about being the luckiest man alive. The crowd cheered and cheered for that. They couldn't get enough of him.

Gene tore his gaze from the ceiling. "You're telling me I have what he had?"

"Yes."

The man in front of the microphone had seemed ghostly, like a vapor. He only lived two more seasons after that speech. By the time the Yankees returned to the mound three years later, the Iron Horse was gone. Like a ghost. Or, like a vapor, maybe.

Chapter Sixteen

The Fireplug

Today's drug deal went down like every other one. Meet outside the school's chem lab, near the broken drinking fountain. Hand over a brown paper sack stuffed with meds and get tens and twenties in return. Sometimes, the customers offered a glossy shopping bag from a store like Gucci, Lululemon, or Saks Fifth, if the buyer was a girl. But not today.

The whole thing took five seconds, max. Unless the client wanted to make small talk, which the girls usually did, probably so they could feel better about the whole thing.

"I don't usually do this," a buyer lied. "But everyone's talking about it."

No one ever questioned the price. Twenty bucks for two milligrams? No problem. Thirty bucks for a brick? Cheap, if you compared it to other cities, like New York or LA. The best customers dropped a full G to stock up for the school year. To help them get through finals or Christmas break or whatever. Something to take the edge off and slow things down. Help them forget about life for a while.

And, really, what difference did it make? Most of them could find this stuff in their parents' medicine cabinets, if they only tried hard enough. Unless, that was, their parents happened to watch *Nightline* or *20/20.* Then, after yet another story about the Opioid Crisis in America, the 'rents hid the stuff in their closets or shoved them into the backs of glove compartments or maybe stashed the pills at work. Imagine all the pills in all the office buildings in all the big cities of America, rolling around in desk drawers, right next to Bics and dayglo highlighters.

The news shows put a serious crimp on supply. They made it harder and harder to find Percs and Oxy and nearly impossible to get Vikes without a note from the Pope. About the only downers still available were Xanax and Norco. But that was enough.

And, again, who really got hurt? It wasn't like customers got heroin, coke, or meth, even, which made people go crazy. It was just a downer, about as strong as a shot of vodka or a coupla beers. Kid stuff. And if the customers didn't get it from a brown paper sack by the chem lab, they got it somewhere else.

Sometimes my friends wondered if it bothered me, the way everything went down. If I could sleep at night, doing what I did. I always told them I slept like everyone else: on my favorite side with a good pillow.

No one ever got the joke.

Chapter Seventeen

Emile Boudreaux

The navy-blue autopsy report stood out from the other folders on the desk for no other reason than its color. The dark cardstock looked like the center of a bruise. Deep and obvious, demanding to be seen.

Emile flipped it open before he remembered the coffee cup at his elbow. Too late, a stream of Folgers spat from the cup and splashed on the report, right next to the name of the deceased.

Elizabeth Nicole Sullivan. The name reeked of old money. While his birth name—Emile—sounded like something a Frenchman named a poodle—this girl's name left nothing to the imagination.

Well-fed? Check. Four years of braces for perfect pearly whites? Check. Trust fund at Merrill Lynch? Probably check, check, and check.

That was what he guessed from the autopsy, anyway. Although her death didn't quite match the description. A girl like that should've been thrown from a polo pony or died when she wrapped her Lamborghini around a light pole. She shouldn't be found wallowing in vomit on the filthy floor of a stash house across the street from her college.

That was why he stayed after work to study the report tonight. Review it a dozen times, if necessary. Try to find something—anything—new, so Cap wouldn't pull the plug and call in the suits from the DEA. It was worth missing a homecooked meal. Even if he sat all alone at HPD headquarters with no one for company but a cleaning crew working two floors above his head.

Maybe he missed something on the first go-round. Let a little detail slip through his fingers, which could mean the difference between nailing the dealer and letting the guy walk. Some guy called the Fireplug, if an accounting ledger found at the crime scene was to be believed.

Funny how these things worked. Most people pictured an overdose as a simple, painless way to go. Pop a few meds, settle in for a nap, and then drift off to never-never-land. Easy-peasy. Lulled by a soft buzz that dulled the edges and turned everything liquid.

Only, that wasn't how it happened. There was a buzz, all right. The minute the opioid entered someone's bloodstream, the heart spewed it to every corner of the body, including the user's brain. Where it touched something called the nucleus accumbens—the brain's G-spot—and the world turned into a very beautiful place, indeed. For a few minutes, anyway.

But then the neurons got fat and lazy on the drug and forgot to tell the lungs to breathe. That was when the real fun began. Without the lungs, the brain went haywire. After four minutes…permanent brain damage. If someone was *unlucky* enough to be revived at that point, she could look forward to sitting around in Depends undergarments and relearning the alphabet.

Sure, the synapses put up a good fight. But every time a person overdosed, the signals had nowhere else to go, so the brain seized up like a rusty, useless gear.

While the rest of the system went into freefall, fluid leaked into the lungs, or saliva pooled at the back of the throat unchecked, so the victim usually foamed at the mouth like a sick cur. Pretty, wasn't it?

After that came the slow, painful process of suffocation. As each organ checked out in turn. Did the person suffer? Hell, yeah. Especially if they choked on their own vomit, which happened more often than not.

So strong was the body's will to breathe, people went crazy without oxygen. Like that case he covered for the Louisiana PD, which put him off the bayou forever and sent him running for the landlocked Houston office.

The case involved a riverboat captain who capsized his boat in a stand of tupelos. One minute the guy was cruising along the Atchafalaya, thinking nothing could be finer than a day off in a brand-new pirogue. The next minute, the poor sap got tangled under a clump of tupelo roots as big as bowling balls. The boat flipped and trapped him under the muck.

They found his body the next day. Minus his fingernails, which he jammed into the underbelly of the boat as he tried to right it. Ripped clean down to the meat. That was how much of a fight a body put up to get oxygen.

And that was why he had to get to the bottom of this case. No one deserved to die like that, and especially not some twenty-year-old kid who could barely vote. Yeah, she went ahead and added a fifth of vodka to the mix, but that didn't give the dealer the right to sell her the stuff in the first place.

He reread the cover sheet, inked with a logo for the Harris County Institute of Forensic Sciences. Nothing new to be learned from the legal mumbo-jumbo. All that stuff about the autopsy being performed pursuant to Article 49.25 of the Texas Code of Criminal Procedure, blah, blah, blah.

Most of it he could guess. The victim appeared well-developed, well-nourished, and average-framed, of course. Any idiot could see that from the autopsy photos. Same with the examiner collecting fingernail scrapings, cuticle clippings, etcetera, etcetera.

Apparently, Miss Sullivan spent a lot of time at the beauty salon, since the ME found two hundred strands of hair weave sewn to the girl's scalp. How was that even possible? She also spent a lot of time at the dentist's office, since her "oral cavity had full natural dentition in good repair." Maybe that stuff about a Merrill Lynch trust fund was true then, too.

The kicker came next, though. Since the ME couldn't detect blunt trauma to the head, neck or torso, foul play went right out the window. And since her heart looked okay for someone her age—"homogeneous, dark red, and firm without pallor, hemorrhage, or fibrosis"—she wasn't a long-term drug user. More like a weekend partier. Someone who wanted to close out her summer in a memorable way.

He spent the next hour pouring over the report. The air conditioner finally clicked off, like he knew it would, around midnight, but he didn't budge.

No matter how many times he read the autopsy, he couldn't see past the mundane details. To him, Elizabeth Nicole Sullivan was nothing more than a sad statistic. An average girl of above-average means who got caught doing something she wasn't supposed to do. At least, not in the quantity she did it in.

For a girl who wanted to end her summer in a memorable way, Miss Sullivan's death was wholly forgettable.

Chapter Eighteen

Skye

They cruised through the parking lot for several minutes before a space opened up near the door to Whole Foods. By the end of the week, families like hers got antsy for the weekend, so they all piled into their Volvos, Priuses, or other kinds of bougie cars and headed to the health-food store to stock up on sea-salt chips, free-trade strawberries, and ginger beer.

Once Dad snagged a space, she tripped out of the Volvo and followed him into the store. She wore her Hello Kitty pajama pants tonight and had pulled her hair into two messy pigtails. It wasn't like she was going to see anyone, so it didn't really matter if she looked like a kid again.

She grabbed a shopping cart with a rusty wheel—*natch*—and rolled it over to the vegetable bin. Together, she and Dad filled the cart with a little of this and a couple of that.

They saved the frozen-food aisle for last.

"You know," she pointed to a certain frosted window, "it'd be a whole lot cheaper to just grab one of those babies for dinner."

Her dad gazed where she pointed. "Frozen pizza? But I thought you liked to make it at the house."

"To be honest, it's a lot of work. And look…this one's made with organic flour and everything."

The pizza on the box looked amazing. Just like a real pizza, with cheese bubbling around the crust and everything. Although, that could've been photoshopped, of course.

"Okay. Whatever you want."

He seemed distracted tonight, so Skye wordlessly tossed a couple of pies in the basket. "I think that's it. Want to head out?"

"Sure. Gotta watch the ol' paycheck, anyway. We're coming to the end of the month."

Then we should be shopping at Walmart, she wanted to say. But that would sound really snarky, and he already looked stressed enough. Maybe it was the craziness of the urgent care center, where things got busier and busier toward the end of the week. At least, that's what he always said whenever he came home late.

They went through the checkout line and lugged the groceries to the Volvo. By the time they finished loading them in the trunk, night had fallen.

"Hey, Skye." Her dad nodded at the store. "Wanna go back inside and grab a beer?"

"But the pizza..."

"They'll keep. Long enough for one beer, at least."

She hated to say no, since he seemed to need it tonight. So, they backtracked into the store and grabbed some stools at the bar. Luckily, most of the other shoppers had disappeared by then, so they had the whole place to themselves.

An older man with a scruffy goatee approached them a minute later. "What can I get you?" He slapped two brown, recycled napkins on the counter.

"How about a chai tea and a Sam Adams." She answered for both of them, since she knew the game by now.

Her dad nodded to reaffirm the order, and the bartender shuffled away.

"So, what's up?" When Skye leaned back on the barstool, she noticed for the first time how bags underscored his eyes. The skin under them looked especially bruised and pulpy tonight. "You seem kinda out of it."

"There's a lot going on at work. It never stops."

"Do you like it, at least?"

He chuckled wryly. "Compared to the med center? Nope. Compared to the unemployment line? You bet."

"You should call the med center and see if you can get your old job back. Maybe they'll do it. You never know."

"It doesn't work like that. Once you leave, you're not supposed to go back. Especially after what they said about me."

"But you didn't do anything, right?" She shot him a sideways glance.

He never did explain what happened at the med center, not really. All she knew was someone in the pharmacy department got busted for taking medicine, along with a few of the internists on staff. Her dad called it a "wide net."

"It was politics," which didn't really answer the question. "That's one thing I won't miss. Going through all those layers to get to the CMO." His gaze bounced up from the counter. "That's chief medical officer."

"Yeah, I know. You told me."

He'd complained about the lady all the time. Called her incompetent and petty. Said she fired people first and asked questions later. Or, something like that.

"You don't like her very much, do you?"

"Nope. No, I don't."

"Here you go." The bartender had returned with a chai tea that he deposited in front of Skye. "And a Sam Adams for the gentleman."

Dad nodded as the beer appeared in front of him. "Let's talk about something else."

The bartender moved out of sight.

"How's your job going?"

"Good, I guess. Turns out everyone wants the same things." She sipped from the tea, pointedly, in case the bartender was looking. "Either people come into the store to copy a key or they want to talk about security cameras. Do you know they make 'em with infrared night vision now? It's true. They're very cool. And they only cost a couple hundred bucks each. We should totally get one for over the front door."

Dad drank from his beer before passing it to her under the counter. "Don't know if we can afford it. And I'm not really thrilled about spending money on a place we don't even own."

She palmed the glass and turned away. A large front window gave her a panoramic view of the parking lot, which had emptied by now. Only a half dozen cars filled the spaces, including their Volvo, a Subaru, and an old Dodge Durango, which hulked inside a handicapped spot.

"Anyway," she gulped from the glass and passed it back, "sometimes people come into the store to check out the gun safes. Houston has a lot of hunters."

"And that's news to you?"

"Not really. But they get in my face about it. They want to brag about the number of points on a buck. Do I look like I'd care?"

"No. But it wouldn't kill you to make a little small talk." He grinned. "No pun intended."

"None taken. Anyway—"

"Excuse me. Sir?" The bartender had returned.

"Hmmm?"

"I'm afraid we've had a complaint."

"Huh?"

"A complaint. From another customer." The bartender pointed to a guy wearing sweatpants, who was lurking by the deli section. "From that gentleman over there."

The jogger pursed his lips, as if he'd just chugged a mouthful of bleach.

"He said you're giving beer to your underage daughter. I'll have to see an ID, miss."

As the silence thickened around them, Skye struggled to think of something to say. But she wasn't quick enough.

"*Nein*," her father spat, breaking the silence. "*Nein. Das ist falsch.*"

The bartender's face blanked.

"*Er ist ein wichtigtuer!*"

The bartender turned to Skye for an explanation. "What'd your dad say?"

All at once, Skye understood what was happening. It was quite brilliant, actually. All she had to do was play along and not blow it.

"He's not my dad." She spoke slowly, to give her brain a chance to catch up with her mouth. "He's my uncle. My German uncle. Just got into this

98

country, as a matter of fact."

"That may be, but—"

"*Hast du nicht mehr alle tassen im schrank?*" Dad pretended to be suitably insulted. His German was pretty good, to be honest, and she had to give him props for speed. If she didn't know better, she'd mistake him for an immigrant fresh off the boat from the old country.

"Calm down, Uncle," she said. "He just made a mistake."

Dad huffed and puffed a bit more, while Skye rearranged her features to look suitably apologetic.

"It's how they do things in Germany." She shrugged, as if she understood why someone might make that mistake. "Kids there drink beer in preschool. Look, if it was up to me…"

The bartender leaned away now, as if he wanted to take it all back. "No, it's cool. I didn't know. Tell your uncle I'm sorry. But don't have any more, okay? Not unless you can give me a valid ID."

"Sure. But don't you think it's cool to learn about other cultures? It's so interesting to meet people from a different country."

Maybe if she added the whole diversity thing, the bartender would leave them alone.

"Oh, yeah. Nothing like getting a different point of view, I guess. Tell your uncle I'm sorry."

Skye turned to her dad. "Uncle…das…uh."

Her father waved the words away, to save her the trouble of coming up with the right phrase. Too bad they weren't speaking French because she could totally nail it in that language.

When the bartender finally left, Skye giggled into her palm. "What was that?" she whispered afterward.

"That was called 'thinking on the fly," he whispered back. "Whew! We could've gotten busted for sure."

"That was something, all right."

"Well, it's not like we were hurting anything."

Skye knew where he was coming from—that jogger totally overstepped the bounds when he ratted them out—but something still bothered her.

"Couldn't he get fired for serving me, though?" Although the guy hadn't gone out of his way to be friendly or anything, he didn't deserve to be fired.

"Nah. He might've gotten his hand slapped." Her dad continued to whisper, just in case.

"But I thought they took away a place's liquor license or something." She seemed to recall a video in phys ed about alcohol awareness. One scene showed an actor in an apron being shoved into the back of a police car for serving a minor. Maybe that was just how Hollywood saw it.

"I dunno. Does it matter? Look, let's get out of here. We've got those pizzas melting in the car." Dad threw some bills on the counter. "Race you."

Skye started to follow him, but she turned before the exit. When she glanced back at the bartender, he stood at the sink with the nearly full tea in his hand. She wanted to run right back and stuff a few bucks into a tip jar, only Whole Foods wouldn't allow its employees to accept tips anymore.

Instead, she waited for the guy to glance up and then she mouthed, "I'm sorry."

You never knew how an evening with Dad was going to turn out. Or, what he thought he was teaching you along the way. As usual, his parenting style was unorthodox, to say the least.

* * *

As it turned out, the frozen pizza she fixed them for dinner wasn't nearly as good as one she fixed from scratch, despite the amazing photo on the box. She refused to give Dad the satisfaction of being right, though, so she ate the last bit of crust without mentioning it.

Dad got to the end of his slice at the same time, but, unlike her, he immediately rose. "Dinner was good, muffin. Thanks."

She watched him shuffle to the counter, where he fired up his computer.

"What're you doing tonight?" she asked, unnecessarily.

They both knew exactly what he planned to do: review his case notes until he couldn't see straight and then he'd shuffle off to bed without bothering to close the program. Skye wouldn't know what to think if she ever wandered into the kitchen and found the counter illuminated by natural light instead of a blue glow from his computer.

"I've got some work to do. Maybe read the paper. What about you?"

"I dunno." She carried their plates to the sink as she considered it. "I haven't had a Friday night off in a while. I didn't really plan anything."

To be honest, it felt weird to have nowhere to go for once, now that classes had ended for the week and Mr. Jacks gave her the night off from the lock shop. At first, she thought she might enjoy a few hours of freedom, with nowhere to go and nothing to do, but now she wasn't so sure.

"How about doing homework?" her dad asked. "Nothing like getting a jump on the 'ol weekend."

Skye rolled her eyes, since he wasn't really paying attention to her anyway. "Nah. My brain's fried. Think I'll start on that in the morning."

The last thing she wanted to do was crack open a book and be reminded of all the assignments she neglected to tackle during the week. That would only make her feel worse about staying home on a Friday night, virtually alone.

"I know," she said, "do you mind if I try to open your safe again?"

The last time she tried, it took her forever to feel the fence drop in the gate, and then she barely got to enjoy her victory before Harper called and summoned her back to the kitchen. But there was no way on earth Harper would call her tonight, given their last phone call, so she didn't have to worry about that now. She might even improve her time.

According to a brochure Mr. Jacks gave her from the Associated Locksmiths of America, which she actually read despite some initial misgivings, the group staged safecracking classes to teach people how to pick up the pace when it came to unlocking a safe. They even staged contests that pitted students against each other so people could try out their skills. Some of the contests sounded so lame—who wanted to win a year's subscription to *Locksmithing Magazine*?—while others paid their first-place winners in cash. There was no way she was good enough to compete against other people yet, but imagine the amazing Christmas gifts she could buy if she was. She could even get her dad a new computer, since he cursed the old one under his breath whenever the screen froze.

"Go ahead and try to open it," he said, reflexively. "I don't mind."

She tossed the dinner plates in the dishwasher and pressed the machine's start button. Once she finished wiping down the table, she stuffed her cell in her pocket and headed for her father's bedroom.

A different stack of laundry sat at the end of his bed this time, and this one was even taller than the last. By the end of the week, he didn't even try to keep his room in order, as evidenced by the wad of dirty underwear he'd piled next to the closet door. She almost tripped over the pile as she opened the door to get at the Sentry safe inside.

She didn't notice a stray jockstrap as she stepped in the closet until it was too late and she tumbled against the wall when her toe snagged on it. That pushed aside the old gym bag she found the first time around, and whatever filled the bag rattled together in a cascade of *plinks* and *plonks*. Although he'd stuffed the bag to the brim, which was obvious by the bag's lumpy shape, whatever was inside sounded light and airy.

Curious now, she lifted the bag off the ground and was surprised by its weightlessness. Whatever her dad brought to the gym weighed about as much as Axl when he was first born.

The *plinks* and *plonks* resumed as she carried the bag to the unmade bed. She turned the duffel over, after first unzipping the main compartment, and let the contents spill on the comforter. A stream of amber plastic bottles, all of them missing their lids, poured out.

In addition to missing lids, someone had ripped off the containers' labels. Every one of them. All except for a lone bottle that teetered at the bed's edge. She scooped that one up and tried to read the paper, but it was too dark, so she flicked on the table lamp next to the bed.

Sure enough, a forgotten label still clung to the bottle's side. Someone had gotten a prescription for three milligrams worth of Xanax, dispensed by St. Sebastian's Healthcare System, where her dad once worked. She struggled to find the prescribing physician's name but couldn't.

Her gaze swept back and forth over the bedspread. Over the dozens of smoky amber plastic bottles. All of them empty. All those protective shells with nothing left to protect.

She tried to make sense of it. She studied the bottles until her eyes watered. Who could need that much Xanax? And why would someone take off the labels?

For her dad to hide the bag in his closet was one thing, but for him to scrub the labels off was something altogether different. It didn't feel right, and she could usually trust her feelings.

She finally scooped the bottles off the comforter in handfuls and stuffed them in the gym bag. By now, she'd forgotten all about the safe and all about practicing on it. Compared to what she found in the duffel bag, it didn't seem so important after all.

Chapter Nineteen

Reef

The streetlamps threw shadows across the curves at the Lee & Joe Jamail Skatepark in downtown Houston, which messed with Reef's vision and turned everything upside-down.

He tried to do a fast-plant at the end of an ollie, but his deck shot out from under him and disappeared into a corner.

"Dude." Kenny scowled as he skated over. "What's wrong with you? That's, like, the fifth time you've bailed tonight."

"It's gotta be the shadows." Reef sat up and searched for his board, which was marooned by the nearest wall. He couldn't exactly tell Kenny the truth. It wasn't only shadows that messed with his mind tonight. Every time he glanced at the fence, he thought he saw Skye standing behind it. When he checked out the bottom of a halfpipe, there she was. He even saw her face on top of a flat-rail, of all things.

"You're skating like a newb." Kenny scowled even more. "Get your head in the game."

"I told you…I can't see straight. This is bogus."

Reef tried to stand, but pain shot through his ankle and made him sink back down again. "Think I gave myself a hot pocket." If it was like his other injuries, the joint would swell like a balloon by morning, which meant no more skating for a few days. Not that he minded. He needed a good excuse to spend more time at the lock shop, even though he'd have to limp through the stockroom and prop his ankle on an overturned box.

"That sucks," Kenny said. "Call it a night?"

"Sure." Reef wobbled upright and went to grab his board. When he flipped it over to check for damage, he couldn't find any, so he painfully followed Kenny to the exit.

They'd outlasted everyone else at the park. Which meant they could saunter through the middle of a halfpipe and not have to worry about some poser sailing over their heads.

"Let me guess," Kenny said. "Girl trouble?"

"Maybe." The right ankle throbbed. "There's this chick I work with. Turns out she goes to Immaculate Word, too."

"Aha. Thought so. Have you bagged her yet?"

Kenny shot him a look, since they both knew it could happen. Reef had nailed a couple of girls he met at college, only none of them were clean enough to bring home to his family. He couldn't exactly walk through the front door with a skank and expect his parents to be happy about it. Especially since they got off on planning the "perfect" wedding for him.

"No...not yet." He couldn't get over the way Skye scowled at him when she found him in the boss's office. Or the way his lungs refused to work afterward. "Not only that, but I found out something weird about my boss."

"What's that?"

Reef paused. It wasn't that he didn't trust Kenny with the truth—the guy was like a brother, after all—but he wasn't sure Kenny would understand.

"Everything's all messed up." How could he explain tax forms to someone like Kenny? Reef barely knew how to read those things, and he'd been doing it for years.

Thankfully, the words came to him a second later. "Turns out my boss made a shitload of money last year. And I'm not sure where all the dough came from."

They stepped onto the asphalt parking lot. Night fell quickly this time of year, and the grassy median had morphed from green to black.

"He even made more money than my dad did," Reef added.

"Seriously? But your dad's a doctor and everything."

"Yeah. And all Mr. Jacks has is that crappy lock shop. He must be printing money in the back or something."

"You need to get in on that action." Kenny snorted. "Get a slice of that pie."

"It's just a saying, dumbass. He's not really printing money in the back."

Sometimes he wondered why he tried. Maybe his mom was right and he should trade in Kenny for a smarter best friend. But every time he considered it, Kenny popped off with something hilarious, and then they'd both fall to the ground laughing.

"He must be getting the money from somewhere. But I can't figure out where."

"So, go ask him."

"Yeah, right."

Kenny made it sound like the most natural thing in the world. Like all Reef had to do was hobble over to Mr. Jacks's office and ask the man to explain his tax forms.

"I can't do it," Reef said. "Not without him getting suspicious."

They stood by Kenny's Toyota Corolla now. Since Kenny never bothered to lock the car unless there was a board inside, Reef yanked open the back door and tossed his deck on the floorboard.

"He doesn't even know I've been in his office." He slid into the car and Kenny did the same. "And I go there almost every day."

"Isn't that, like, breaking and entering?"

"Not exactly. The lock's busted on the guy's door. So, technically, I'm not breaking into anything."

"Gotcha. But I don't know why you care. It's not your money."

"Because it's weird. I mean, it's gotta come from somewhere, right?"

"So, go ask him. Go up to your boss and say, 'Yo...boss. What's with the dough? Gimme some.'"

Kenny laughed even harder as he whipped the Toyota out of the parking space. While he shredded on a skateboard, he sucked at driving, so the Toyota pogoed in fits and starts to the exit.

The guy didn't even bother to turn on his headlamps when he drove. He just maneuvered the car in the pitch black toward the glowing billboards on

Westheimer.

"Can't do it, my friend," Reef said. "He's not supposed to know I was in his office, remember? He'd freak out. The girl did, the first time she saw me there."

"See? It always comes back to a chick. Think she's gonna rat you out?"

"Nah." Reef shook his head, although Kenny couldn't see him in the dark. "She's too busy being his buddy to worry about me."

"She doesn't sound like your type then. Not if she's hanging out with some old guy. Not when she could have herself some prime Reef."

"It's not like that. He's trying to teach her something. They work on safes all the time. And I mean, all the time. That's something else I don't get. It's like she's his daughter or something."

"He hired his daughter to work at the store?"

"Seriously, Kenny? Are you even listening to me? She's not his daughter. She only acts like it. They don't even notice me when they get together."

He couldn't forget the first time he caught Skye and Mr. Jacks huddled beside a safe. He'd gone to the showroom to retrieve a pen, but then he heard a noise by the back wall, so he inched over to the counter. What if a customer needed help?

Only, it wasn't a customer. He peered over the counter to see Skye and Mr. Jacks staring at an open safe. His boss sat on his haunches, right next to the safe's door, while Skye sat cross-legged on the ground beside him.

The old man raised his fingers in the air, as if he wanted to show her something. Maybe he did it on purpose, but his hand fluttered like a bird. Like a sparrow, right? Like the one his dad told him about when he was trying to get Reef to take the job.

His dad said Mr. Jacks would take Reef under his wing and teach him everything he knew about the lock business. Fat chance. There was a sparrow, all right. But the sparrow wasn't Reef...it was Skye.

As he watched them in the showroom, Skye mimicked the twirling motion with her hand, only her fingers didn't shake. She looked like a puppet, while Mr. Jacks worked the strings. Reef couldn't stop staring, even when his knee banged the counter with a *thwack!* and Mr. Jacks jumped up, like he'd been caught doing something he wasn't supposed to.

"Hey there, Reef. Whaddya need?" He sounded gruff, like he was trying to hide his surprise. Like it was Reef's fault he'd stumbled across their little tea party.

"I, uh, was looking for a pen." Reef couldn't look away. The old guy looked so comfortable with Skye, as if he was having a picnic with her, right there on the floor. Until Reef came along and spoiled it, like a big hairy ant they'd found on the food.

He backed away from the counter then, little by little. He never did get the pen, which didn't matter, since he forgot why he needed it in the first place.

The second time it happened, Reef swore he wouldn't go into the showroom again. If he needed a pen, he'd ask Ted. Although, that could be like asking a cop to share his gun, since Ted didn't like to loan any*thing* to any*one*. But if it meant avoiding an awkward silence when he stumbled across Skye and Mr. Jacks, it might be worth it.

"You should just quit." Kenny's voice brought him back to the car.

"What?"

"Tell your old man you don't want to work there anymore. It's not like you need the money."

"True. But I can't leave yet. Not 'til I figure out what's going on. Where the guy's getting his dough."

By now, they'd arrived at Westheimer, where Kenny managed to hit every pothole in the road. Even the ones by the curb.

"Let me get this straight." Kenny randomly checked the rearview. "You like this chick, only she's too busy hanging out with your boss to notice you're around. That's messed up."

"It's not like I care or anything."

"No?"

"Seriously," Reef said. "I've only talked to her a couple times. She could be a total dweeb for all I know."

"So, write her off and find someone new. Someone who wants to hang out with you and not some old guy."

Yeah, but that old guy made more than two million bucks last year, he wanted to tell his friend. Two million bucks from a crappy lock shop in a rundown strip center.

Something was up. The only question was, What?

Chapter Twenty

Skye

The house was dark by the time Skye got home from work a few days later. Between her shifts at the store and lessons with Mr. Jacks afterward, it happened all the time now.

She spied her dad's silver Volvo already in the driveway when she rounded the last corner before the house, its hood swathed in purple moonlight.

She'd gotten used to seeing the parked car; to hearing the squeak of hinges as she threw open the front door and snuck inside; to gliding through darkness toward the kitchen.

"Skye? That you?"

Light suddenly flooded the room. "Sorry, Dad. Didn't mean to wake you."

He shuffled across the hall, his face bleary with sleep. Thankfully, he always wore sweatpants and a long-sleeved Ironman T-shirt to bed, so every inch of his dad-bod was covered.

"What time is it?" He squinted at her as he walked into the kitchen.

"Late. After midnight." She opened the fridge and grabbed a beer, which she held up as a peace offering. "Want one?"

"After midnight? You should've been home hours ago. What happened?"

"Mr. Jacks wanted to give me another lesson." She popped the top off the beer and handed it to him. "He says I have a real knack for safecracking."

"Safecracking? What're you talking about?" He took the bribe and folded onto one of the barstools by the counter.

"I told you about it...it's really cool. There's a bunch of people who get together to crack safes and stuff. They have clubs and everything where they race each other." She grabbed a second beer and joined him at the counter. After spending four hours huddled in front of a safe with Mr. Jacks, she deserved the Pilsner.

"I don't like you coming home so late." He sounded more coherent now, unfortunately. "You've got classes tomorrow."

"I know, I know. I'm sorry."

To be honest, she never thought she'd have to worry about coming home late from work when she first took the job. She only took it for Christmas money and as a way to avoid the Symphony Showcase, right? It wasn't supposed to be anything she actually looked forward to. Not like this.

When did that start?

Somehow, little by little, she'd gotten used to the place. Used to the smell of polished brass, old keys, and red honeysuckle air freshener in the bathroom.

The way Mr. Jacks praised her when she did something right? Amazing. When he took her advice and actually used it? Awesome. *Move that Master Lock display over a foot,* she'd said, and he'd moved it. *Lower the pink keys for the ladies.* Done. Just like that. Like she had something worthwhile to say and he wanted to hear it.

She liked being a cashier and all, but that wasn't the only thing. Sure, she enjoyed ringing up customers on the ancient Royal and figuring out the math in her head. But the minute she mastered the register, Mr. Jacks gave her more to do. Before long, she was signing for shipments and tracking down wayward orders, figuring out payroll for the guys in the back, and calling the power company to get a lower rate for every kilowatt hour.

Granted, it was only a dinky lock shop, and she earned less than nine bucks an hour after taxes. But Mr. Jacks trusted her enough to leave her in charge of something. And when he got back from whatever doctor's appointment, or medical test, or drugstore run he had to make, he was more anxious than ever to teach her about safecracking. He gave her a lesson every day now. Like he'd become obsessed with it or something.

At first, she felt kind of bad. It wasn't like he ever spent time with the other employees at the shop. Then again, *they* weren't the ones giving up their free time to learn this stuff. *They* weren't the ones staying after work to finetune their way around a dial. And *they* didn't practice until they could feel the fence drop in the gate before it even happened.

That first lesson, she closed her eyes to block out everything else, and now she did it all the time.

"Skye?"

Her eyes popped open again.

"Are you even listening to me?" Her dad wore a deep frown that crinkled his forehead.

"Sorry. I was thinking about work."

"That's the problem. You said this job wouldn't interfere with your classes. Now look at you. Coming home in the middle of the night when you've got school tomorrow."

"I know. I said I'm sorry." She quickly focused on the beer so he couldn't read the truth in her eyes. Couldn't figure out how important this job had become to her. Last week she wrote an econ paper on her computer and forgot to turn it in. She missed the deadline by two days, which meant an automatic thirty-point deduction on her score. But the worst part? She didn't even care.

Then there was yesterday's French test, which she didn't remember until the teacher slapped a scantron on the desk in front of her. Even Harper noticed she could barely stay awake through her classes now.

"Frankly, I'm a little disappointed in you." Dad seemed to have found his rhythm because his voice rose. "You've never been this distracted before. You've always managed to handle your schedule."

"I'm not *that* distracted." She tried to sound neutral, which wasn't easy.

Dad was the one who encouraged her to take the job in the first place. He was the one who agreed it would look good on her resume.

"Oh, really?" His tone was challenging. "How are your classes going now, Skye?"

"Look…you said it was okay for me to take the job. It's not my fault my boss wants to teach me something new. You're always telling me to try new things."

"Oh." Little by little, the scowl melted. "Now, don't get me wrong. I'm not telling you to quit your job. But I want you to get home at a decent hour. Got it?"

"Sure, Dad. Whatever you say." As long as it ended this conversation, she'd agree to anything. Promise him anything. "No more getting home after midnight. Got it."

"You need to come straight home after your shift. No more overtime."

"Yes, sir. No overtime. Except..." Her voice trailed off. She'd been meaning to ask him something, only she never quite found the right time. Either he was too busy, or she was, and now Mr. Jacks needed an answer by tomorrow. It was now or never.

"Well, um, my boss wants me to do something." She purposefully avoided his eyes. "There's this contest, see, and he thinks I should enter. But I don't want to do it behind your back."

"What do you mean, a contest?"

"Remember how I said they have clubs and stuff for people who like safes?"

"Yeah. So?" It sounded like he wanted to end the conversation, too, only she wouldn't let him.

"Well, there's a big contest coming up next week. A really big one." She spoke quickly, before he could. "It's in Houston, and I wouldn't even have to travel or anything. At the Marriott downtown."

"I don't think I'm following you."

"Okay. I'll start at the beginning." She took a deep breath. "Mr. Jacks wants me to enter a safecracking contest next week. He doesn't think I'll win, but he wants me to try."

That last part stung a little. Mr. Jacks warned her not to get her hopes up. She hadn't been practicing for years, like a lot of people who entered the contests.

She blundered on, "It's in the ballroom, on this big stage. Everyone has to open a safe, and the one with the fastest time wins." Come to think of it, this wasn't any different than quidditch, or speed chess, or symphony tryouts, even. The person with the best score, time, or audition won. Dad could understand that.

"He really thinks you're ready for this?" He sounded curious now.

"He does. I've been working super hard. I might not win, but I want to try. And they give out prizes and everything."

"Prizes? What kind of prizes?"

"Money. First prize is ten thousand dollars. Cash money."

"Cash money?" Finally, a hint of a smile. "Well, whaddya know."

"Cash money" was a joke between them. They used it whenever they wanted to brag about something. As in, "I found twenty dollars on the sidewalk today. Cash money."

"Yep. The person who wins the contest gets ten grand. Cash money," she said.

"Well…what about the entry fee? How much would you have to pay up front?"

"Nothing. Mr. Jacks promised to take care of it for me."

"And he really thinks you're good enough?"

"He does. He said I'm a fast learner. I must get that from you."

"You don't have to butter me up." Thankfully, the hard edge was completely gone by now. "And I'm serious about the overtime. If Mr. Jacks wants to train you for this thing, tell him you have to do it during your shift. No more coming home so late."

Little did he know, but she often came home this late. He just wasn't awake to find out.

"Aye, aye, Captain." She threw him a mock salute. "No overtime. *Nada.* I'll tell him tomorrow. And thanks, Dad. You're the greatest."

"Yeah, yeah, yeah." He rose and lobbed his empty beer bottle in the trash. "I'm going to bed. You should, too. And don't forget the light."

She started to rise as well, until she remembered something. She lingered in the kitchen until he disappeared, until the house fell silent again, and then she pulled her cell from the pocket of her jeans. The ringer vibrated only a second ago, only she couldn't pull it out in the middle of her dad's lecture.

Surprisingly, the text was from Harper. It even sounded upbeat, despite their last telephone conversation: *Give me a call,* chica. *Big news!!*

Of course, with Harper, there was no telling what qualified as "big news." It could be anything from an A on a bio test to something she read about in *People.* But at least they were on speaking terms again.

She punched a number on her speed dial and waited for the call to connect.

"Y'lo?" Harper sounded fully awake, unlike her father earlier.

"Hey, I got your text. What's up?"

"Only the most amazing thing ever. And I mean, like, ever."

"Let me guess. Ricky Martin finally got divorced?"

Harper chuckled. "I wish. No, it's not that. Although, I wouldn't be surprised if he did. You know, those Hollywood marriages never last."

Skye was about to remind the girl to focus, but she didn't want to rock the boat so soon. "Anyway. You said something big happened. What?"

"Are you sitting down? You should be sitting down for this."

"Close enough. What's up?"

"You'll never believe who's coming to the Symphony Showcase next weekend."

"Next weekend?"

It took her a moment to realize what Harper was talking about. When she did, a strange feeling washed over her. It was the same one that settled on her shoulders the night Harper mentioned Alexandra's friends. "Please don't tell me you're talking about that whole clique thing again."

Harper squealed, right in her ear. "*Eeeiiieee!* They all want to come to the show. Sort of like my own personal cheering section. Can you believe it?"

"Oh, Harper."

"Everyone's coming." The girl wasn't even listening to her. "And they want to sit right next to my section!"

"And you're seriously excited about this?" *Please, God. Please don't let her be serious.*

"I thought you'd be happy for me, Skye. Why aren't you happy? People actually want to come to one of my concerts. Even my parents don't want to do that. They say they do, but I know they're lying."

"Then what makes you think this group is any different? It's a trap."

Nothing but silence for a beat or two.

"Well?"

"I should've known it was a mistake to tell you," Harper said.

"I'm just being realistic."

"Well, stop it. They're all taking me to dinner afterward. Oh my god, I don't have anything to wear. I'll have to work on that."

It's no use. Harper wasn't listening. She was too blinded by the thought of Alexandra and her friends to pay attention to anything else. "Harper?"

"Look, I've gotta go. Forget I said anything. It's not like we see each other at school or anything anymore."

"What do you mean?"

"Everything changed after you took that stupid job. It's like you dropped off the face of the earth. By the way...don't even bother coming to the showcase. I don't want you there."

"Good, because I'm not going." No need to mention she had something else planned for next Saturday. Harper wouldn't know, or care, about a safecracking contest.

The conversation ended the same way as the last one: with a whoosh of dead air.

Judging by the eerie feeling in her chest, Skye was right about one thing. She didn't know how, and she didn't exactly know when, but the worst was yet to come. Too bad Harper couldn't see it that way, too.

Chapter Twenty-One

Gene

The concrete fortress of HPD headquarters looked like every other building in downtown Houston: white, blocky, impenetrable. Only one thing was different...the flags. Three of them jutted from a transom above the door, like golf flags waving from a sand trap.

The Stars & Stripes he recognized, of course. Same thing with the Texas flag. But what the hell was the third one? It didn't look familiar. The cloth was white, centered by a splat of blue, which made it look like a postage stamp for one of those tiny European countries nobody cared about. Liechtenstein maybe?

Gene shook his head as he walked under the flags and into the building on Travis Street. It could've been the medicine talking. Ever since he started taking riluzole—twice a day, every day—he felt gassy and bloated and pissed at the world. Things that never used to bother him before now loomed large. Like the way Ted bitched about having a girl around the shop. Or how Reef couldn't string a sentence together without using the word "dude." And now the HPD headquarters looked like the damn embassy for Liechtenstein.

A bored cop stood behind a counter right inside the door, running interference. It was the same routine every time. Pass through a metal detector, sign a book, hand over his Texas driver's license...blah, blah, blah. The cop knew him well enough to pass Gene through without any additional rigmarole, so the whole thing only took a few minutes. Then Gene rode the elevator to the sixth floor, which was home to the homicide unit.

The elevator's doors whooshed open on a warren of cubicles that looked like an insurance agency, not a homicide squad. Gene sidled up to a cube in the back and rapped his knuckles against its cloth side.

"Surprise, surprise." He reflexively shoved his hand in his pocket, as he entered Boudreaux's cube, so his friend wouldn't notice the tremor.

"Hey, Gene." The cop waved a Taco Bell burrito in greeting. "Long time no see."

"Is that breakfast?" Although Gene had been known to spread Cheez Whiz on a Ritz and call it a meal, the sight of a dripping, greasy burrito so early in the morning made his stomach churn. Although, that could've been the riluzole talking again.

"'Fraid so." Boudreaux wiped some hot sauce from his chin. "I've been here since six, so it could be my lunch."

"Tasty. Just don't offer me a bite."

Boudreaux chuckled, since they both knew he never would. "Whaddya doing here?"

"Thought I'd pay Cap a little visit."

He settled into the only available chair. Between him, Boudreaux, and the burrito, there wasn't much room left over, but that didn't stop Boudreaux from splashing about a month's worth of file folders across his desk. The black folders dribbled over the side and puddled onto the industrial carpet like spilled ink.

"You're out of luck." Boudreaux rubbed his chin again, but the sauce was gone. "He had a press conference today and they're all still downstairs."

The building's first floor held a special room for press conferences, with extra outlets, a colorful backdrop of Houston's skyline, and an official-looking podium. The police chief liked to squeeze the podium's sides together whenever he gave a press conference, which made him look like a cop trying to collar a criminal.

Like everything else in the cubicle, the chair under Gene's keister was regulation beige, with metal legs and a frayed seat cushion. He perched on its edge, since there was no telling who'd been sitting there before him.

Murderers, pimps, arsonists…all manner of Houston's finest had been in Boudreaux's cubicle at one time or another.

The detective shoved his fist into the pile of black folders and magically pulled out one colored navy blue. "Check this out." He casually tossed it to Gene.

The top sheet wore the official seal for the Harris County Institute of Forensic Sciences. Under it was a case number, which happened to be ML14-477, and then the name of the deceased: Elizabeth Nicole Sullivan.

"What's this?" Gene kept his hand under the folder, so his traitorous fingers wouldn't betray him.

"The autopsy report for that kid who died a coupla weeks ago. Remember? The room behind the master closet?"

"And you're just now getting the autopsy?" That seemed late, even for the HPD, which was known to have a hefty backlog.

"Nah. I got it a few days later. I even stayed after work to go over it. But you haven't exactly been around, so I couldn't show it to you."

How could he argue with that? Gene hadn't gone anywhere for a couple weeks. Ever since the doctor dropped the bombshell about ALS and put him on a merry-go-round of medical appointments, blood tests, and MRIs, he kept to himself.

Normally, he liked to contact Boudreaux at least once a week, even if it was only for a quick call on his cell during a cigarette break. But the last few weeks had been anything but normal. His life had shrunk to the size of the cubicle they sat in: everything stripped down to the basic, the simple, the threadbare.

"Yeah. Sorry about that. I've been busy at work." He wasn't ready to tell Boudreaux the truth. Especially since he hadn't told the captain yet.

"Medical Examiner ruled the girl's death an overdose," Boudreaux said. "And get this…he called it 'accidental.' That's the kiss of death for a tox report. That means we won't get it back for a least six weeks."

Gene blinked. "Accidental? Really? I thought for sure the ME would consider homicide, since you found her at a dealer's house."

"Yeah, but there was no trauma and no needles." Boudreaux pointed at the papers in Gene's lap. "Her liver was inflamed, so you've got your alcohol poisoning. And her eyes looked bloodshot, so she suffocated. That happens a lot with an OD. But we're probably looking at prescription meds here. We found an empty Xanax bottle in the girl's purse, which she still had, by the way. She hadn't traded it away for drugs. Witnesses said she came to the dealer's house that night to party it up before school started."

Gene scanned the first page of the report. Sure enough, alongside "cause of death" was one word: overdose. Beside "manner of death," the assistant deputy chief medical examiner had simply typed "accidental."

Gene reread the first page. "Did they even consider suicide?" He'd been around long enough to know sometimes an "accidental" overdose was anything but.

"Nah. Parents didn't want that stuff on the report, and neither did we. No need to insinuate the kid purposefully ended her own life."

"You told me the parents were out of town. So, how'd they know?" Even though he couldn't remember many details about the case—he hadn't been around for weeks, after all—he distinctly remembered Boudreaux telling him Cap had to give the bad news to a maid.

"Parents got it off the internet," Boudreaux said. "One of her friends posted something on Facebook."

"Ouch."

"Yeah, and then Mr. Sullivan turned around and got his lawyer involved. They didn't want the word 'suicide' anywhere near the report."

"I don't blame them. When did you say you'll get the tox?"

"Not for the full six weeks now. But it'll definitely verify the levels, and maybe then we can figure out who was supplying. These street pharmacists all have their own favorites, you know."

"Charming." Gene slid the report back on the desk. "Any idea when Cap'll be back?"

"Could take another hour." Boudreaux glanced at his desktop calendar. "Hey, we're playing poker again this weekend. Do you want in?"

Gene waffled. Not because he didn't want to go. If anything, he needed a night out so he could drink beer, scratch, and breathe stale cigarette smoke with the men in blue. Anything to feel normal again. But Dr. Fischer warned him to take it easy. Told him to get to bed early. Which wasn't as easy as he made it sound, since Gene had been spending so much time with Skye on her lessons.

"I don't know." He could only imagine the shit he'd catch if he nodded off after the first shuffle.

"Why not. What else do you have going on?" Boudreaux shot him a funny look, as if he couldn't imagine anything more important.

"Some stuff."

"What kind of stuff?"

"Look, I've got things to do. Okay?" He didn't mean to bark at Boudreaux, but leave it to the cop to turn a poker game into a matter of life or death.

"Okay, okay. I get it." Boudreaux threw up his hands. "No skin off my nose."

Gene finally slid into the seat with a sigh. The least he could do was give Boudreaux something to hang his hat on. "Look, I'm getting a kid ready for a contest next weekend. Okay? A manipulation contest. And she's pretty good. Green as all get out, but she's a natural."

"Really?" That perked Boudreaux up. "You're telling me you found a mini-me to go to those safecracking conventions with you?"

"Hey, at least it's not some Comic-Con crap." Gene lowered his voice, since there was no telling who could be sitting in the next cubicle over. With his luck, it'd be a cop who liked to dress up as Wonder Woman or Han Solo on the weekends. "It's an actual contest, with cash prizes and everything. It takes talent to crack those safes."

"Um-hum."

"I told you...she's really good." Which felt strange to say. He'd seen a lot of lockpickers come and go over the years. Usually, the ones with talent couldn't focus and the ones who could focus had no finesse. But this girl was different. She had both. She was a musician, which was obvious by the way she moved her fingers. And her mind clicked through combinations like a computer. There was no telling how far Skye could go.

Boudreaux leaned back. "Look, if you want to spend your time babysitting some kid, go right ahead. We'll miss you at the table."

"Thanks. I think." Gene slowly rose now, exhausted by the banter. How could he last through six hours of poker if he couldn't bullshit for five minutes? Besides, he liked to spend time with Skye. She reminded him of Marilyn, especially when she worked a lock. She'd stick her tongue out without realizing it—like a tiny, pink eraser on the end of a number-ten pencil—and she'd hold it there until she finished. Just like Marilyn, whenever she made one of those needlepoint samplers for him. Or whenever she read a particularly good article in *Seventeen*.

"See you around." Gene pointed to the autopsy report for Elizabeth Nicole Sullivan. "Call me when you get the kid's tox back, okay?"

"Sure. And don't forget to let me know if run across anyone called the Fireplug."

"What?"

Boudreaux shot him a funny look. "The Fireplug. The nickname I told you about. Could be the guy who gave the Sullivan kid the drugs that killed her."

"Oh, yeah. That's right." To be honest, Gene had forgotten about the nickname, but he didn't have the heart to tell Boudreaux.

He waved goodbye and walked back to where the elevator door stood open. Thankfully, a cop approached the empty car ahead of him, so Gene wouldn't have to work the buttons on the control panel to lower the car to the first floor.

He couldn't exactly trust his fingers to do that anymore.

Chapter Twenty-Two

Skye

By the following Friday, Skye was so exhausted she woke up even later than usual. She stumbled around the bedroom for a good five minutes before she found her jeans on the floor, next to the white wood desk. Then she threw on an extra-warm hoodie, bleach stains and all. She'd grown so used to being groggy in the morning, she could navigate her way to the coffee machine with her eyes closed now. She even remembered to put a to-go cup under the downspout this time, unlike yesterday. *What a mess.*

Once the coffee finished brewing, she grabbed the full cup from the machine and tossed some kibble to Axl before she dashed down the walk, coffee sloshing everywhere.

The rest of the day went pretty much the same way: no matter how hard she tried to wake up and get her act together, she couldn't. The fog lasted through econ class, where she wasted ten minutes looking for a scrap of notebook paper before she finally clawed one from the bottom of her backpack. She barely survived the next two classes, both of which passed in a blur.

Things only got worse at lunch, when she had to settle for a bag of M&Ms from the vending machine because she forgot to bring enough change for a sandwich. Now that Harper wasn't around—the girl switched out of Econ 201 a while ago—she didn't have anyone else to bum money from.

The weeks of neglect had finally taken their toll, and not just when it came to little things like notebook paper and spare change. Now, her professors used terms she didn't understand in their lectures. She dutifully copied everything they said, but the words didn't make sense. Her notes had started to resemble hieroglyphics; something even she, the author, couldn't recognize.

The last class was the worst. She finally stopped taking notes when the person next to her got up to leave. She rushed to the exit along with everyone else, clutching the lit book to her chest as if it could protect her from the teacher's glare.

She paused on the stairs to stuff the book in her backpack before she threw the hood over her head and tumbled down the steps. Ever since November's arrival, a cold wind sliced the air, which made the walk home seem ten times longer.

She set off for the house, like always, with her head down and her thoughts a million miles away. She only stopped when she rounded the last corner before the property. There, standing on the landing, which the landlord euphemistically called a "front porch," was a stranger. A middle-aged woman with close-cropped hair and baggie khaki shorts that exposed her legs to the wind.

Skye didn't recognize her at first. But that wasn't what troubled her. What troubled her was seeing *anyone* on the front steps of her house. That never happened. And when it did, the stranger always wore a delivery uniform, or at least a gimme cap with the name of a restaurant splashed across the bill.

This stranger wore neither. And something about her posture struck a chord. Like the way the woman rounded her shoulders against the cold. The pigeon-toed stance, with both heels splayed wide. The crook of her pale arms, which she folded against her chest.

"Mom?" Skye forced herself to walk forward, since she had little choice in the matter.

The woman finally noticed her. "Hello, Skye."

Her smile stopped Skye cold. Oh, she still felt her heart beating against her ribs, of course, but nothing else moved. How could her mother reappear on the front steps after five years—a quarter of Skye's life so far—and then smile?

"What're you doing here?" she asked.

"Let's go inside." Her mother sounded confident, as if she already knew Skye would say yes. "I'm freezing my ass off."

Skye didn't reply. She couldn't work her tongue now, and her brain refused to help. Maybe because she had dreamt about this day for so long. Thought about it for so long. She'd pictured the scene so many different ways. But never like this. No, it always took place on a warm summer's day, under a glaze of hazy sunshine. Never on a stark, blustery day, when everything—her mother included—looked harsh and brittle.

"What...what are you doing here?" she repeated.

"C'mon, Skye. I'm freezing."

Skye couldn't move, though. And when she replayed the scene in her mind later that night, she wished more than anything she had stopped everything right then and there. That she had turned around and jogged back to campus, leaving her mother to shiver on the front porch. That was what she should've done.

Instead, she nodded. "Okay."

She realized, too late, she'd forgotten to check the driveway before she spoke. Although she didn't expect to see her dad's Volvo parked at the house so early in the day, it would be just like him to suddenly appear in the middle of an afternoon when he wasn't expected.

He'd be furious, of course. But he'd furious with Skye, and not with her mom. He'd yell at Skye because she'd allowed the woman to enter their house, while he ignored the person who caused all the drama in the first place. Not because he cared about Skye's mom, but because he didn't. Why should he waste his breath on someone he no longer cared about?

Skye slowly moved to the front door and turned the house key in the lock. Maybe she could pretend everything was normal. That today was nothing special, nothing different. Just one more Friday in a whole line of Fridays.

Too bad her fingers didn't agree, because they trembled as she worked the lock.

"Thanks, Skye." As soon as the door swung open, her mother darted into the house before Skye could move. Even the back of the woman's head looked different now. Instead of brown silky waves, like Skye remembered, or imagined them to be, anyway, this woman's hair was dishwater brown and spiked in every direction. The strands looked stiff and unforgiving, like bristles on a hairbrush. Like Skye could cut her finger on one if she wasn't careful.

"What a great place." Her mother stood in the living room. "Real nice. Your dad did pretty good for himself."

Finally, Skye found her voice. "Yeah, well. He wanted to get some new stuff. It's all from IKEA."

She failed to mention her father dragged her to the massive furniture warehouse one Saturday morning when they both realized her mother wasn't coming back. That he ordered an entire roomful of furniture—fake houseplant included—in less than thirty minutes.

In fact, anyone with a decent enough credit score could order this exact room from page twenty-six of the IKEA catalog. For all she knew, every neighbor on the street had one exactly like it.

"Wait a minute." Her mother's appraisal stalled when she realized something. "What happened to the piano?"

It was an accusation, of course, but Skye shrugged it off. "No one used it after you left. Dad, uh, donated it."

She also failed to mention her father was going to drag the piano to the curb for the trash pickers until Skye stopped him. She had no idea what happened to the piano once the Goodwill truck pulled away from the house.

"Why would he do that?" Her mother looked genuinely confused. As if she couldn't understand why anyone would give away a perfectly good piano.

Where to begin? Did she really want to know Dad still flinched whenever he heard someone play the instrument? That he purposefully sat as far away from the baby grand as possible whenever he came to one of Skye's concerts, back in high school?

They never talked about it, of course, but his face changed the moment a pianist walked on stage to perform. Even with bright stage lights, Skye could see the way his features shifted. See how his eyes narrowed whenever a pianist sat down to play. She'd be crazy not to notice it, even with the blinding lights.

"Well?" Her mother wouldn't give it up. "Why did he give it away?"

"I told you. No one was using it." She didn't apologize—didn't even feel like apologizing, really—but she had to say something.

"Your grandmother gave me that piano. You were supposed to get it someday."

"Look, I'm sorry. Can I, um, get you something to drink? A Coke?" Anything to change the subject. Anything to buy some time.

"Hmmm." Finally, her mother nodded. "Maybe a glass of water would be good."

"Sure." Skye shrugged the backpack from her shoulders and let it fall to the ground. She felt like a tour guide in her own house as she headed for the kitchen, with her mother on her heels. As if the woman expected her to explain the sights along the way, which Skye refused to do, of course. That she even invited her mother into the house was more than enough. More than most people would've done, probably.

Skye pried open a cabinet and reached for a red Solo cup. "I only have tap water. Hope that's okay."

She didn't turn. Partly to block her mom's view of the messy counter, but partly to buy herself even more time. As long as she kept her hands busy, she wouldn't have to deal with this. Whatever *this* was.

It worked for a few minutes, at least.

"Thanks again, Skye, for letting me in."

"No problem. Why did you say you're here?" Skye watched water overflow the rim of the cup, unchecked, as she asked the question for the third time.

"Look, can we sit down and talk? I don't want to talk to the back of your head."

"Sure." Skye slapped off the faucet. "I guess."

She gave her mother the drink and watched as the woman picked out a chair in the living room. Which happened to be the Grönud armchair in vintage beige, also available in taupe and gray, if anyone wanted to know.

"Now," her mother said. "Let's see. Maybe I should start at the beginning. Want me to start at the beginning?"

What Skye wanted was to yell at her mother to shut up, but that wouldn't help anything. Not when her mother made it sound as if she'd only just returned from a run to the dry cleaners with a bag of dirty clothes.

For some reason, her mother mistook her silence for agreement. "Of course, you do. Now, I have to say that it's complicated. Things got pretty bad there for a while, you know. Not that your father didn't try to help me." She spoke quickly, as if she knew Skye would defend him. "Because he did."

"Help with what?"

Skye vaguely recalled an unease that had settled over the house in the days leading up to her mother's disappearance. Of cold silences and colder glares. Of a whole weekend when her mother wouldn't talk to her father. She always assumed it was because of money. Or, rather, the lack of it. Although her dad was a doctor, he never made the big bucks because he insisted on working at community clinics or halfway houses, where he could help the most people with his medical degree. Outside of that troubled stint at St. Sebastian's Healthcare System, he never made more than a hundred grand a year, if she had to guess.

"He tried to help me at first. With the panic attacks."

"What panic attacks?"

"You know." Her mother rolled her eyes. "Don't tell me you didn't know. And your dad tried to help me. He really did. He brought home a bagful of medicine from the hospital. But after a while, even that didn't work."

Her mother didn't blink, as if Skye should understand everything now. Only, she didn't. Although she'd found the husks of pill bottles in her father's bedroom closet, the rest of the story didn't make sense. She had vague memories of her mother starting her mornings with a cup of coffee and a few pills next to it in the saucer, but she never thought to ask her about it. Why didn't she ask her about it?

Maybe because her father seemed okay with it. He always called her mom "quirky." That was what he'd said whenever her mother obsessed over a tiny detail no other mother cared about. Like the way she folded the napkin in Skye's lunchbox just so all through elementary school—always quarters, never halves—and placed it in the exact same spot by the Thermos. Every time. She even followed Skye onto the school bus once to make sure she'd done it correctly. Which didn't help Skye's popularity any, but it seemed to make her mother feel better.

Later, when Skye graduated from elementary school and moved on to junior high, her mother insisted on color-coding the homework folders they passed out at Back-to-School Night. Not because Skye wanted them that way but because her mother did. That way she could check Skye's homework at night, long after Skye had gone to bed. Granted, all that hard work earned Skye a place on the honor roll, but that was beside the point.

"You weren't that bad," Skye lied.

"What about the time I took the washing machine apart?" Her mother's eyes clouded at the memory. "I used your dad's best screwdriver. Boy, was he mad. He found me on the floor in the laundry room, trying to shove the nuts and bolts back where they belonged." She tried to chuckle, but it, too, was brittle "For some reason, I thought the machine was getting grease on your clothes. That's when your dad started bringing home the medicine."

"But why did you think you had to leave?"

"Well, he told me…"

At that moment, a loud *cccrrreeeaaakkk* sounded on the other side of the wall.

"Shhh!" Skye's head whipped around. "Did you hear that?" The sound was rough and rusty, and suspiciously car-like.

"I didn't hear anything."

Her mother probably thought she was faking it to get out of their conversation, but Skye didn't care. "Well, I did. C'mon, you have to leave."

Skye turned and took her mother's arm—so thin, Skye's fingers reached all the way around the bicep—and then she pulled her to her feet. "You've got to leave. Now."

Her mother tried to break free, only she wasn't strong enough. In the next instant, Skye maneuvered them both into the kitchen, where she nudged her mom through the back door and onto the steps.

"I'll call you later. Okay?"

There wasn't time for more. By now, the mechanical cough had grown louder. Skye quickly slammed the door shut, remembering too late she didn't have her mother's telephone number. One problem at a time, though. One problem at a time.

She hurriedly rushed back to the front door, where she wiped the surprised look off her face and yanked the panel open. There, out on the lawn, she saw...nothing. Nothing but the spindly tree, its last remaining leaves quivering in the wind. The brown crabgrass, the furthest thing from green or lush. A car, slowly wheezing its way down the road in fits and starts, its muffler hovering an inch above the asphalt.

She leaned against the doorjamb then. Finally, when her breathing leveled and she felt steady enough, she went back inside the house.

Maybe it was a dream after all. Everything looked the same. Over there sat the Grönud armchair with its overstuffed cushions. The perfectly green houseplant with the uniform leaves. Even the coffee table looked the same, with a slick white surface that mirrored the sun.

But the Solo cup...that was new. She only gave it to her mom because she knew she'd have to throw it away afterward. She couldn't afford to let her father see three dirty cups in the sink. After five years of doing life in multiples of two—two forks, two spoons, two cups—seeing a third would upset him.

She scooped the cup from the table and hurried to the kitchen. She blindly shoved the trash in the can, her thoughts a million miles away. What did her mother say? Something about medicine. Something about getting medicine from the hospital.

So, that was what was in the gym bag. All those empty pill bottles rolling around on her father's comforter. At least that part of the story made sense now.

Chapter Twenty-Three

Gene

Gene woke up at nine the next morning, Saturday. Before the diagnosis, he stayed in the sack until almost nine-thirty—weekends, too—because he didn't have to be at the shop until ten.

But that was before the doctor delivered the gut-punch about ALS. Now, he felt guilty if he didn't rise and shine at a decent hour. Always up and at 'em by nine, so he could play ball with Knox, enjoy a second cup of coffee, or take a nice, long shower if he felt like it. The world was his oyster, but only if he got his ass out of bed to enjoy it.

Everything felt different now. Now, when his eyelids opened in the morning, they snapped to attention instead of sludging apart bit by bit.

It was the drinking, of course. Since he stopped drinking a six-pack every night, his head wasn't stuffed with cement and his reflexes worked like they should. That was the upside to all of this. He didn't want booze anymore. He barely had enough energy to make it through the day without it, so he could only imagine how much damage a six-pack or two would cause.

In the end, he quit cold turkey. It wasn't anything dramatic, or heroic. He simply quit. He refused to make drive-bys to the Stop-N-Go after work. Substituted Dr. Pepper for light beer with dinner. Avoided the kitchen altogether after midnight. Simple things like that.

Hell, if he knew it was that easy, he would've quit years ago. Though he'd never had such a compelling reason before.

Even Knox noticed a difference. Now, he bounded into Gene's bedroom at the slightest squeak of the bedsprings, and then he dropped a slobbery tennis ball on the area rug. Leave it to Knox to angle for a game of catch first thing in the morning, before Gene had even had a chance to roll out of bed.

Sure enough, the bedroom door creaked open a second later, and Knox appeared in the doorway, with an aggressively yellow Prince tennis ball clutched in his jaws.

"What? You wanna play doubles this morning?" Gene reached down so the dog could deposit a wet tennis ball in his palm.

He gripped the ball, dog spit and all, and sat up again. Every move he made now took a second longer; every action required a few more steps. Walk to the sink to wash his hands? Now he had to walk the long way around and grip the edge of the kitchen counter for balance. Move a box from one shelf to the other in the closet? It all depended on the box's size, weight, and height, not to mention the time of day. He could carry more weight in the morning than he could at night.

Throw a tennis ball down the hall? That took a bigger-than-usual wind-up so the ball had enough *oomph* to reach the living room.

He cocked his arm back and let the ball sail. The minute Knox chased after it, the doorbell rang. A peal of cathedral bells, which rippled down the musical scale. Just like the bells they used at Westminster Abbey.

When Gene first installed it, a few decades ago, he chose the ringtone for Marilyn's sake, since she loved everything and anything having to do with Britain. Given the choice between a simple ding-dong and a princess-worthy fanfare, it was no contest.

"What the...?"

He rolled out of bed and stumbled into the hall. Before he threw open the front door, he automatically paused by a nearby mirror. Luckily, he slept in gym shorts—a holdover from his Army days—and the Space City Lock Shoppe T-shirt didn't look too bad, either, since it had no discernable stains on the front. A quick pass to smash his hair flat and he was ready to greet the visitor.

"Hello."

It was Skye, of all people, standing on the landing. She held an extra-large Starbucks coffee cup.

"I, um, noticed you left this at the shop." She quickly whipped her other hand forward to reveal a wallet. She moved nervously, as if she worried he might snatch the wallet from her hand if she didn't move quickly enough.

"Where'd you find that?"

"You left it on the counter yesterday. I thought you'd be worried if you didn't know where it was."

"Huh. Well, whaddya know." He cautiously accepted it. "Did you get my address from the driver's license?"

"No, Google. You can find out anything there."

Which didn't make him feel better, but she didn't seem to notice.

"I also found an old dry-cleaning slip in there that had your address on it. By the way, you might want to pick up that sport coat."

He chuckled, since he had no idea what she was talking about. The last time he wore a sport coat was to some banquet for the HPD. No telling whether that dry cleaner was even in business anymore. "Thanks. I'll do that. Well, goodbye."

He moved to shut the door, but she beat him to it. She braced her palm against the panel and softly pushed it back. "Can I come in a minute?"

His first reaction was to say no. He didn't like the idea of employees knowing where he lived, and especially not this one. People might jump to the wrong conclusion if they spied a pretty college student in his house, and he didn't need that kind of gossip.

"I don't think that's a good idea." He began to close the door again, more forcefully this time.

"Come on. No one's even out here. And I really have to go." She jiggled back and forth from one foot to the other, until he finally caught on.

"Oh, right. You need to use the bathroom."

He waved her in, and she quickly hopped onto the Mexican pavers.

"Thanks," she said. "It'll just take a second." She furtively glanced around the living room as if searching for something.

"It's down the hall." He pointed left, toward the bathroom.

"Thanks."

Gene reluctantly moved away from the door. He might as well look for Knox in the meantime, since he'd ignored the dog in favor of the doorbell. Come to think of it...where was the dog? Knox never laid low if he could sniff someone new.

It didn't happen very often. But, every once in a while, a Girl Scout would appear on the porch with boxes of Thin Mints or a neighbor would show up with a flyer for a missing cat or a FedEx driver hustled up the walk with a purple-and-orange package. Then Knox tripped all over himself to check out the newcomer.

Gene moved to the kitchen, where he found the dog trying to free the tennis ball from under the counter. Instead of pawing it, like a smarter dog, Knox just stared, as if he could hypnotize the ball into doing his bidding.

"I've got news for you." Gene bent and pried the ball loose. "This thing ain't going anywhere until you grow some thumbs."

He plucked up the ball and tossed it into the living room. On second thought, he didn't want Skye to be scared out of her wits when she ran across a strange pit bull, so he followed Knox over there. The bathroom door stood wide open across the way, but the room was empty.

"Skye?" Maybe she misunderstood, although his directions seemed simple enough. Maybe she took a wrong turn.

"Yes?" It took a moment for her voice to reach him. She sounded surprised. Either that, or confused.

He couldn't tell. He could barely understand a young person on a good day, and it didn't help when he couldn't read her face.

"You okay?" He walked to the end of the hall, where it came to a T. On the right side sat his bedroom, in all its messy glory. And to the left? That was where he spied Skye, standing in the doorway, with her fingers splayed across her lips. Like she wanted to say something, but she was too afraid to speak.

Something snapped in him then. That door wasn't supposed to be open. Skye wasn't supposed to see that room. Except for a once-a-week cleaning, he never ever went into it. No one did.

"I'm sorry..." Her voice dissipated as he joined her at the doorway. She looked awestruck by the Barbie-pink bedspread with matching shams. By the shiny medals from the Associated Locksmiths of America draped over the mirror. By the poster of President Clinton and his saxophone hovering over a four-poster bed. By everything she wasn't supposed to see.

He immediately turned her away from the room and nudged her into the hall. Then he slammed the door shut behind them, to block out the memories.

"Please don't be mad." Her eyes were wide. "I didn't mean to go in there."

"Then why did you? Do you always go places where you're not supposed to be?"

"But I didn't know."

He guided her toward the kitchen. Each step drained the anger a bit more, until it was all gone.

And really, what difference did it make? It was a free country, right? He probably left the door open by mistake and she couldn't help but notice Marilyn's Barbie-pink bedspread.

He couldn't blame Skye for being curious, now could he?

Only, he did blame her. He blamed her for dredging up a memory he spent all day, every day, trying to forget. A memory that ruined most mornings, before the day even began. All by glancing into his daughter's empty bedroom.

They were so much alike. When Skye waltzed into the lock shop that first day, wearing her faded blue jeans and Buddy Holly glasses, he saw Marilyn all over again.

The way Skye squinted over the frames when she didn't understand a question? Vintage Marilyn when she couldn't figure out algebra. The way she looked up to him, like he knew all the answers? Marilyn did that, too, even when he didn't have a clue. The way she worried about his health? Just like Marilyn, who always nagged him to get more sleep.

No wonder he tried to drown out the memories for thirty years. Only alcohol could soften the pain and buff the jagged edges smooth again.

Everyone said it would get easier with time. Time would soften the edges and lessen the ache. But it didn't work like that for him. Why didn't it work like that for him?

"I said I'm sorry." Skye sounded closer now. "Why didn't you ever say anything?"

"Because you didn't ask. By the way, her name was Marilyn."

And she should be the one here with me, he wanted to say. She should've been the one to take center stage next weekend at the contest and open the safe. It wasn't Skye's fault. He knew that. And he'd never hurt her feelings by saying so.

Why should both of them be in pain?

Chapter Twenty-Four

Skye

One peek at the girly-girl bedroom in Mr. Jacks's house, and she was hooked. A frothy pink bedspread rippled across a giant four-poster bed, and then it spooled onto the carpet in a rosy swirl. It reminded her of strawberry frosting on a vanilla birthday cake.

She'd never seen such a prissy bedroom before. Not that she had a lot of experience with that kind of thing, since it was just her and Dad at the house now. But this was a candy maker's dream come true. She wanted to lick the frosting right off the bedspread, taste the mint-colored polka dots on the wallpaper, and slurp up the Kelly-green carpet like Jell-O through a straw.

The room swirled in pinks and greens and baby blues. Colors that shouldn't go together but somehow did. Even the famous guy in the poster over the bed wore a baby-blue tie.

That wasn't the only poster, either. Not by a long shot. Whoever decorated the room hung up at least six more, and all of them showed the same group of singers bunched around a standing microphone. Four African-American guys in pastel sweater vests and skinny ties. Hair buzzed high in identical flattops. Whoever lived there had a major crush on some group called Boyz II Men.

Her gaze traveled south from the posters, down to an enormous dresser that hugged the opposite wall. The white dresser wore a thick slab of glass on top, and someone had arranged a bunch of those old-timey Instamatic pictures underneath it, from what she could see.

For some reason, she felt drawn to the photos, like iron magnetized to steel.

She forgot all about the Kelly-green carpet until it was too late. Fresh vacuum cleaner tracks carved neat rows into the carpet, but she smashed those flat as she walked across it. Which meant there was no turning back now. Anyone could tell a visitor tiptoed across the room.

If it wasn't for the footprints, she could've hightailed it out of the bedroom and into the bathroom, where she was supposed to go in the first place. Then she could pretend she never stumbled across the princess bedroom with its four-poster bed and pictures under glass. But it was too late for that now.

So, she leaned over the dresser and studied the pictures. Right away, she noticed the same girl appeared in every one. Always front and center, so there was no missing her.

And oddly enough, the girl looked just like her.

Same college sweatshirt, like the one Harper talked her into wearing for homecoming. Same strawberry-blonde hair pulled into a messy ponytail. And the glasses! While Skye always thought her frames looked modern, now she could see they made them in the seventies, too. And they looked right at home in that time and place.

In one of the pictures, the girl wore shorts and balanced on a rock, her face turned to catch the sun. In another, she wore sandals, jeans, and a huge medal around her neck, like a show pony in a winners' circle.

Skye glanced up from the dresser. There, dangling from a corner of the mirror, hung the same medal that appeared in the photo. Time and light had bleached the blue ribbon purple, but it looked exactly the same as the one under glass. Same gold banner with Associated Locksmiths of America printed on it. Same stylized torch in the corner. Same everything.

She didn't have time to think about it, though. Just then, Mr. Jacks called out, so she hot-footed it back to the doorway and hoped he wouldn't notice the footprints on the carpet. She almost made it, too. But he appeared in the doorway a heartbeat ahead of her.

"I'm sorry..."

He wouldn't look at her. His gaze ping-ponged around the room, desperately, as if he was seeing it for the first time, too. But that couldn't be right. The vacuum cleaner tracks looked fresh and everything made of glass sparkled. Someone had cleaned the room recently.

But he still wouldn't look at her. Instead, he reached for her shoulder and softly pushed her into the hall. She was so surprised, she almost stumbled. The next thing she knew, he closed the door behind them and the girly-girl bedroom disappeared.

"Please don't be mad..."

What else could she say? He caught her fair and square. She'd been snooping around in his house when she was supposed to be using the bathroom.

She wanted to push the rewind button and go back in time. Unsee the pictures under glass. Forget all about the girl who looked just like her.

If she hadn't stopped by Starbucks that morning—or at least ordered a large decaf—she might've been able to hold it until she got back to her own house. Then she could return to work on Monday and slide his wallet back on his desk, where it belonged. But it was too late for that now.

"I didn't mean to go in there."

"Then why did you?" He steered her toward the kitchen. "Do you always go places you're not supposed to be?"

"But I didn't know."

Mr. Jacks fell silent for a while.

"I said I'm sorry." She moved closer. "Why didn't you ever say anything?"

"Because you never asked. By the way, her name was Marilyn."

"We look alike." She didn't want to get him mad all over again by talking about the girl, but her curiosity got the best of her. "Don't you think we look alike?"

"Maybe." He shrugged. "I never noticed. It doesn't matter. She's not with us anymore."

With anyone else, she would've dropped the subject right then and there. She would happily let sleeping dogs lie, as her dad used to say. But this wasn't just anyone. This was Mr. Jacks. "What happened to her?"

"She was killed by a drunk driver." Sadness dimmed his eyes. "Guy fishtailed his work truck into her car. That's what the cops said, anyway. Could've happened to anyone."

It wasn't so much the words that surprised her but the way he said them. As if the accident happened yesterday, when she could tell by the bedroom it happened a long time ago.

"Did they ever catch the guy?"

"Oh, yeah. His company shelled out millions. Gave me enough money to start a second company, as a matter of fact. But it doesn't matter. Money can't bring her back."

"No. Of course not." Another thought immediately came to her, but it was dangerous, too. "What about her mom?" All this time, Mr. Jacks never said one word about a wife...a girlfriend...anything.

"She left me. Right after Marilyn was born. Couldn't handle it, I guess."

"That sucks. I'm so sorry."

"Me, too."

To be honest, she didn't know what else to say. Anger, she could deal with. But this...this was something different. This was a grown man who looked ready to cry.

She finally settled on the one thing that didn't feel too weird. She lightly touched his shoulder until his face relaxed, and then she purposefully kept it there a moment longer.

It all made sense now. The way he took Skye in so quickly. The way he trusted her from the start, with no questions asked. How was she to know it was because she happened to look like someone else? That she reminded Mr. Jacks of a daughter he lost a long time ago?

What would he think if they didn't look alike? If she wore dresses instead or cut her hair short or had a different pair of glasses? Would he care about her then? She was almost afraid to ask.

"What you don't know can't kill you," her father liked to say. Maybe he was right. Maybe it was better to stop, because otherwise, she could end up asking the wrong question and getting an answer she didn't want to hear.

Chapter Twenty-Five

Gene

I t took Gene a moment to recover after the scene in the kitchen. He didn't mean to get all weepy when he found Skye in Marilyn's room. That wasn't how he usually acted. *Damn riluzole.*

Ever since he started taking the drug, he couldn't keep his emotions in check. He'd see a sappy commercial on television or hear a certain Beatles song on the radio, and bam! Cue the waterworks.

He padded down the hall once Skye left, and then he hooked a right at the door to his bedroom, where he threw on a Space City polo and his Saturday jeans. He headed back to the kitchen, where Knox was gnawing on the aggressively yellow tennis ball.

"I told you not to lick that thing. Am I going to find yellow crap all over the house now?"

The dog didn't fess up, of course, but Gene reached over to scratch behind Knox's ears anyway. It wasn't the dog's fault. It was no one's fault, really.

Gene was in the painful process of straightening when the cell in his pocket buzzed.

"Y'lo," he mumbled into the phone.

"Hey, Gene."

It was Boudreaux again. Why was the guy calling him? They spoke to each other only yesterday.

"What's up? And you've gotta stop stalking me like this. People will talk."

"Very funny. It's not like I'm dying to call you every day, either."

"Then why are you?"

"I forgot to tell you something else down at the station." Boudreaux burped softly, under his breath. Probably the aftereffects of another burrito.

"Yeah? What's so important you had to call me at the house?"

"Remember that autopsy report you saw yesterday? The one for the college kid named Sullivan?"

Gene squinted. "I think so. You said you wouldn't get the tox back for a while, but the autopsy showed meds and booze. I already knew that stuff."

"Yeah, but I forgot to tell you something else. It was about the meds in her purse. She carried a huge one, and she had pills rolling around on the bottom, like Tic Tacs."

"You already told me that, too. Said she was carrying Xanax." Gene glanced at Knox, who couldn't care less about the conversation happening in front of him.

"Not everything." Boudreaux cleared his throat. "The investigator found some Oxy, too. But it wasn't your normal dose. You know…ones and twos. That's what we usually see on the street. Kids pay about a buck a milligram for that stuff; sometimes more. Two mils go for twenty bucks if the buyer's desperate. Anyway, that's not what they found."

"Look, I'm not a pharmacist," Gene said. "So, all this suspense with the meds is lost on me. Just give it to me straight."

"Fine. Jeez, you're crabby this morning. Anyway, this kid had some Oxy in a three-milligram dose. It's called a green brick, even though it's a triangle. Go figure."

"Okay, Boudreaux. You're still losing me. I don't have to time to play cat-and-mouse this morning." He glanced at Knox. "Sorry, buddy."

"I'll tell you why it means something." Now it was Boudreaux's turn to sound testy. "Street thugs don't usually sell three mils. They normally sell them in ones and twos, 'cuz they're easier to get. Up it to three and we're talking hospital-grade, or at least something that comes from a doctor."

"Whaddya know." A light finally clicked on in his brain.

"Yep. The girl got the meds from a doc. Or, that's what it looks like, anyway.

Maybe a doctor, a drug rep…whatever. Which means the guy had to know someone on the inside. That's what I'm trying to tell you."

"Got it. Someone on the inside. Anything else?"

"Isn't that enough?" Boudreaux sounded miffed again.

"Yeah, that's enough. How about if I call you next week?"

"Good. Make sure and run the name by your people again. The dealer called him the Fireplug. See if it means anything. Gotta get the captain off my ass."

"I'll let you know. Wouldn't want you to get that skinny ass of yours chewed up."

"Ha, ha. And don't be such a stranger."

Boudreaux hung up before Gene could say more. Probably just as well, because he had nothing left to say, anyway.

Somewhere, someone knew what happened to Elizabeth Nicole Sullivan in the house across the street from Immaculate Word. Only, no one would talk. Why did everyone want to protect this creep?

Chapter Twenty-Six

Reef

The lock shop looked a lot different on a Saturday afternoon than it did during the week. For one thing, mom-and-pop SUVs filled the parking lot and people actually milled around in the showroom.

He wasn't supposed to start his shift until two, but he didn't have any other place to be. He couldn't go to the skate park, since he'd jacked up his ankle, and Skye didn't expect him at her house until six, which was five whole hours away.

Thank god he finally worked up the nerve to ask her on a date yesterday. It was pretty late by the time he screwed up his courage, but he asked her anyway. And, much to his surprise, she said yes.

Just like that…she moved him from the friend zone into something much better.

They'd start with dinner first. Kenny offered him the Corolla, as long as Reef gassed it up, and he told his parents his shift lasted until ten, so they wouldn't bother him. A cooler set of parents would wonder why a lock shop needed to stay open until ten on a Saturday night, but his parents didn't even question it.

The dinner wouldn't happen for a while, though, so he had a whole afternoon to kill. He'd called Mr. Jacks to see if maybe he could come to work early, and the old guy agreed.

When he sailed through the entrance of Space City Lock Shoppe, he hoped

Skye would be sitting behind the counter, but Mr. Jacks was the one to greet him.

"Hey, Reef."

"Yo, boss. What's up?"

The man pointed to a customer by the Master Lock display. A guy there held two small locks, as if he was weighing them. "Can you help that guy out?"

"Sure. No problem." Reef tucked the board under his arm and hurried over to the customer. Ever since Skye started working at the store, Mr. Jacks never asked him to help out in the showroom anymore. Like he didn't trust him or something.

Reef moved in before his boss could change his mind. "Um, can I help you?"

"Maybe." The customer gave him the once-over first, like he didn't believe Reef actually worked there.

"It's okay. I'm an employee. My nametag's in the back." Reef jerked his thumb over his shoulder to prove it.

"Okay, then. I'm supposed to get a lock for my kid's bike, only I don't know which one to pick. What do you think?"

He held out the two locks. One took a key, while the other ran on a combo system.

Ka-ching! If he'd learned anything from the skate park, it was that you could never be too careful with your board. Especially the pros. They always used two locks on their sick-looking decks: one for the nose and a different one for the tail.

"You should probably get both locks," Reef said. "People have to work twice as hard to steal your stuff if you've got a keyed lock and one with a combo, too."

"Yeah, right." The guy looked skeptical again. "You're just saying that to beef up your sales. What...are you on commission or something?"

"No, that's not it. It's just smart. You lock the back wheel with a combo, and then you use a keyed one on the front. People who know how to jack one kind don't usually know how to mess with the other. So, either way, you're covered."

"Really?"

"Totally. And go with the smallest chain link you can find. It makes it harder to wedge a file between the links."

"Huh. You learn something new every day. Thanks, kid." This time the customer actually smiled. "I'll take both of them, then."

"Cool. My boss will help you at the cash register." Since he'd aced the sale, he might as well go for broke. "And have a nice day."

The guy headed for the counter, so Reef grabbed his board and dodged around some other customers who clogged the aisle. By the time he reached Mr. Jacks, his boss was ringing up the purchase.

"Pretty cool, huh?"

Mr. Jacks shot him a funny look. "That customer gave you a rave review. Said you really know your way around the store."

"No biggie." No one had ever complimented him at the store before, though, and it felt surprisingly good. "It wasn't that tough."

"You're something, kid. Didn't know you had it in you."

"A lot of my buddies use two locks. Makes it harder to jack with the shackles."

"The shackles?" Mr. Jacks snorted. "Where'd you learn to call it a shackle?"

"Um, the stockroom?" After spending so much time in there, sorting parts in the dim light, he'd be stupid not to know what to call it. Not only that, but a giant poster from Sargant & Greenleaf hung over the door and it showed model eight-oh-seven-seven in all its silver glory. Every part was labeled, including the shackle. While other stores lined their stockrooms with posters of chicks in bikinis, he got stuck working at a place with posters of hardware. *Go figure.*

"Good to know you're paying attention," Mr. Jacks said. "Maybe I should move you out of the stockroom and into sales. Maybe you could improve our revenue."

"Really? I thought this place was a gold mine. Thought you sold, like, a couple million bucks worth of stuff every year." Reef immediately slapped a hand over his mouth.

CHAPTER TWENTY-SIX

"What'd you say?"

"Uh, nothing. Just talking to myself."

Mr. Jacks wasn't buying it, though. "You said something about a gold mine. What makes you think that?"

"I dunno."

"Yeah, you do. Otherwise you wouldn't have said it. Have you been poking around in my office?"

"What? No. Of course not." He cheesed it with a smile, which probably looked about as phony as it felt. "I never go in there."

"And I don't believe you. What've you been up to?"

Reef's mind blanked. He wanted to say something—anything—but his voice refused to work.

"Reef...I'm gonna ask you one more time. Have you been poking around in my office? It's a simple question. Yes or no."

"Not exactly." The old guy had him by the balls. But just when he was about to confess, he thought of something. "I know the store's a gold mine because, well, I see all the packages that come through here. And that means you're selling a ton of stuff. Right?"

"Oh." He could almost hear Mr. Jacks's mind whirling. "You *do* see all the stuff that comes through here, don't you? Well, I have a little confession to make." His boss glanced over his shoulder. "All those packages you get through the back door? They're not all for the shop. Most of them get sent across the street, to a warehouse I've got. It's my side hustle on the internet. That's where I make the big bucks."

"You're kidding." Reef had never, ever, seen anyone shuffle stuff from the store to a warehouse during all the time he'd been there.

"Yeah, it's true. I've got a night crew that fills orders at the warehouse. So, I've got two businesses going at once."

"Cool. So, you're, like, this big internet dude."

Mr. Jacks chuckled. "Hardly. I can barely work the computer in my office. But, yeah, we get most of our sales off the internet. A lot more than we do from this place."

Reef glanced around the dinky showroom at the few people who milled around the displays, taking their time as they read the packages. To be honest, he should've guessed something like that was going on. While products dangled from every pegboard on the walls, there weren't enough pegboards in all of Houston to make the kind of money that showed up on the store's tax return.

"Gotcha," he said. "It's cool you have another business. That makes sense. So, can I clock in now?"

"Sure. Get out of here. And thanks again for helping that customer."

Reef spun around before Mr. Jacks could change his mind. At least the guy's Form 1040 made sense now. At least he understood how a dinky lock business could make so much cash. And it wasn't because of anything illegal.

Although his dad would be happy, Reef felt only disappointment. It would've made Mr. Jacks so much cooler.

Chapter Twenty-Seven

Gene

By the time Reef sailed around the counter, still looking like Knox with that goddamn tennis ball, another customer approached the cash register. But this one held a small box instead of two different kinds of Master Locks.

The customer was an older gal with silver hair and a ring finger that sported an enormous diamond.

"You want me to explain that to you?" Gene gently took the package from her. It was a padlock with a Bluetooth receiver built-in. Top of the line lock. Real snazzy.

"That's okay. I thought I'd ask my grandson to help. He takes care of my computer for me."

"You're lucky then." Gene turned to ring up the purchase. "He can probably figure this thing out in no time flat. Those teenagers are hardwired to understand this stuff."

"Tell me about it." The lady leaned closer, as if she wanted to let him in on a secret. "Half the time I don't understand what he's talking about. I just nod my head anyway."

When she smiled, two rows of perfectly white teeth gleamed back at him. Too bad about the rock on her finger. She was a real looker.

"I get it," he said. "Kids today have no fear of technology. They'll take gizmos apart if they have to."

"I'm always afraid I'll break something." Her laugh reminded him of tinkling crystal in a china cabinet. "This generation is beyond me."

"You got a lot of grandkids?"

Thankfully, she stayed put, even after he handed her the receipt. She smelled good, and her perfume lingered in the air. Something made with flowers. The good kind.

"Oh, my. Yes. Six grandchildren. All ages, too. I never thought I'd have so many. I'll tell you what, though...I wouldn't trade them for anything. They can be a handful, of course." Out came the pearly teeth again. "But I love them all."

"I never had any. Wouldn't know what that's like."

"Dear me. I'm so sorry." Her smile sagged at the admission. "Everyone should have at least one grandchild. I don't know what I'd do with myself otherwise."

"Yeah, I suppose. Guess it wasn't in the cards."

"I guess not. Well, I'm sure you have plenty to do around here." She gestured at the merchandise all around them.

"I guess so." He wasn't ready to end the conversation, though, so he struggled to think of something else to say. Something to make her stay. It wasn't like talking to Ted or Albert or Reef, even. This gal was nice to him even though he wasn't her boss.

His body instinctively relaxed. Lulled by the tone of her voice and the smell of her perfume.

"Say, do the grandkids need locks for their bikes or anything?" He gestured to the Master Lock display. If it worked for Reef, it might work for him, too. He didn't care about the sale, though. What he really wanted was to keep the smell of flowers in the room.

"No, I'm afraid not. And my grandson's waiting in the car for me. Brendon—he's the oldest—always drives me around on Saturdays. We'll go for cappuccinos next. My treat."

"Good for you." Gene reluctantly handed her the purchase. "You go have fun with that grandson of yours. And come back if you ever need anything else."

"I'll do that." She smiled shyly. "Never know when I might need something else."

Gene watched her walk away, and her backside looked just as good as her front. Too bad ladies like her didn't come into the store more often. They softened the place up. They took his mind off the WD-40 and oiled brass, and they made him think about something else for a change. Things like grandkids. And flowers.

Course, he heard the stuff about grandkids all the time. But he usually heard it from Albert, who shoved a cell phone under his nose at the start of every work week and made him look at pictures from the weekend. Birthday parties, pee-wee soccer games, first steps. That kind of thing. To hear Albert tell it, his grandkids were perfect. Never fussy. Always angels.

Of course, when Albert herded the boys into the store once, it looked like a hurricane had whorled through the place afterward. But Albert didn't seem to notice. He was too busy showing the boys where paw-paw worked.

Gene leaned his elbows on the counter, the customers gone for a moment. No, he never did have any luck in the grandkid department. Though he would've made a helluva grandpa. He could picture a kid playing in the stockroom out back with a pile of empty delivery boxes. It was a kid's Nirvana, actually. All those cardboard boxes and not a mom in sight. They could build forts or pirate ships or—

"Excuse me." A snap sounded by Gene's ear.

He turned to see some guy in a red windbreaker standing next to him.

"Hello? I asked you about the security cameras."

The guy had some nerve to snap his fingers. All he had to do was clear his throat, for godsake. No need to get snappy. "They're over there." Gene pointed brusquely to a line of security cameras that filled a shelf. "They're arranged by size. Biggest to smallest."

"Got it."

When the snapper left to study the cameras, Gene leaned on the counter again. Yep, he would've made a helluva grandpa. He could've handed the business down to a little mini-me and kept it in the family. Lock, stock, and barrel. He could've taught him—or her, since it was the twenty-first century, after all—the lock business from the ground up.

He could see them totaling sales receipts at the end of a night or doing inventory in the warehouse in matching polos. He might even change the name of the shop to include the grandkid. Maybe "Gene Jacks & Sons" or "Two Jacks Lock Shop."

Then again, with his luck, a franchise would come along and snatch the place up when he was gone. Those places usually changed the name, anyway. They always went for something generic, like Locks R' Us, the Lock Spot, or One-Stop Locks. Something with no personality. Then they'd rip out the carpet and oak in the showroom and replace it with laminate and glass. Make it look all shiny. Too shiny. They'd take whatever personality he managed to create and kill it with disinfectant. He didn't want to think about it, although he probably should at some point. He only had a couple of years left, to hear Dr. Fischer tell it, and—

Snap. "Hello, again. I need you to get down the big one. I'm in a hurry."

Gene rolled his eyes. At that moment, he wished more than anything he had scheduled Skye to work the afternoon shift. She'd know what to say, and how to say it, to this guy. How to play nice. Gene didn't.

He immediately doubled the price of the camera in his mind and left to help the customer.

No, too bad he couldn't pass the guy off to Skye. She had the patience of a saint. Unlike him, she would play nice and charge the guy the correct amount. She was everything he wasn't, and maybe that was he liked her so much.

Chapter Twenty-Eight

Reef

Traffic had lightened by the time he picked Skye up for the date, and they had the whole road to themselves as they drove to the restaurant.

Once they arrived at the parking lot, though, it was a different story. Reef whipped Kenny's Corolla onto the asphalt at Brenner's, but the valet ignored them to help another customer. Between the shiny beemers and glossy G-Wagons, the dusty Toyota stood out like a sore thumb.

Reef waited for the guy to finally take the keys before he rushed over to Skye's door and opened it before the valet could.

"You look really good," he said as she climbed out of the car.

"Thanks."

For once, she'd traded in the ripped jeans for an actual skirt. Something high and tight that showed off her legs.

"Nice restaurant." She shimmied the skirt down when her feet hit the ground.

"Yeah." He wanted to make a big first impression. As his friends always said, 'Go big or go home.' "My dad told me about this place." Not that his dad would eat at Brenner's, since it billed itself as a steakhouse. But Reef didn't care about that. Not like the rest of his family did.

"You know I'm vegan, right?"

"What?"

"Just kidding." She playfully punched his arm. "That was too easy."

He tried to think of a funny comeback, only his mind blanked. For some reason, he couldn't remember how to talk to her once they left the store. Instead, he studied the ground, the sky, the hostess stand—anything else, really—while he tried to ignore the silence.

It seemed a lot more chill at the shop. There, it was easy to make small talk about creepy Ted and how he freaked them out or they whispered about Mr. Jacks's hands or they imitated a clueless customer who didn't know which way was up when it came to locks. All that flew out the window, though, the minute they stepped into the real world. Somewhere like this.

"So, how're your classes going?" he finally asked.

"They're okay. Economics is a pain, but I'm doing better than I thought I would."

"That's good."

And, just like that, the conversation stalled again. If it wasn't for the hostess, who luckily called them over to her stand, he might've had to come up with another lame question.

The hostess looked kind of familiar, come to think of it, so he ducked his head and pretended not to notice. He didn't want Skye to get the wrong impression of him on their first date.

"Raynesh, party of two?"

"What? Oh, yeah." He usually remembered to use his American name whenever he made a reservation. Hopefully, Skye wouldn't notice.

The hostess and Skye walked ahead of him, into the restaurant.

"Raynesh?" Skye had turned around at the last second and her eyes were laughing.

He pretended he couldn't hear her. He gazed around the room, which had wood-paneled walls and beams across the ceiling. It looked like someplace a hunter would hang out. Like a mountain lodge but without the stuffed animal heads. Or the mountains.

Instead, the place had sparkly crystal chandeliers and real cloth napkins on the tables. And it was quiet. That bougie kind of quiet. A place where a guy could spend two bills, easy, on dinner. But it was all okay. Skye was worth it. And he had plenty of cash, so that wasn't a problem.

He'd spent hours trying to work up the courage to ask her out yesterday. Usually, she was busy or he was, and their schedules never jelled. But that didn't mean he couldn't sense it when she came into the shop. The air changed. It crackled every time she stepped into the showroom.

That was how he knew he wanted to date her. Because no matter what else was happening—he could be cutting a key, logging inventory, talking to the delivery guy—the skin on the back of his neck goose-pimpled whenever she landed on the property.

And now, here they were, in one of Houston's most expensive restaurants on a Saturday night. *Go figure.*

The hostess waited for him to push in Skye's chair before she handed them menus. Luckily, he didn't know the girl, after all.

"Blake will be your server tonight." Her voice was flat, since she'd probably delivered the same speech a dozen times already. "Enjoy your meal."

"Thanks." He opened the page and automatically glanced right. Yep…two bills, easy.

Skye gaped at him. "This place is spendy! How much money is Mr. Jacks paying you?"

"Not enough. But don't worry about it. I've got it covered."

She looked suspicious, but at least she didn't ask any more questions. Which was good, because he didn't want to talk about it. He wanted to talk about her.

"So, what's new?"

"Well, something weird happened to me this morning." She put down the menu and leaned over the table again. Every time she did that, he could almost see down her sweater. Almost.

"Really?"

"Yeah. I found Mr. Jacks's wallet, so I went over to his house."

"You went over to his house? What's it like?"

"Okay, I guess. Nothing fancy. Kind of like a grandpa's house."

He set the menu aside, too. "Why'd you go there?" He knew they were close, but that seemed a little extreme.

"I told you…I had to give him back his wallet. Did you know he had a kid at one time? A girl. But she died."

"Really?"

"Yeah. He keeps her room super clean and everything. Like she never left."

"Sounds like a bad movie. I hope you didn't find a skeleton in the closet. You know, boo!"

He threw up his hands to startle her, and it worked.

She fell back against the chair with a laugh. "You're such a dork. No, I didn't find a skeleton. But I did find pictures of his daughter. And she looked just like me. Glasses and everything."

"I like the glasses." Which was true, and he didn't care if she knew it. "They make you look smart."

"*Ookkkaaayyy*…but I'm talking about Mr. Jacks here. He got all mad when I went in her room. Like he didn't want me to know about her."

Reef reached for a water glass while she spoke. He didn't want to be a douche or anything, but he was glad she told him the real reason for her visit. Forget about the dead chick; he felt better knowing nothing weird was going on between her and Mr. Jacks.

"Don't you think that's a little strange?" Skye asked. "I mean, we could've been twins or something."

"Maybe that's why he wants to hang out with you. Because you look like his dead kid."

"Maybe."

He knew by her tone, though, she didn't believe it.

"Or, maybe he just thinks I'm doing a really good job," she added.

"Yeah, right. That's it. That's totally it." Time to change the subject. "What'd your dad say when you went over there? Didn't he mind?"

"He didn't know. He—"

Just then, a server appeared at their table. The guy named Blake stopped short. "You guys old enough to drink?" He sounded disappointed. "We've got sodas and lemonade, too."

"I'll take a Diet Coke," Skye said. "No ice."

"Got it." The waiter gave Reef the same bored look. "You?"

"Me too. And I think we'll start with the fried calamari." He spoke loudly, so Skye would notice. "Make that two, actually."

Not surprisingly, the order perked up the waiter, and he straightened. "Okay, then. Good choice. I'll have them right out."

Skye leaned over the table again when the waiter disappeared. "Look at you. Ordering the apps. You're like Bill Gates or something."

"Hardly. But I hate it when waiters get all pissed because they can't sell you drinks. Like you shouldn't be sitting at their table."

"He's a jerk. Anyway, I still can't believe Mr. Jacks never told us he had a daughter."

"Maybe he doesn't want to talk about it. You said she's dead, right?"

"Yeah. She died a long time ago."

He couldn't quite picture Skye standing in Mr. Jacks's house. It felt as surreal as seeing her now, leaning across the table from him in a fancy restaurant. "You started to say something before we got interrupted."

"Oh, yeah. My dad didn't know about it. He always works Saturdays, so he wasn't home to find out."

"Hey…my dad works Saturdays, too. He's a psychiatrist."

"Mine has to work Saturdays *and* Sundays. He's a doctor at one of those minute-clinics by the freeway."

"Which one?" The hot pocket never did heal on its own after he fell, so Reef went to an urgent care center near the beltway. By then, the ankle had swollen as big as a grapefruit, and the doc on duty gave him a lace-up brace and some anti-inflammatories. How weird would it be if it was Skye's dad?

"He works at the one outside the loop, near the beltway."

"Sounds like the same one I went to. I jacked my ankle at the skate park, so the guy set me up with a bandage and stuff."

"Could've been my dad. He only started working there this summer. He used to work at the med center."

At that moment, a Diet Coke magically appeared at Reef's elbow. Without ice. "Why'd your dad leave that job? I thought everyone wants to work at the med center."

"It's kind of a long story." She picked up her drink and took a sip. "Have you ever eaten here before?"

"Wait…are you changing the subject?"

"I don't know. Maybe."

"If you don't want to talk about it, it's no big deal."

"Fine. He got fired, okay?" She set her glass down. "It wasn't his fault, though."

"That sucks." Time to backpedal, big time. No need to piss her off so early. "That's totally bogus. I'm sure it was a mistake."

"It's true. Someone started taking medicine from the pharmacy long ago, so they did this whole sting operation. In the end, they blamed my dad. They thought he was selling it."

"Couldn't he hire a lawyer?"

"Not really. No one wants to get on the med center's bad side. Dad said it was better just to take a job somewhere else and let the whole thing blow over."

"He was probably right. Houston is crawling with clinics and stuff. I think that's why my dad wanted me to go to med school."

"But here's the really sucky part." She leaned forward one more time, and he almost forgot what they were talking about. "They could've taken away his medical license, too. Only they didn't. So, I know they really didn't think he was dealing."

"Huh." He tried to keep his gaze on her face, which wasn't easy. What was he supposed to do? Not look?

"And now he's got to work at that place near the freeway," she said. "It's kinda small, don't you think?"

"A little."

That dulled her smile. "But—"

"There's nothing wrong with it," he quickly added.

"You don't have to say that. I guess I'm just sensitive because he's a really good doctor. He even works on his case notes at night. They shouldn't have fired him. They didn't know the whole story."

"That's completely bogus. And the clinic wasn't that bad. They had free coffee and stuff."

He worked hard to stay on her good side after that. He completely avoided anything that would remind her of her dad. By the time he ordered baked Alaska for dessert, she was totally into him. He could tell.

"What do you want to do after this?" she asked.

"I don't know." He knew exactly what he wanted to do after this. "I thought we could cruise around for a while."

"Drive around? You don't mean park somewhere, do you?"

"What? No, of course not. I don't mean that. I just thought we'd go for a drive. Since we have my buddy's car and all."

"Good. That's better. I was hoping you weren't one of those guys."

"Those guys?"

"You know. The kind that takes you out to a fancy dinner and then thinks they'll get something afterward. I hate that."

"What idiots. That's bogus."

"I didn't think you were like that. How about if we check out the Galleria?"

"The Galleria?" He immediately pictured the enormous shopping center with three layers of stores, all of them closed by now. People wandering around like zombies because they had nowhere else to go. Maybe a few girls taking quinceañera snaps by the staircase. Which was not his idea of a good time. "Sure. I guess so. Why not."

"Great." She smiled again. "It's kinda cool to walk around and check out the stuff there. Do you skate?"

"Of course." It took him a moment to realize what she meant. "Oh…you're talking about ice skating."

"What did you think I meant?"

"I was hoping you were talking about the skate park. Hey…I could take you there. Show you where I skateboard."

Maybe he could salvage this date after all. Especially if they didn't have to walk around a closed mall with a bunch of other people, like zombies.

"That sounds good. Teach me?"

"Sure. I'd like that."

He could picture her on a skateboard, and he liked what he saw. She'd totally rock it. If he couldn't get her in the backseat of Kenny's car, at least they'd be somewhere that didn't totally suck.

"It's a plan, then." She sounded happy again. "And we'd better eat all the dessert when it comes. It's super expensive."

Reef nodded along, even though his thoughts were a million miles away. So what if things didn't move forward tonight. There'd be other times. Other dinners and other desserts.

Like his skate buds also said, "Every win has to start with the decision to try."

Chapter Twenty-Nine

Gene

The day before the twenty-fifth annual International Safecracking Competition—or the ISC, for those in the know—started out like any other: a half-dozen walk-ins at the shop, a few deliveries, and then a wave of phone calls to trace a misplaced order. Today, it was a boxful of Emsec knobs that somehow ended up going to a shop in Pearland. Gene spent half the afternoon trying to locate the missing order and the other half trying to convince the FedEx driver to bring it back to the right address.

By the time he rose from his desk at six-thirty, his feet had swollen to twice their normal size. He shuffled to the door and wearily leaned against its frame. His body was betraying him. Little by little, just like Dr. Fischer said it would. What used to take five minutes now took twice as long and sometimes required a rest stop in-between.

He listened for signs of life in the shop. He expected to hear Ted at the machine or maybe Reef with a box cutter, finally unpacking the wayward order. But the only sound that reached him came from an overhead light, which threw off a low, subconscious buzz that barely registered.

Maybe he'd look for Skye and start in on their final lesson before tomorrow. That would give him something to do until the other guys got back.

He slogged toward the showroom. When he emerged through the doorway, though, he realized the front of the shop was just as quiet as the back. Thank goodness no customers lurked around, since nothing bothered him more than to see a customer disappear through the exit because no one was around to help him.

Gene paused next to the Master Lock display. They all must've gone to dinner at the same time, which he'd warned them not to do. He told them the shop would look like a ghost town if they did, but they didn't listen. They never listened. Though, once again, that could've been the riluzole talking.

His gaze pinballed around the place. Just when he was about to give up and go back to the paperwork on his desk, something banged at the rear of the store. Like a door slamming shut. Like the back door, which led to the alley.

He cursed Reef under his breath as he made for the door. The kid was supposed to lock it behind him any time he accepted a delivery. Was it that tough? Otherwise, anyone could wander into the shop. One time, he found a homeless guy relieving himself in the corner, and he had to chase the guy away with a socket wrench when he wouldn't leave.

Sure enough, the door to the alley swung back and forth on a breeze. Maybe he should check out the rear landing before he locked it, just to be safe. You could never be too careful.

He shuffled outside. Just then, something flashed to his left. He could've sworn he saw someone duck behind a thick palm at the end of the property. The landlord had planted it there to spruce things up, only no one ever watered it, so the tree topped out at five feet. Brown fronds dripped to the ground and shrouded some figures crouched behind it.

"Please don't!" A girl's voice rippled over the asphalt. "Don't kill him!"

Leather soles scraped the pavement. Then, the pop of fist hitting bone.

"I mean it, Reef! Stop it."

He recognized Skye's voice then. He hurried over to the palm just as a body spun around and slithered to the ground. He didn't know what was worse: the look on Skye's face or the way blood dribbled from Ted's mouth.

"What happened?" he shouted, as soon as he reached them.

One look at Skye and the torn blouse, and he knew exactly what happened.

The girl didn't seem to hear him, though. She was too busy watching Reef, who stood nearby. The kid shook his fist in the air, as if it was on fire.

Probably the aftershock of his knuckles meeting a rock-hard jaw.

"Skye?" Gene repeated.

But it was no use. Skye couldn't hear him. She only had eyes for Reef. And that was when his memory drifted.

Back in time, to another night just like this one. To another pretty girl with a ruined blouse.

It was Marilyn's freshman year at Immaculate Word. The very same school Skye attended now. It seemed like only a few weeks ago. Maybe a year at most.

His daughter didn't know a soul at the college when she enrolled, but she met a guy soon enough. The guys always hung around the library, she said. It wasn't like they wanted to check out a book, though. They wanted a date for a football game, a fraternity party, whatever. Like the place was a meat market made just for them and the girls were the special of the day.

Marilyn hated it. Until, one day, a certain guy noticed her. A guy who seemed different from the rest. He even helped her get a book from the top shelf when she couldn't reach it. She was so grateful, she agreed to go to a party with him the following weekend.

Gene refused to let her go at first, since she didn't even know the guy. That was one of the worst things about being a single parent. He had to play both bad cop and good cop, and sometimes he didn't know which one to be.

When Marilyn started to cry, she took the decision out of his hands, anyway. He'd do anything to make her happy. Anything to dry the tears. So, in the end, he relented, of course, and he told her to have fun and be home by midnight.

She putzed around in the bathroom for a whole hour the night of the date, and when she reemerged, he didn't recognize her. Gone were the glasses and ponytail, replaced by contacts, hair she'd straightened on the ironing board, and feet that wobbled in sky-high leather wedges.

She looked amazing. Prettier than he'd ever seen her, and she was a beautiful baby to begin with.

The hours dragged by once Marilyn left for the party. When she didn't come home at midnight, he tried not to worry. Told himself at least she had some friends now and he should be grateful for that. Maybe she just lost track of time. He wasn't drinking back then, though, so the worry gnawed at him more and more, until the telephone finally rang at twelve-thirty.

"Marilyn?" Desperation crept into his voice.

"Daddy? I need a ride home. Can you come get me?"

What was worse...the way she called him "daddy," which she hadn't done for a dozen years, or the way her voice cracked on the last word? Maybe it was neither of those. Maybe the fact she called him, instead of a girlfriend, told him everything he needed to know.

By some miracle, he didn't get pulled over by the cops as he sped to the address she provided, even though he pushed seventy all the way there. He raced past house after house, looking for the one with a party out front, until he spotted an open garage door and a gaggle of kids on the drive.

His car fishtailed to a stop before he hopped out. When he realized Marilyn wasn't part of the gang on the driveway, though, he kept walking. Everyone backed away from him as he passed, once they realized it was someone's dad. He could've heard a pin drop as he walked from the driveway to the house, where he paused at the foot of the stairs.

He spotted someone sitting at the very top, all alone. The girl had stick-straight hair and sky-high leather wedges.

"Marilyn?" He hurried to her side and wrapped his arm around her. He dried a tear with his other hand, which trailed mascara down her cheek. That was when he noticed the ripped blouse.

The world stopped. And in the silence, when he wanted to put his fist through the nearest wall, or the nearest face, he stuffed the anger down and drew her closer. He tucked her in tight before he helped her down the stairs and through the crowd, all the way to the car door.

This time, the kids on the driveway pretended not to notice him as he hurried along. That wasn't what he remembered most, though. What he remembered most was the look on Marilyn's face when he drove her away from the party. It was a look of pure relief, tinged with wonder. The same look Skye gave Reef now. He understood it implicitly.

Only, this was Reef's show, not his. The best thing he could do was get

Ted's carcass off the pavement and make sure the guy never went anywhere near Skye again.

It was a good thing Reef was the one who found Ted and Skye, instead of him. This time he would've killed the bastard. Even with fingers that shook.

No matter what, he would've found a way.

Chapter Thirty

Skye

She couldn't catch her breath as she made her way into the shop. She went to the front counter, where she slapped her hand on the display case. She needed to feel cool, solid glass beneath her fingers. Anything to jumpstart her lungs.

She didn't want anyone to see her like this, and especially not Mr. Jacks. He'd think she couldn't handle herself. That she needed a big, strong guy to save her. Someone like Reef.

To be honest, there was no telling what Ted would've done if Reef hadn't come outside when he did. She tried not to think about it, or about the look on Ted's face when he grabbed her, but it was impossible. Her memory snagged on the ugly snarl and the darkness in his eyes.

Breathe in, breathe out.

And so it went, for at least a minute. Gradually, her vision sharpened, the empty store aisles came into focus, and she felt the grit beneath her fingertips.

How could she have been so stupid? Ted never asked her to do anything for him. She should've known something was up when he asked if she could carry a box to his car.

In fact, he'd barely spoken to her before. When he did, it was in monosyllables, like a caveman. *Yeah. No. Uh, uh.*

But that didn't mean he didn't stare. She should've paid more attention to that. She should've noticed the way her skin crawled whenever he looked at her. That whenever he threw a sideways glance at her—he must've thought she wouldn't notice—the skin on her arms goose-pimpled. Especially when he didn't look away. He acted like it was his right to stare. Like it was his right to give her the willies when she never asked for the attention.

After a while, she pretended not to notice him. Why did she do that? Why didn't she say something then? She should've told Mr. Jacks about it, although she knew it would be her word against his. Since she only started working at the shop last month, and not ten years ago, like Ted, people might not believe her. They might tell her Ted was harmless or lonely or just horsing around. Maybe *she* was the one with the problem. No, it was better to lay low and let Ted enjoy his little peepshow. It couldn't hurt anything. Right?

She'd have to tell Dad when she got home, of course. He'd notice the ripped shirt, and he'd want to know how it happened. How many times before had he warned her about guys like Ted? Told her to stay away from greasy old men who puckered the skin on her arms and made her neck tingle? He'd be so mad at her. And disappointed she hadn't listened to him.

Not to mention, what about all those stranger-danger movies she saw back in high school? Every year, they played the same one in gym class. And, every year, a narrator told them the best way to fend off an attacker laid right in their palms. Literally. All she had to do was crook her wrist back and jam her palm into the guy's jawbone. Simple. It would be like hitting a punching bag. Only, a punching bag like Ted could hit her back.

Maybe it was something on her face. Was that it? Could Ted tell by looking at her that she wouldn't fight back? That she wasn't a stranger-danger-type person who would deck him with the heel of her hand?

Now, the look on Ted's face when Reef came after him…that was a different story. Skye surprised herself by laughing out loud. It was impossible not to. The minute Ted realized what was happening, his eyes bulged, like he was SpongeBob SquarePants on a sugar high. Like the guy could see his life flashing before his eyes and he didn't necessarily like the show.

She laughed harder as she pushed against the counter. When she finally sobered up, she realized she'd knocked aside an old practice lock Mr. Jacks made for her.

He'd gone to so much trouble. He'd taken an old lock and sawed it in half to expose the inside. The wheels, the fence, the gate, the random screws, the pilot holes. She lifted the lock and carefully turned it over, front to back. She had no idea how he did it, but he laid bare all the stuff that made a lock work. He even superglued a piece of Plexiglass on top, so she wouldn't jar the fence from the gate by accident.

"You okay in here?"

The voice startled her. "Yeah. I think so."

"Sorry. Didn't mean to scare you." Mr. Jacks walked into the showroom, his hand raking what little hair he had left over his scalp. "Though I understand why you'd be jumpy."

"It's okay. I'll get over it."

"Really?"

"Really." Although, there was no telling how long *that* would take. How long before she heard a noise and didn't flinch? Saw a shadow and didn't duck? Before the thought of someone asking her to go outside didn't cause her to cringe? Right now, all she wanted was to bask in the bright lights of the showroom and feel safe again.

"Ted's gone." Mr. Jacks made another pass at his hair, but his fingers wobbled so much it didn't do any good. "You don't have to worry about him anymore. I fired his ass."

"He's lucky Reef didn't kill him. I really thought he would."

"Reef's a smart kid. He knows Ted's not worth it."

Her boss moved closer. But he didn't try to touch her or hug her or do anything else awkward. Instead, he joined her at the counter and leaned against the plate glass, just like her. "My buddy would call him a regular POS."

"Excuse me?" She'd heard him on the phone sometimes, talking to a friend during a cigarette break. She knew the guy on the other end was a cop by the way the acronyms flew: IFR. MO. And now, apparently, POS.

"Piece of shit," he said. "I thought that's what you kids called it."

"Um, no." She wanted to laugh again, but that might hurt his feelings. It was funny when he tried to sound cool. It reminded her of Axl trying to wiggle into an old Kleenex box that was much too small for him. They both thought they were something they weren't.

"I've got a great idea," he said. "Why don't we practice with the locks? It'll take your mind off things." He nodded at the halved lock in front of her. "C'mon. You've only got a few hours left until the big show tomorrow."

"Sure. I guess so." She gratefully reached for the jerry-rigged lock, thankful to have something to do with her hands. "Or...I could try one of those." She pointed to a tall safe that leaned against the wall.

A gleaming silver model from Original Safe and Vault, it had four wheels, instead of three, which meant it was a hundred times harder to open. It also had removable shelves for jewelry and stuff. Customers always seemed surprised when she told them that. When she rattled off the accessories, UIL rating, door thickness, fire grade. As if she was too young to know that stuff, let alone care about it.

"They won't give you a four-wheeler at the contest," Mr. Jacks said. "It'd take too long, and no one wants to sit through that. But if you insist."

He moved around the counter, with her on his heels. Before they reached the back wall, though, he suddenly stopped.

"I forgot. I've got a trick to get you ready." With that, he pivoted and disappeared through the side door again.

She waited while he scrounged up whatever he was looking for. When he returned after a second, he held his arms behind his back, as if hiding something.

"What're you doing?"

"Nothing. Let's go see about that four-wheeler."

They moved around the counter again and walked to the wall. She knelt beside the Original safe, and he did the same. Like always, she closed her eyes before she touched the dial, and, like always, she waited for the numbers to talk to her.

It sounded cheesy, but each safe told her something different. Gave her a clue about what to do. She couldn't explain it, and, even if she did, no one would believe her. So, she reached for the cold-rolled steel, but her eyes flew open when something loud blared next to her.

"You ain't nothin' but a hound dog..."

Mr. Jacks crouched beside her with an old-timey boombox on his lap, the volume cranked to high.

"What're you doing?" she yelled.

He grinned but didn't turn it down.

"...cryin' all the time."

"Could you please turn that thing off?" Her voice was shrill, but she felt ridiculous. If he was trying to help her, he was going about it all wrong.

He kept right on grinning, though. He seemed to think it was funny to hear Elvis bounce off the shop's walls. She rolled onto her heels and waited for him to finally knock it off. She'd been embarrassed enough for one night.

"Okay, okay," he mouthed. He reached for the volume and killed the music. "I want to work on your concentration. It's an old trick I learned years ago. Hell, you probably weren't even born back then. Someone taught me to practice with music on. It'll help you focus, no matter what else is going on around you."

"But Elvis Presley? Really?"

"Elvis. The Police. Whatever. It doesn't matter." He gestured with his free hand, and she noticed the tremble again. Like the music never stopped playing. Like his knuckles danced to a backbeat that wasn't there anymore.

It was getting worse. Over the past month, the quiver in Mr. Jacks's hands had grown to a full-blown quake, and she noticed it all the time now.

"Mr. Jacks?" She wanted to say something before, but she didn't know what.

"Yeah?"

"Is everything okay? I mean, with your hands and stuff?"

"Hmmm." His fingers slipped off the boombox. "Why do you ask?"

"Because you seem sick. Are you?" Even though he never talked about it, something was obviously wrong.

"That bad, huh?" He shrugged. "Wasn't sure how long before you'd notice."

"Oh, I noticed."

He lumbered to his feet, and then he moved to one of the stools behind the counter and plunked down the silent boombox. "Guess I should've told you sooner."

"You don't have to keep stuff from me. I'm not a baby, you know."

"I know. But I figured if I told you, you'd feel sorry for me. And that's the last thing I wanted. It all began about a month ago."

Time stood still as he told her the story. Tears slowly filled her eyes, even though she knew it was the last thing he wanted. She couldn't help it, and neither could he.

Chapter Thirty-One

Reef

The minute his fist bounced off Ted's jaw, the old guy dropped to the ground like a bag of rocks. One pop to the mouth—rapid-fire, like a gunshot—and the guy's head snapped back from his spine. After that, Ted did a three-sixty on the pavement and collapsed on the ground.

The nerves blazed in Reef's hand so he shook it, but it was no use. His knuckles throbbed and burned. All the stuff that happened when bone met bone with nothing to get in the way.

The only reason he didn't slaughter Ted was because of Skye. The way she screamed at him to stop. She sounded hysterical, and he didn't want to make things worse by decking the guy again.

He never meant to be a superhero. He only did it because of the way Ted trapped Skye behind the palm tree, like an animal. It reminded him of all those times back in junior high, when he first got to America, and the eighth graders penned him beside his locker. The guys laughed at the wild look on Reef's face when he realized he couldn't get away from them. He was trapped behind a wall of flannel shirts and blue jeans, worn by guys who desperately wanted him to go for it. Because, if he went for it, that gave the jocks the right to pound him into the pavement.

He finally stepped away from Ted's body and shook his fist one last time.

"Crap. That hurts." But he threw Skye a smile, too, because he wanted her to think he did it all for her sake. And he'd do it all over again.

"Here. Let me see your hand." She reached for it with trembling fingers. She didn't seem to notice the rip in her shirt, which showed off a lacy pink bra. It was shiny and frilly, and something he didn't expect a girl like her to wear.

"Your hand's all red. We should put ice on it or something."

"Or something," he said, all casual like. Let her think he got in fistfights all the time. That this wasn't only his second one. And the first? It happened when one of the middle-schoolers got tired of stalling and took a swing at him.

"I'm so glad you found us." She began to rub his knuckles, awkwardly.

"I thought I heard someone back here. What was that guy thinking?" He threw a disgusted look at the lump on the ground. It was anyone's guess what was going through Ted's mind when he hit on Skye. The perv had to know it wasn't going to end well.

"He asked me to come out here and help him load a box in his car." Skye shook her head, as if she couldn't believe how stupid she was. "I should've asked you to do it. But I had no idea he was going to jump me like that."

"He ruined your shirt."

She finally noticed the gap and then she quickly pulled the ends together. "I know. The big jerk. Now I have to throw it away."

"Here." He pulled his hand from hers and shrugged off his black hoodie, which he threw over her shoulders. "You can wear this."

Her eyes widened, as if he'd tossed a mink coat over her shoulders and not an Under Armour sweatshirt.

"Thanks. It's kinda cold out here."

For some reason, she kept looking at him. As if she'd forgotten all about the body lying at their feet. Maybe she could pretend it never happened that way, and pretty soon Ted would wake up from a nap or something.

Meanwhile, the guy gasped for air, like a beached carp.

"See?" Reef kicked Ted's shoulder with his tennis shoe. "I didn't kill him."

"No, but you could've. How'd you learn to fight like that?"

"Guess I picked it up at the skate park. You've gotta hustle for what you want out there." No need for her to know he was a nerd when he first showed up in America. That his father was the one who taught him how to throw a punch so he wouldn't get cornered after school again. "It's no big deal."

Even though it was kind of a big deal, if he thought about it. Chick in distress and all that.

"It's a huge deal." She leaned forward and softly kissed his cheek. "I owe you one."

Ka-ching! A light bulb went off in his head, like the bare bulb in the stockroom that brought the dark corners to life. A moment he'd been waiting for. Maybe now he could finally get her to loosen up. After all, she just said she owed him one. Right?

Chapter Thirty-Two

Gene

A major cold-front swept through Houston overnight and lowered the temperature in the house by twenty degrees by the time daylight broached the bedroom window. He rolled off the mattress and pulled on a black fleece pullover, black jeans, and equally dark Adidas. He purposefully chose a getup that would make him look and feel like a Secret Service agent. A wall of black everyone would notice but no one would be able to place. At least, not the newcomers.

Old-timers would remember him, of course. The guys who went back decades. They were the ones who conjured a whole safecracking industry out of nothing. Back then, in the early seventies, he could walk into a boring conference room for a contest—no fancy-schmancy ballrooms back then—and hear whispers lash behind his back like a bullwhip sluicing the air. *That's him. Are you sure? Gotta be.*

He owned those early contests, when people treated him like royalty. When they watched his every move and followed his every step. Their eyes widened whenever he walked into a lobby or hall. They shyly approached him and asked for his "secret" to cracking a safe. The smiles faded, though, when he told them there was no secret. Just hours and hours spent practicing with a dial, training his fingers to feel something most people couldn't, and blocking out everything but the call of the wheel.

But that was then. Now, he stood in his bathroom and tried to flatten his hair with wobbling fingers. He even added a little Brylcreem on top to grease the cowlick down.

If the past was any indication, he should finish up pronto and get to the J.W. Marriott as quickly as possible. Not that being early would change anything—she'd still face the same competitors, no matter what—but he wanted time to gauge the scene first. Help him acclimate to the surroundings so he wouldn't be distracted by things that didn't matter. The sideshows. The lights and noise. Things that tempted weaker men and made them forget why they were there in the first place.

A lot of people went to the contests to be entertained. To mingle in the lobby and cram their pockets full of free stuff, which they'd never, ever use. They couldn't get enough of it, because they finally found themselves in like-minded company. Surrounded by people who understood the pull of safecracking and the lure of anything that came with a combination lock.

The British guys would be there, of course, wearing skinny jeans and collared shirts, and the ones from South America, who seemed to think chunky gold chains never went out of style. Lots of Asians, who also wore black to feel stealthy when they walked down the halls. A few girls—women, actually—but none as young as Skye. Mostly wives and grown daughters of lock-shop owners, who came by their love of safes honestly.

Gene finally exhaled when he pulled up in front of the hotel. Good thing he'd instructed Skye to meet him in the lobby, since she'd only make him nervous on the drive over by asking too many questions and getting too distracted. He knew she'd be overwhelmed—there was no question about that—but maybe he could calm her down if he got his own head in the game first.

The hotel would be bustling by now. Vendors always arrived early to watch the union guys assemble their displays like giant Legos. The workers connected the structures pole by pole, bracket by bracket, until a sky-high display emerged that paid tribute to the latest gizmos and gadgets in the lock industry.

Next, the sales guys would arrive. They would fan glossy brochures on every available surface and wait like vultures for their customers to walk through the entrance.

It was all a sideshow, really. Something to give people a breather between classes in the conference rooms. The classes were the "official" reason for the event. The reason they used in their ads, anyway. Classes all day long, tucked into nondescript conference rooms that orbited the flashy Grand Ballroom. Classes on locksmithing, stun guns, business accounting, you name it. Real-world stuff, which they sugarcoated with the tacky giveaways, free booze, and disco lights.

He drove toward the flat-fronted hotel, which anchored an entire corner of pricey downtown real estate. Coated wires crisscrossed overhead, creating a grid for the electric trains that cruised through Houston. The train wires fractured his attention for a moment and pulled his gaze sideways, but he still managed to swerve into an empty parking lot at the last second and pop a twenty into the meter, which guaranteed all-day parking.

Cold air greeted him as he left the lot and walked into the hotel.

The minute he stepped into the lobby, things changed. It felt as if he'd tumbled through a snow globe and landed in a wonderland of silver confetti and smooth jazz.

Uniformed attendants milled around with shiny placards: Conference Bookstore. Visitors' Lounge. Judge's Area. Only one sign read Check-In, so Gene headed for that one.

Once he signed in, he accepted a Kelly-green tote bag stuffed with brochures and a plastic nametag, which he trashed. The people who needed to know his name already knew it, so what was the point? Only then, when he'd squared everything away, did he pull out his cell and call Skye.

She picked up on the first ring. "Where are you?" She sounded desperate.

"Okay, now. Slow down." He didn't expect the nerves to kick in so early. It was going to be a *looonnnggg* day. "I'm in the lobby. Where're you?"

"We just got here. Reef's parking. Oh, my god...the hotel is huge!"

"It's that not huge," he lied. Of course, it was all a matter of perspective, and to some people, maybe it seemed small. Just not to Skye.

"I don't think I can do this..." She hadn't stepped one foot in the hotel and already she'd become her own worst enemy.

"Listen to me, Skye. You can do this." He hated to state the obvious, but he'd do it all day long, if that was what it took. "This is what you've been working for. Just park the damn car and come inside. I'm standing next to the registration desk."

"Okay." Her voice had fallen even more.

He had to do something. "You know, I haven't seen any other girls here yet." Some people might call the ploy sneaky, but she didn't really give him a choice. "No one wants you girls to be here, anyway. You should leave it to the big boys."

"Excuse me?"

"You know what I'm saying." He gazed around the empty lobby. "Right now, it's just me and some fellas. Why don't you turn around and go back to bed? Get some beauty sleep. Let us guys have our fun."

"I'll be there in a minute." Finally, an edge crept back into her voice. "Don't go anywhere."

That's more like it. He smiled as slipped the cell in his pocket. If she only knew how much like Marilyn she sounded. How his daughter's voice hardened, too, whenever someone told her she couldn't do something. Then she channeled the fear into motion and put one foot in front of the other until she got where she needed to be. She took all that nervous energy and funneled it into something useful. Just like Skye.

A second later, she slipped into the lobby, with Reef close behind. She looked like a waif in black: skinny jeans, checkered tennis shoes, and a chunky sweater that stopped at her collarbone. *Perfect.* The only thing missing was the Buddy Holly glasses, which normally covered the top half of her face.

"Yo!"

At first, she froze at the sound of his voice. But once she spotted him, she slumped to his side, her shoulders stooped for some reason.

"Don't do that," he snapped.

"Do what?"

She looked surprised, but he didn't have time to worry about her feelings. He'd have to make it up to her later.

"Don't slouch like that. You have every right to be here. And what'd you do with the glasses?"

"I…I thought I'd wear my contacts instead."

"You thought wrong." He clipped his words on purpose. She needed a little tough love right about now. It was the only way she'd make it through the day. "The glasses give you an 'in.' Something for people to talk about, remember you by. Everyone will know you after a while as the girl in the glasses. Put 'em back on."

She fumbled around in her pocket until she found the chunky frames. "Okay. Fine. I'll put them on after I take out my contacts. By the way, you didn't even say good morning to Reef yet."

She gestured behind her, where Reef stood waiting.

"Hey, Reef." Gene nodded at him.

The kid wore slim-fitting sweats with no pockets and a matching hoodie. He'd even slicked his hair back to keep it out of his eyes today. "Looking good, son."

"Thanks. This place is huge."

"It's all just smoke and mirrors." Gene frowned, since he needed Reef to be on his side today. He didn't need Reef to make Skye feel even more nervous than she already did. "It's really not that big."

Luckily, Reef got the message. "Oh, yeah. You're right. This place is dinky compared to others."

Gene returned his attention to Skye. "Here's what we're gonna do. We're going to let everyone else waste their time in the lobby. We're going straight to the ballroom. I want to show you what it looks like."

He walked away before she could protest. When she caught up to him, her head wobbled back and forth, like a goldfish attracted to anything shiny. She gaped at everything and anything, including a giant roulette wheel embedded with hundreds of tiny LED lights. A camo-colored pinball machine next to it advertised gun safes. Not to mention the sparkly velvet ropes that marked the passageway like something from a Hollywood movie premier. He didn't slow down for any of it, though, until someone stopped right in front of him.

"Gene, my man!" A stranger clapped Gene on the shoulder, the *thwack* echoing down the hall.

The man was huge, and he wore a Super Bowl-size ring on each finger, thumbs included.

Gene finally remembered his name. "Hey, Reynaldo. Guess they're letting anyone in these days."

The giant smiled, which exposed a diamond in his front tooth. "I thought you died, man. Haven't seen you around in a dog's age."

"Then you weren't looking in the right places." He never did like Reynaldo, to be honest. The guy was a showboat, and he only distracted the media with all the bling. Took the focus off the art of safecracking. A poser, was what kids today would call him. He'd have to remember to use that term when he talked to Skye and Reef later.

"Look, I'm kinda busy," Gene said. "See you around."

"Not so fast." The poser turned to Skye. "This guy your uncle? You know you're with a legend, right? The one-and-only Gene Jacks. The king of safecracking."

To Gene's everlasting relief, Skye rolled her eyes. "Yeah, that's what he tells me. He's a legend in his own mind."

"See?" Gene feigned resignation. "Kids. What're you gonna do?"

He moved around Reynaldo's massive frame. He didn't have time for this. Guys like Reynaldo wanted to waste his time talking about the past. They couldn't forget the attention and they still thirsted for the fame.

It was your typical story: bozos like Reynaldo chased after the limelight, even after it dimmed, while the rest of them got on with their lives.

Once he finally broke free of the man, Gene headed for the ballroom, with the teenagers on his heels. A pair of closed doors greeted them. No one ever locked hotel doors, though, since workers needed to dart inside to set up tables and chairs. Sure enough, one of the doors swung open when he twisted the knob.

The room was even bigger than he imagined. Unlike a lot of places, the Grand Ballroom lived up to its name. A Volkswagen-size chandelier hung from the ceiling, its sides draped in gold fabric that stretched from one corner of the room to the other. A platform took center stage under the chandelier, and hundreds of chairs with chrome legs and padded seats circled it. The place looked like a wrestling arena in Vegas, complete with velvet ropes to separate the crowd from competitors. As a final touch, a television camera blocked the back entrance, probably a local sports channel that had nothing better to do on a Sunday afternoon than film a safecracking competition.

After a second, he realized what was missing: the sound of anyone behind him. He turned around to see Skye and Reef, who were frozen in place.

Skye broke the silence first. "You're kidding, right?"

Gene waved it all away. "This is nothing. You should've seen the hotels back in New York. Now, *those* were ballrooms."

It was another lie, of course. When he first started out, the year Nixon took office, professional safecrackers stayed at fleabag motels with names like the Oasis and Del Rio and Hiway Hacienda. It took decades for the venues to get better.

"Whoa, dude." Reef sounded like a six-year-old at a McDonald's PlayPlace. "This room is ginormous."

"It's not that big, Reef. And it's kinda tacky, don't you think?"

Thank goodness, Reef caught his drift again. "Oh, yeah. It's cheesy. Low-key cheesy. Like, when's the next bar mitzvah?"

But Skye wasn't buying it. She continued to stare at the shiny fabric that fell from the chandelier and the sea of purple chairs under it. "They're expecting this many people? They put out five hundred chairs."

"Nah. There's not that many." Gene tried to sound nonchalant, but he knew she was right. Skye could work numbers backward and forward, and she could estimate anything in the blink of an eye. "Lots of folks won't even show. I mean, c'mon. Would you rather watch some strangers work a dial or stay in the lobby and get free stuff? They only put out that many chairs to impress the TV people."

"TV people?" Her eyes widened even more. "What do you mean, 'TV people'?"

What could he say? She was bound to find out anyway. Better for her to know everything now than get blindsided closer to the contest. This way, there'd be no surprises.

"Sometimes a local TV station will film it. Kind of like a human-interest story, I think they call it. You won't even notice them."

In fact, Gene never noticed the cameras when he competed. He focused on the brand-new lock in front of him and did his job. So intent on feeling for the fence, it startled him to hear the audience break into applause whenever he cracked open a safe.

He'd squint at the news reporter afterward, dumbfounded, whenever one thrust a microphone under his nose. Say a few words for the folks back home? To be honest, there wasn't anything to say. He was faster than anyone else when it came to cracking a safe. End of story.

Just when he was about to physically turn Skye away from the camera, something jangled in his pocket. He cautiously pulled out his cell and checked the screen.

Uh-oh. It was Boudreaux. Calling him bright and early on a Sunday morning. Didn't the guy have a poker game last night? That would mean—what?—he got three hours of shut-eye, maybe? The guy should be sleeping it off instead of bugging Gene with a phone call.

"Aren't you going to answer it?" Skye asked.

"Nah. I'll call him back. Let's go see where they put your chair on the stage."

No need to distract Skye with the telephone call. Right now, it was time to focus on the here and now and block out everything else.

"C'mere." He quickly waved her forward.

Seven chairs marched along the stage, their seats padded for the contestants' comfort. Next to each chair sat a brand-new Sentry safe, set at an angle for the camera's benefit.

Each chair wore a laminated card on its backrest. The names read like a roll call at the United Nations.

First up was Sergei Ivonovich. No doubt a refugee from the former Soviet Republic, odds were good the Russian couldn't last more than an hour without a cigarette. Ivonovich would lose his focus pretty quick without a Sobronie between his teeth, which would only help Skye in the long run.

Beside Ivonovich was a chair for Jose Castro, who might've come from South America. The boys from Brazil always brought along an entourage of nephews, uncles, and whoever else happened to be nearby. Midway through the contest, the group would start chanting, as if they were at a soccer game instead of a safecracking competition.

His gaze moved farther south. Like a bettor at the racetrack, Gene handicapped the missing competitors by their names alone. Apparently, someone by the name of Chaz Lee earned the third seat on the stage, which was as close to the center as possible. That one could be a real problem. The name sounded young, and young ones always had a lot to prove, since they wanted to show their families they hadn't screwed up their lives by choosing safecracking over a safer, saner career, like medicine or engineering.

Finally, at the very end of the row, he found a chair marked for Skye. Next to the video camera and the farthest seat away from the middle. Might as well have been Siberia.

In his experience, the audience always focused on the middle. Skye could fall asleep out there on the end, mesmerized by a dial that went around and around, instead of feeding off the energy of the crowd. No, it wouldn't do at all.

He made a mental note to find the manager later and get him or her to make the switch. He'd give some bullshit story about how Skye's eyesight required a middle placement. Peripheral vision and all that. He'd moved his own chair plenty of times when he was competing, and now it was his turn to stack the deck in Skye's favor.

His experience had to count for something, right? If it couldn't help Marilyn, at least it could help Skye.

Chapter Thirty-Three

Skye

She'd never seen a room so big, or so empty. It looked like a football field, with fabric walls joined at the seams that went on and on and an enormous light above her head that glowed like a scoreboard.

She felt like doing cartwheels down the carpet. She wanted to whisper her name to the walls and hear it echo in return. Throw one of her Vans at the fancy chandelier above her head to see if she could hit a crystal and make it dance.

But what was with the television camera? Mr. Jacks never said anything about that. Then again, she might not have believed him if he had.

She knew stations filmed stuff like poker tournaments, video-game contests...that kind of thing. She saw the shows sometimes when she flipped channels on her way to *Jeopardy*. All the tournaments looked the same to her, a bunch of dorky guys in dark sunglasses who turned their baseball caps sideways to look cool.

But that was different. The camera next to this stage looked professional. Like it belonged to a big-time TV station. One of the regular ones that actually broadcast its shows during the daytime.

A cold fear swept over her again. The same fear that consumed her when she arrived in the lobby that morning. The room was stuffed with shiny furniture and pricey lights and industrial steel beams that looked like sculptures in an art gallery. Something that was way out of her league.

Too bad Dad wasn't here. He'd probably whistle under his breath and say something corny, like "Holy cow!" Then he'd wander off to check his phone messages, of course, but for a moment, at least, he'd be impressed.

Her gaze fell to the carpet. "It's freezing in here, Mr. Jacks." Good thing she wore a sweater, because cold air blew around her legs.

"It'll warm up." He waved her forward. "C'mon."

He sounded so sure of himself. Instead of answering his cell phone a minute ago, he stuffed it in his pocket. She'd never seen him so serious.

"C'mon," he repeated. "Go check out the stage."

For some reason, she felt keenly aware of the holes in her jeans and scuff marks on her Vans as she walked to the stage. What with the mirrors, she couldn't make a move without seeing her reflection bounce back a dozen times over. So, maybe Mr. Jacks was right. Maybe it was a good thing she put the glasses back on. People would remember her, all right, but the glasses also helped mask her fear.

She broke away from the others and headed for the platform. Plastic chairs fanned out in four quadrants, separated by wide aisles that led to the stage. She cautiously approached the nearest one. The aisle ended with a temporary set of stairs that climbed higher and higher, until they reached the platform.

She gripped the stair's flimsy handrail out of habit, but it wobbled. Apparently, they made it with cheap aluminum. She'd have to remember that when she went on stage later. The last thing she wanted was to fall on her face in front of all those people or land in some poor guy's lap in the first row.

She carefully climbed the stairs and set her backpack on the ground. Then she looked up and took a slow turn, gradually spinning faster and faster, until the glow of the chandelier became a continuous thread of light. She kept spinning until the room tilted sideways, and then she only stopped to catch her breath.

"So cool." She couldn't think of anything else to say. The beige fabric on the walls swallowed her voice, so it didn't echo like she expected. It did, however, attract the attention of Mr. Jacks, who stared at her as if she'd lost her mind.

"Are you finished yet?" He threw up his hands, as if he didn't know what to do with her.

"Not yet." She'd never been on a stage like this. All those times she played in the symphony, they crammed the musicians onto risers that left no room for anything but instruments and music stands. But here, she had all the space in the world. Space to do more cartwheels than she'd ever done before or give a high kick, like one of those dancers in the Rockettes, or twirl around and around, like a kid in a three-way mirror at the Houston Rodeo. It felt freeing, to say the least.

"Okay, then." Mr. Jacks still stared at her as if she'd lost her mind. "I think you've got the hang of it."

Reluctantly, she moved to the edge of the platform. Just when she was about to rescue her backpack from the floor, a door banged open across the way. An old lady in a white apron bustled into the ballroom with a tray of shiny water glasses. She scowled at Skye before she set the glasses on a table.

"What're you doing up there?" She seemed surprised to find someone onstage.

"Uh...I dunno."

"Get off," the woman snapped. "You're not supposed to be up there."

Normally, Skye would grab the backpack and go, since the lady was, like, fifty years older than her, but something about the lady's tone tickled the hair on the back of her neck. She wasn't hurting anything. The stage could take way more punishment than what she was giving it. The old lady was just being mean.

And mean people sucked.

"Excuse me?" she asked.

"You heard me. Get off." The lady took a step closer, as if she planned to push Skye off the stage if she didn't move.

Skye quickly glanced at Mr. Jacks. Why didn't *he* say something? He was the one who told her to get up there in the first place. He should be the one to tell the worker to back off.

But he didn't. He acted like it was her problem and she'd have to handle it.

So, Skye said the first thing that popped into her head. "It's okay. The general manager told me he didn't mind. I'm in the contest this afternoon."

Well, that came out quickly. For some reason, the lie just rolled right off her lips. But only because the lady in front of her was being mean, and she shouldn't boss around teenagers like that. It was true…mean people sucked.

"Oh." Whether the woman actually believed Skye or not, the lie took the wind from her sails. "I didn't know. Sorry."

"That's okay. There was no way you could know." Skye even tossed off a smile, to prove she was being the bigger person.

"Mr. Roberts didn't tell me. He never tells me anything. But if he said it's okay, then I guess it's okay."

"No problem. I'm done here, anyway." Skye reached for the backpack and flung it over her shoulder as she hopped off the stage. She didn't even bother to grab the flimsy handrail this time. "Please thank him for me. He's a nice guy."

She walked back to where Mr. Jacks stood with his mouth agape. She didn't apologize to him, either, or explain herself. She did what she had to do. Right?

After all, she'd learned from the best.

Chapter Thirty-Four

Gene

Watching Skye lie like that was a revelation.

Usually, kids like Skye couldn't keep a straight face when they did it. At least, that was what he found with Marilyn. The few times she tried to lie to him, she started out strong but then cracked a smile halfway through, which meant the gig was up.

The best liars? Definitely the cops he played poker with. They all lied. Only, they called it bluffing, and the lies stopped the minute they turned in their chips. At least, that was how it was supposed to happen.

This time felt different, though. Skye didn't blink when she said she knew the general manager, as if she believed it herself. Her face betrayed nothing, and that was what worried him.

Yeah, she would've made a helluva poker player. Or, a great con. Neither of which made him feel particularly proud at the moment.

After all, what did he really know about her? She never invited her parents to come and visit the shop, even though he reminded her several times. For all he knew, she lived on her own in a rundown apartment building on Westheimer. Sort of like that kids' book he got Marilyn for Christmas one year. The one with a girl and her horse, where the kid—she had a funny name. Poppy, maybe?— ran roughshod over the grownups when they tried to question her.

Skye seemed fine in every other way, though. And it sounded like she finally regained her confidence, which was the most important thing. He needed her to be okay with everything today: the cold air-conditioning, the enormity of the ballroom, the chaos outside in the hall...all things that could distract her otherwise. So, she had that going for her.

"Hey." Skye reached for his arm when they walked into the hall. "I have to go to the bathroom and take out these contacts. Have you seen one?"

"Nope. I've never been here before either, remember? But maybe you and Reef can find one. I've gotta return a call, anyway."

"Sure," Reef said. "I'll bet there's one out front. C'mon."

Once Skye and Reef took off, Gene pulled the cell from his pocket and checked his recent calls before tapping on Boudreaux's name. His buddy answered right away.

"That you, Gene?" Boudreaux's voice sounded soft and muffled, as if he'd stuffed a wad of food in his cheek again.

"Yeah, it's me. You called earlier?"

"Um, hmmm." Boudreaux paused, probably to drop whatever he was eating and wipe the sauce from his chin. "Got some bad news last night. Another girl died in that stash house across from the school."

Gene squinted. It took him a moment to realize what Boudreaux was talking about. When he did, he pictured a giant pile of designer handbags, with a smaller clump of candy-colored computer notebooks nearby. "You mean the house with two safes?"

"Yup. That's the one."

"I thought you closed that place down."

"We did. Only they found a body outside this time, in the bushes. The gardener went out there yesterday to mow the lawn, and there she was."

"You don't say. Overdose?" It was an easy guess, since why else would a college girl show up dead in someone's front yard?

"Same as last time. Another kid with prescription meds in her purse." Boudreaux paused to let Gene catch up with him. It was a little too early for either of them to think clearly or to put two and two together and hope to come up with anything close to four. "Did you ever ask any of your contacts about that guy called the Fireplug?"

Gene pursed his lips since he'd forgotten all about it, to be honest. In his defense, he had a lot going on. "Nah. I never did hear anything. Okay, I didn't ask. But my clients aren't exactly the right market for a drug dealer."

"Never said they were. But we need to nail this guy before it happens again. Cap's calling the DEA today if we don't."

"Wish I could help you, buddy. I really do. But I don't know anything. Look, I've gotta go. Keep me posted, okay?"

Gene grunted goodbye and clicked off the line. To be honest, so many thoughts swirled through his brain, he didn't know what to say. Since the conversation didn't affect him right here and right now, he'd have to deal with it later. Once he got Skye up on that stage and after they got this show on the road.

Everything else could wait until then.

* * *

By the time the contest rolled around, every seat in the Grand Ballroom was taken. Even some extra chairs they'd added to accommodate the overflow crowd.

The new chairs messed up the tidy little rows and turned the seating area into a giant blob, with no discernable pattern. Skye didn't seem to have a problem with it, though, because she threaded her way through the crowd and bounded up the stairs to the stage. She didn't even bother to grab a flimsy aluminum handrail on the makeshift stairs, as if she couldn't wait to reach her seat.

Which Gene had managed to get moved to the center of the stage. Unfortunately, for the poor guy from South America, that meant someone else had to sit in Siberia. But better the soccer player than Skye.

The organizers had staged everything for maximum effect. A DJ kicked off the event with some snazzy music, and then an announcer bellowed out each contestant's name and hometown. The crowd went wild for the local girl from Houston, and they cheered and cheered until she finally acknowledged them by pumping her fist in the air.

And, just like that, the contest started. The competitors locked gazes on their wheels and never glanced away. Their fingers blurred as they twirled the dials around, like they were frantically trying to unscrew them from the tempered steel.

The quirks came out pretty fast. Chaz Lee, the one who sounded so young, tapped his foot obsessively while he worked, while a pale European next to him snapped his gum in time to the music.

Skye was a maniac. She never glanced left or right. If anything caught her eye—anything at all—no one could tell. She worked the dial like she'd been doing it every single day of her life, and not just for the past few months.

When she handed him her backpack earlier for safekeeping, Gene automatically accepted it, happy to have a job to do. But now it felt like a lead balloon in his lap, so he dropped it to the ground and pushed it aside with his ankle.

After a while, the sounds around him dimmed, and Gene's mind drifted off to another time and place. To a nondescript room at the Tropicana Gardens, north of Dallas. A clear summer's day. Not that anyone would know it by walking around the conference rooms, since the conference center didn't have windows.

Even back then, he wore black clothes when he competed, to make a statement. It helped him blend in and stand out at the same time. It was the last contest Marilyn attended, as it turned out, and he wanted to look extra sharp for her.

Out of all the people in the audience, and there were dozens in the crappy conference room, she was the only one who mattered. When he popped open the safe and stood, Marilyn placed her hand over her heart and beamed at him. In that moment, he forgot about the prize money, the applause, anything else. She was proud of him. That was enough.

Now, it was Skye's turn. She worked the dial like Marilyn did, with her tongue poking through her teeth like an eraser on a number-ten pencil. Like it always did whenever she concentrated.

Would Skye be able to see him, though, if she happened to glance away from the dial? Probably not. Since the person in front of him pulled out a giant wool cap with a puffball on top and plunked it on her head, he'd be blocked from Skye's view. So, Gene tapped Reef on the shoulder and pointed out two chairs closer to center stage, which somehow managed to stay empty, even with the crowd.

Gene picked his way across the row to the seats. He had to step over an entire line of people to do that, so he vowed not to get up again when he finally reached the seat. However long it took, he would sit in Skye's sightline, like Marilyn had done for him, and silently will her to win.

Although she wouldn't acknowledge him, she'd be able to feel his presence. It was the least he could do.

After a moment, though, something fluttered against his ankle. Reef was gone—ostensibly to visit the bathroom again—so Gene lifted Skye's backpack from the floor and plunked it on Reef's empty chair. The vibration came from a side pocket sewn into the bag. One of two pockets on the outside.

It vibrated like a cell phone. He almost turned away, since he had no business answering anyone else's phone. But, then, what if Skye's parents were calling? She never said anything about them coming to the contest. Of course, they'd want to be there, right? Marilyn wouldn't have missed it for the world, and neither should Skye's mom or dad. No parent or family member would want to miss something this important. And if they did, they'd probably want to call the contestant to make up for it.

He didn't reach for the phone right away. But when the vibration was about to falter, he yanked the cell from the bag and stared at the screen. Someone was calling Skye from the seven-one-three area code, which meant it had to be her parents. Maybe he could finally talk to her mother or say hello to her father. He might even invite them to visit the store later. It was worth a shot.

"Y'lo?" He spoke loudly, since the caller would never be able to hear him over the music otherwise.

"Uh, yeah. I'm looking for the Fireplug."

The girl's voice cracked on the last word. She sounded young, hopelessly young. And scared. Everything fell away as Gene stared at the phone, stupid with shock.

"Come again? Who—"

The line went dead. Apparently, the caller had hung up, too spooked to say anything more.

Gene glanced at the stage, where Skye worked the dial around and around, like a machine. A machine in glasses that hid whatever emotion lurked behind them. She looked like a black robot up there. Not quite human. Someone, or something, he didn't recognize.

"Hey." Reef had returned from the restroom, and he wiped his hands on his skinny pants while he waited for Gene to move the backpack off his seat. He'd have to wait a second longer.

So many questions fired through Gene's mind. The who, what, and where of it all stalled in his throat, unasked. Even when the crowd began to cheer around him and Reef gave him a strange look, Gene didn't say a word. It was as if someone had muted the sounds around him until all that was left was his breath and the puzzled look on Reef's face.

"You okay, Mr. Jacks?"

"Yeah." Gene finally dropped the phone to his lap, where it laid like a spent revolver.

"She did it." Reef beamed at him. "Skye opened the safe."

"What?"

"She did it." The kid sounded so excited.

Gene slowly shifted his attention to the stage. By now, Skye had moved in front of the safe, and she had a huge grin. She wasn't the only one...the kid stuck in Siberia also had his door open. It was anyone's guess who actually finished first, but Gene couldn't focus on that at the moment.

All he could focus on was the voice of a stranger coming through the telephone. A voice that sounded much too young and much too scared to be asking for a drug dealer.

He returned the phone to the backpack before he bolted from the chair. He stumbled across the row of people, and then he wove drunkenly through the crowd until he reached the back door.

He barely heard the panel crash against the wall. He was too busy running

193

away from a small, scared voice on the other end of a cell phone. Running away from a question he couldn't bear to ask, and one he couldn't bear to have answered.

Chapter Thirty-Five

Skye

M r. Jacks looked so confused when he jumped up from his chair. He sat in a different spot now, since he switched seats right at the start of the contest. She couldn't help but notice when he moved, although he told her to keep her gaze front and center.

She watched him sneak to the middle of the new row, her purple backpack dangling from his wrist like a kid's balloon.

Something had changed, though. He wouldn't look at her after she won. Why? Second place was still good, right? Just because she didn't come in first…some guy named Castro beat her to it by a few minutes…she could still be proud of it. It meant a five-thousand-dollar check, and Mr. Jacks never expected her to win the contest in the first place.

She couldn't stop him from leaving, but she had to know why. So, she started to leave the stage, but then the DJ stepped in front of her and stuck a real check in her hands, which had more zeroes on it than she'd ever seen in her life. So, she stood there, mesmerized by the numbers on the paper until it was too late.

By the time she managed to look away, Mr. Jacks was gone. No doubt, he left through a side door. But not Reef, though. Reef waited for her at the edge of the stage, looking awkward, with so many people rushing around him.

She finally broke free of the crowd and worked her way toward him. To the wobbly stairs with the flimsy handrail that led to the ground below. She wanted to reach Reef before he weirded out on her, too, and tried to run away, like Mr. Jacks.

As her fingers curled around the paper-thin metal, she glanced up one last time and froze. Someone new stood on the outskirts of the crowd. A middle-aged woman in baggy khaki shorts and a white t-shirt, with hair that looked like a wire brush.

Once again, her mother's face was pale and drawn. But this time, dark shadows bruised the skin around her eyes.

"Mom?" Skye mouthed the word, utterly confused.

Meanwhile, her mother scanned the crowd, her gaze flitting from one stranger to the next.

Skye couldn't walk away. Even though her mother had no right to be in the auditorium, no right to share in Skye's big moment. But it didn't matter. There she was. And, although it defied logic, Skye felt compelled to walk toward her.

She moved over to where her mother stood, with the check clutched in front of her like a kindergartner with a first-place ribbon.

"Can you believe it?" She thrust out the check, which only added to the chaos all around them.

Her mother looked startled until she recognized Skye.

"Oh, there you are. I couldn't find you. Where did all these people come from?"

"They came for the contest, Mom. This is a really big deal. But what are *you* doing here?"

Her mother leaned forward, and with her came the acrid scent of stale cigarette smoke. "I wanted to see you again."

"But why?" Skye lowered the check. "Why now? I tried to write you, you know."

"I know."

Skye squinted. "You couldn't know. The post office sent the letter back. They ruined the envelope, by the way." Funny how she remembered such a tiny detail after all this time.

"Your father told me. Don't worry. I've been keeping up with you."

"Keeping up with me?' *What does that even mean?* There was no way her father would go behind her back like that. "I don't believe you. He told me not to talk to you anymore."

"I know. We both thought it was for the best. That we waited until I got better."

Skye fought the impulse to roll her eyes. She didn't mean to be harsh—really, she didn't—but she couldn't help herself. "I know, I know. The anxiety attacks. So, are you?"

"Am I what?"

"You know…better."

Judging by the way her mother looked, Skye already knew the answer. But it wouldn't hurt to ask, since it overshadowed everything else between them. Her mother acted as if she had no voice in what happened to her over the last five years.

"I'm getting there," she said.

Her mother looked hopeful, as if she expected Skye to congratulate her. But she couldn't do it.

"By the way," Skye said, instead, "you missed my high-school graduation."

The peevishness was gone; now all she felt was resignation. Skye knew she should be angry. That she could easily list a dozen milestones her mother had missed. But she couldn't. Not without reminding herself in the process. So, she left it at that.

"I'm sorry," her mother said. "Your dad told me it was real nice. But things are different now."

Skye's response was automatic. "I'm different too, Mom. And I wasn't alone all that time, you know. Other people helped me."

Her mother winced. "I'm sure they did. I'm so sorry. How can I make it up to you?"

Again, Skye no longer felt angry. Even about the long-overdue apology.

"You can't make it up to me. But it's okay. Like I said, I was never alone. I've gotta go now. I don't want to lose my friends in this crowd."

With that, Skye returned the check to her pocket. It was time to find Mr.

Jacks. Show him what she won. What *they* won. Because his was the only opinion that mattered right now. Not her mother's, not the crowd's, only his. Everything else could wait until that happened.

She began to walk away. She didn't stop until something touched her arm.

"Good job." It was Reef, who slung his arm around her shoulders in a show of support.

She leaned into him, grateful for the distraction. "Thanks. Can we get out of here now?"

"Of course."

They started to move past the front row, where she spied her backpack on the ground. She walked over it, ready to claim it, but Reef beat her to it. He swept the bag up and took something from the side pocket.

"Just a sec. I stashed my phone in your bag." He pulled out the cell and cradled it in his hand, since he didn't have anywhere else to put it. "You were in the bathroom and I thought you wouldn't mind."

She didn't. She actually liked knowing he felt comfortable enough to keep his stuff in her bag. Like they were a couple or something. After that first date, she worried maybe he'd dump her because she wouldn't ride around with him in his buddy's car.

And then it happened again, right after Reef decked Ted in the alley, so she knew it was over. But apparently, none of that mattered now, because Reef tenderly placed his hand on the small of her back and guided her through the ballroom.

Yep, she had a new set of friends now. Just like she told her mother. People who cared about her. People who would never hurt her, or betray her, like her mother had.

Chapter Thirty-Six

Reef

Than *hat was close. Too close.* As soon he got back to the ballroom and saw the phone in Mr. Jacks's hand, he knew what had happened. Someone must've called his cell while he was gone, and whatever the caller said turned Mr. Jacks pale as a ghost. The man was an albino to begin with, but now he looked pale *and* shaky. Like he didn't know what to do with himself.

Look, it wasn't his fault. Mr. Jacks never should've answered the phone in the first place. It took balls to do that. The guy had no business touching something that didn't belong to him. How would Mr. Jacks feel if Reef tried to answer the boss's phone? He'd hate it, especially since he didn't want Reef to go anywhere near his office in the first place.

So, it wasn't really his fault. And, to be fair, a lot of people were doing it. Since he couldn't handle all the business at Immaculate Word, he even enlisted a partner to help him with deliveries. So, technically, he was only half the problem this time. He supplied the drugs, and the other person handled logistics. It was a great business model, when you stopped to think about it, because every legit business needed someone to fill orders, while someone else handled deliveries.

Only, he couldn't afford to get busted over it. His dad already thought he was a screw-up, and now he'd have proof. His parents had no idea he was stockpiling the prescription meds his dad gave him and selling them to other college students.

Plus, Mr. Jacks really liked Skye. If he thought she was getting calls about drugs in the middle of the day, he'd find a way to forgive her.

He'd never turn her over to the cops. Not after the way they acted at the store. All those times Reef walked in on them practicing with the safes. Like they were a family or something. They sat so close together, he knew they were a team.

So, maybe everything would stay cool, after all. What with the chaos, and Skye winning that big check, and everyone crowding around her, wanting a piece of her, Mr. Jacks couldn't possibly remember one stupid phone call.

And if he did? If Mr. Jacks made a big deal out of it and wanted to find out who called? Reef would just quit his job at the store and tell his dad it didn't work out. That Mr. Jacks wanted him to miss school or something and his grades were too important for that. His dad would understand.

Reef placed his hand on the small of Skye's back now and gently guided her to the exit. No harm, no foul. She'd just won a five-thousand-dollar check, which was about as much as he made in a whole semester of dealing, so they were even, in a way.

He had to work even harder for his cash, too. Customers always wanted to pay for the stash with designer purses, Mac notebooks, or something else he'd have to turn in for dough. Luckily, the guy at EZ Pawn never questioned it when Reef brought in a Neiman's bag stuffed with something new. He always gave the guy the same excuse, anyway. My girlfriend...mother... aunt...wanted to sell this. And, just like that, the clerk would play along, which was smart on his part, since the guy paid a couple hundred bucks for stuff worth three times that amount. Like he always said, no harm, no foul.

Things would stay cool, as long as his dad didn't ask where the money came from. Money for a brand-new Yocaher whenever Reef wanted one, with custom trucks and polyurethane Pig wheels. All the pro gear that kept him skating. Hand-painted brain buckets and tool kits that cost two hundred dollars a pop. No one ever said going pro would be cheap, or even looking like a pro, until he could make it onto the circuit.

That was the end goal. To take all this stuff and get so good at skateboarding he could kiss Houston goodbye. Maybe move to California, Florida, or Hawaii, even, where they took longboarding seriously. Somewhere people didn't yell at him to get off the sidewalk and they didn't put up signs threatening him with a ticket if he rolled through a shopping center's parking lot. Somewhere skateboards showed up on the roads about as much as bicycles or cars.

And if he didn't get a sponsor? He'd continue to make skateboarding videos. People posted videos all day long of insane tricks no one else would try. Things like half-backfoot flips, Ollie Impossibles, or switch backside flips. Tricks designed to make a skater famous. Or kill him. Whichever came first.

So, that was the plan. To get in good with guys who made videos in Santa Monica or Miami or on the Big Island. In the meantime, he had to graduate from Immaculate Word to keep his parents happy and make sure they kept him on their MasterCard account. And he couldn't do it with an arrest on his record. For that, he needed to stay clean.

At first, he thought maybe Skye was into him. Maybe she liked him as much as he liked her. That was the only reason he gave her two chances; both of which she blew. He'd never do that for another girl. And look what it got him. Nothing. That's what.

He kept his mouth shut as they walked away from the ballroom now, his hand planted on her back. He kept guiding her forward, even when a stranger tried to stop and congratulate her on the win. He was on a mission: check out the lobby and find Mr. Jacks.

Only, Mr. Jacks wasn't in the lobby by the time they got there. Oh, a few stragglers came and went, but Mr. Jacks wasn't one of them.

"Hey, Reef?" Skye finally moved out from under his hand when they reached the registration desk. "Did I do something wrong? Mr. Jacks wouldn't even wait for me."

"I don't know." He shrugged. "Maybe he had somewhere else to go. I wouldn't worry about it, though. He'll catch you Monday."

She seemed to think it over. "You're right. Thanks for staying with me. You're such a good friend."

Luckily, she had no idea what went down. And he planned to keep it that way.

Chapter Thirty-Seven

Gene

He drove through the streets of downtown Houston aimlessly, under a spider's web of train wires, one-way street signs, and freeway overpasses. It was all a blur, drowned out by the voice of someone much too young and much too innocent to call a drug dealer in the middle of the afternoon.

To be honest, he couldn't deny that some small part of him always wondered whether Skye knew about the drug dealing at Immaculate Word. She was so smart and so intuitive. He thought maybe she knew the people who ran the stash house. He never dreamed she'd be one of them.

By the time he arrived at the lock shop, a headache pounded behind his ears. He parked in the same spot as always—next to Albert's busted jalopy—before he stepped into the sanctuary of the store. The only place he could relax.

Albert stood by the display counter, helping a customer with a stun gun. That happened more and more often now. Once Gene let Ted go, the rest of the crew had to pick up the slack. He didn't expect them to be so good at each other's jobs, but he was grateful for it.

Albert glanced up when the door whooshed open and Gene entered the space. "You're back."

"Yeah, I'm back." Gene nodded at the customer as he passed. He didn't feel like yakking it up today. He didn't feel like doing much of anything, to be honest. The only way he could function was to barrel through the store. To put one foot in front of the other and never slow down.

"Hey, Boss. We're running a sale on this gun. Right?" Albert pretended to look confused, although Gene knew it was all an act. Albert was obviously faking it for the customer's sake, to make the guy feel like he was getting a good deal. The unspoken assumption being that Gene would happily put the gun on sale for this one-and-only customer.

"Whatever you say." He barely glanced at the product.

"A sale." Albert egged him on. "I told my friend here we might be able to cut him a deal. On account of his being such a good customer and all."

"I don't know." Gene couldn't care less about the gun, or the customer, to be honest. Any other day, he would've played the game with Albert and bantered back and forth. But today he wasn't in the mood, and his head hurt like hell. "You make the call."

He waved away the conversation as he walked. For all he cared, Albert could give the damn gun away. As long as he didn't make Gene think about it anymore.

Gene finally ran out of room when he reached his office. Then the silence turned deafening. Without the whine of the key-cutter, or the shuffling of boxes in the stockroom, the place felt hollow. Abandoned. As if no one had ever worked in the back and nothing would ever be the same again.

Damn. Why did I answer the phone? He turned into his office and slammed the door shut. Watched as the panel bounced back and forth once it hit the busted deadbolt. A metaphor for the day, apparently. A day when nothing worked like it should and the odds were stacked against him.

The office chair squeaked as he sat. He stared at the telephone on his desk, the only landline in the whole store. It seemed to take up half the desk, but that couldn't be right because it shared the space with a stress ball, an ashtray full of quarters, and the good ol' Compaq computer. He ignored all those things as he reached for the landline and automatically dialed the number for HPD.

"Hello?" Boudreaux's voice came through loud and clear now, without noise from the hotel to get in the way.

"Hey." Gene tried to run his hand across his eyes, but he missed and he ended up hitting the bridge of his nose. One problem at a time, though. One problem at a time. "What're you doing?"

"Closing up that case we talked about." Papers shuffled in the background. "Cap's giving it to the guys from Washington. He's not happy about it, and neither am I. But what are you gonna do?"

Gene pictured Boudreaux sitting in his cube with a stream of black folders that flowed across his desk, pockmarked by one colored navy. A pile of old Taco Bell wrappers in the wastebasket. Maybe the cubicle felt like home to Boudreaux, like Gene felt about his shop.

"So, you're off the case, then?" he asked.

"Looks like it. Why? Didja find out anything?"

Gene studied his hands for a moment. His fingertips twitched on the desk, as if the surface was hot to touch. Now was the time to say something. Anything.

Only, he couldn't.

"Nah. I don't know anything. Say, you want to come over to the house later?"

It was a gamble because he'd have to hold his tongue when Boudreaux reached his house, but he didn't want to be alone tonight. He wanted to drown out the silence with Boudreaux's chatter and maybe down a six-pack or two. Listen to the guy's crazy Cajun sayings and hear him badmouth the other cops on the force. Maybe joke about Sarge's bad combover or the guy's incessant paranoia. Anything to make the silence go away.

"Really?" Boudreaux sounded surprised. Then again, it'd been years since Gene had invited him over to the house. "You mean it?"

They usually met in Boudreaux's cube at headquarters or at some icehouse or another neutral spot. The house seemed way too personal, and they never got personal. But maybe it was time.

"You got anything else better to do?" Gene asked.

Boudreaux gave one of his belly laughs. "How can I say no when you put it like that? Sure. What time?"

Gene leaned back, suddenly exhausted. He couldn't focus anymore, but he had to say something. "Seven? Seven-thirty? You pick it. And can you bring the beer?"

Before his buddy answered, Gene glanced at his hands again. He took a good, hard look at the way the digits shook, as if they had a mind of their own. Up and down, up and down. As if divorced from the rest of his body. Boudreaux would notice it, of course. He'd be crazy not to.

"Uh, on second thought…maybe tonight's not such a good idea." Gene's voice sounded soft now. Too soft. Boudreaux would think he was crazy… inviting him over and then taking it back. But he didn't care. He was too tired to care. Too tired to think about anything else but putting the day behind him.

What *was* he thinking? Boudreaux would notice the shake, and then he'd start asking questions. Or, even worse, he'd ask Gene how he spent his day. Whether he talked to his customers about a drug dealer called the Fireplug. Somebody Boudreaux probably pictured as a dirty thug with tattoos covering his neck. Not a pretty college coed who bore an uncanny resemblance to Marilyn.

"I forgot," Gene said. "I, um, already have plans tonight."

"Okay, whatever." Boudreaux tried to sound good with it. "No skin off my nose. Hey, I've gotta go. I'll see you around."

"Yeah. See you around, buddy." Gene slowly hung up the phone, the fingers of his right hand drumming the plastic.

He'd just guaranteed himself another night of loneliness. With nothing for company but Knox and his thoughts. The things he didn't want to think about.

Like how to fire Skye. He'd have to let her go, of course. But he maybe he could call her during the day, when he knew she'd be in class, surrounded by other students. She'd never be able to answer the phone then. He could leave a message for her and tell her not to come in anymore. Tell her goodbye.

Besides, Knox wasn't so bad, and the dog loved it whenever he stayed home. Maybe he could grab a six-pack of Miller Lite from the Stop N' Go before he got to the house. He didn't need Boudreaux for that. Maybe he'd grab two. What difference did it make now?

He wearily rose from the desk. It didn't make a difference. And *that* was the problem.

Chapter Thirty-Eight

Skye

She and Reef walked briskly through the hotel's lobby, past the bank of elevators. Reef had taken his hand off her back, but she still imagined the warmth of his skin on her T-shirt.

Like Reef, she couldn't find Mr. Jacks anywhere. By the time they got to the lobby, no one was left but an employee doing paperwork at the hotel's registration desk. Mr. Jacks hadn't even bothered to congratulate her before he took off. He didn't even have the decency to stay with her and celebrate. Only Reef did that.

She shook her head as they walked. It was his loss. Right? That was what people always said whenever *she* decided not to do something. Like when she skipped auditions for the Symphony Spectacular and her dad said the concert wouldn't be the same without her. Or, when she gave up on the quidditch team and Harper predicted they'd never win another game.

She finally glanced up from the ground when they passed the last elevator in the bank. The door to the car yawned open, ready to swallow another load of passengers. Huddled against the wall was the old lady from the ballroom, the one who yelled at Skye to get off the stage.

This time, the lady carried a stack of folded tablecloths instead of water glasses. She draped the material over her arm, as if she was the great Zolinski, about to pull a rabbit from a hat.

If Skye didn't hurry, the elevator doors would close again and the woman would disappear forever.

"Hey, Reef?" Skye stopped short.

"Yeah?"

"Can you give me a minute? I need to talk to someone."

"Sure." He shrugged, which sent a piece of hair freefalling into his eyes, since the mousse had long since worn off. "No problem. I'll wait for you outside."

Skye quickly slid into the elevator, just before the doors closed. The lady frowned when she realized who was with her now.

"Hello, again," Skye said.

"What floor do you want?" The old lady wouldn't look at her. Instead, she jerked her head toward the control panel, which held an amazing number of buttons. Skye knew the hotel was big when they arrived there that morning, but she had no idea how big. Apparently, the building soared forty stories into the air.

"How about forty?" she said, off the cuff, since she wanted to make sure the ride lasted as long as possible.

"You want the penthouse?" The old lady sounded surprised.

"Sure. Why not?"

With a shrug, the woman stabbed the top button. "Suit yourself."

From this angle, the server looked even older than before. Skye tried to be discreet as she stole a look or two while they traveled up the shaft.

The skin on the woman's face was translucent, too thin to cover a web of tiny blue veins that crisscrossed underneath.

She'd stenciled some eyebrows on either side of her nose, too, but the lines were too thick and too obvious for the rest of her face. They made her look startled, or like a puppet with a mouth that opened at the pull of a string.

To be honest, Skye had never seen someone so old wearing a hotel uniform. "Um. How do you like it here? Working for the hotel, I mean."

The woman shot her a funny look. Like she didn't expect any more conversation once they'd settled on a floor.

"It's a job." She shrugged. "It pays the bills."

Which didn't really answer the question, but it seemed like the old lady didn't want to talk about it, anyway.

Funny, but Skye could feel exhaustion rolling over the woman's shoulders and spine. Given half a chance, the lady looked ready to drop the tablecloths on the floor and curl up on them for a nice, long nap.

"Look, I wanted to say something about what happened this morning. You know, back there in the ballroom." Her voice faltered. She felt like she was talking to a wall, since her companion stared straight ahead.

"Remember?" Skye prodded. "When I was on the stage?"

After a moment, the woman gave a slight nod. "Yeah, I remember. What about it?"

"I didn't really talk to your general manager. I made that part up."

The silence was deafening.

"I hope I didn't get you into trouble. I shouldn't have done it." Skye's face warmed, even though cold air slipped through cracks in the walls as they moved past the floors. For some reason, the hotel must've turned up the heat, and Skye wished more than anything she could peel off the black sweater and drop it to the floor, too.

"That's okay," the lady said.

"Well, um, I wanted to tell you I'm sorry."

"Yeah, well. I knew you were lying."

Skye squinted. "What do you mean?

"Look, we don't have a general manager anymore."

"Huh?" That didn't seem right. She'd seen the look on the server's face when Skye mentioned knowing the guy. It changed the lady's whole posture. Made her finally back off, as if she didn't want to push Skye from the stage, after all.

"I didn't want to embarrass you in front of your grandfather," the stranger continued. "But the hotel fired him last week. So, we don't even have a general manager."

"Oh." A twinge of shame fluttered in her chest. "I'm sorry. I didn't know that."

"Of course you didn't. Look, it's none of my business, but you really shouldn't make it a habit. Lying, I mean. You young people seem to think it's okay. That it's no big deal. But it *is* a big deal. It makes everyone wonder what else you're hiding."

The woman frowned again, which slanted the penciled brows together. "I mean…what's the point? Doesn't seem worth it to me."

Skye didn't know how to respond. Maybe the woman was right. Maybe Skye had blurred the line between truth and fiction so many times she couldn't tell the difference anymore.

To be honest, it was all she knew, growing up like she did. Her dad always said a lie didn't count as long as no one got hurt. But if that was true, why did Skye feel so small right about now? Why did she want to melt into a pool of black on the elevator's indoor-outdoor carpet?

The stranger shifted her load as the elevator doors opened on the tenth floor. She left the car without saying a word. But she didn't have to say more. She'd already said enough.

* * *

The parking lot was only a quarter full when Skye arrived at The College of the Immaculate Word a few hours later. She never did find Mr. Jacks at the hotel, so she had to be content to leave him a note at the lock shop before she headed for the school and the symphony concert.

She invited her dad to come with her, but he said no, of course.

"Sorry, muffin. I've got a rude headache tonight. Think I'll stay in."

"It's okay. I get it." She pecked him on the cheek as she left. "Don't wait up."

How could she blame him? How many times did he have to sit through her symphony concerts and pretend to be impressed, even when the musicians massacred Bach, Beethoven, or Handel? He met her at the edge of the stage afterward and always found something nice to say, even if he didn't exactly mean it.

She took a program from an undergraduate as she walked into Nguyen Auditorium and scanned the crowd. Colorful posters hung from the ceiling tonight, no doubt painted by the same student council girls who hijacked

Antibullying Week.

Boogie to Bach! Get Down with Grieg! Do the Mozart Macarena!

The signs all had cheesy sayings like that, which no one would ever believe, since no one would ever use an exclamation point to describe one of the concerts.

A couple dozen people sat under the banners, and Skye walked to the auditorium's midpoint before she chose a seat. She purposely shied away from the front, but she also didn't want to hide in the back and make Harper think she was embarrassed for her.

She busied herself with reading the program as the minutes ticked by. At some point, Alexandra and her friends burst through the back doorways and laughed their way down the main aisle, as if propelled by their birthright.

She purposefully slid lower in the chair as they passed and pretended to find something extra interesting in the program. *Well, look at that. Some guy named Elliott won a summer scholarship to Julliard. Good for him.*

Thankfully, Alexandra's group didn't even notice her as they hurried forward. When they reached the first row, they dawdled at the lip of the stage, where the stage lights highlighted their every move. Amazing what fresh hair extensions and a thousand dollars' worth of designer clothes could do. Not to mention the mink coats—no such thing as PETA for those girls—which only added to the luster. The girls threw the pricey coats on the ground as if on cue and settled into their seats.

Skye watched them for a bit, until a grandmother entered her row, which forced her to turn sideways. She hadn't even bothered to change clothes before she came to the concert. She still wore the same black sweater, Gap jeans, and scuffed Vans she wore to the safecracking contest. Only now, the clothes smelled like Dial antiperspirant and Reef's cologne.

After a moment, the musicians filed onto the stage with their instruments. They took their seats and patiently waited for the conductor to arrive.

Skye couldn't sit still. She didn't know how, and she didn't exactly know when, but something was about to happen. She could feel it. Even though she didn't believe in premonitions or women's intuition or any of that voodoo stuff, a faint discomfort set her teeth on edge and made it impossible to concentrate on the program anymore.

At least she'd be there afterward to help Harper deal with the mess. She'd make her way down the aisle to the stage, where she'd comfort Harper and tell her everything was going to be okay. She'd act like Dad and find something nice to say, no matter what the clique did to Harper.

After a moment, the conductor approached the podium and signaled for quiet from the audience.

It felt strange to hear a concert from this angle. To sit *behind* a conductor for once. The musicians looked so small, compared to the proscenium arch. A huge velvet curtain ringed the arch and dwarfed even the tuba. Meanwhile, the houselights haloed the musician's heads, as if they were part of a heavenly chorus singing glory to God in the highest.

Amazingly, everyone managed to stay on key through the first few songs. By the halfway point, though, a French horn came in too late for a solo, which threw everyone off.

Then the house lights blazed, signaling intermission, and the grandma next to her finally woke up. Skye used the break to visit the bathroom and when she returned, the old lady was gone. She must've realized she could hang out in the lobby—or sleep there—and no one would notice.

Skye eased into the suddenly open row and fidgeted through five more songs. Was it always this boring? Her eyelids felt leaden, even when Harper played a fairly decent clarinet solo. Just when she thought she couldn't take one...more...second, the houselights flared again and the musicians rose to take a bow.

It was now or never. Skye hurriedly clapped, and then she bolted from the chair. If anything was going to happen, it would happen now. With the crowd on its feet and the musicians oblivious to anything but the sound of applause.

Skye sucked in her breath as she moved forward. Poor Harper. She looked like a baby animal up there, so innocent compared to the pack of wolves in the first row. She even gave the crowd a big smile, her innocence breathtaking.

Before Skye could reach the stage, Alexandra appeared out of nowhere.

"Hey!" the girl called out. "Good job, Harper!" She stuck her thumb triumphantly in the air and waved it around. "You killed it on the solo!"

Skye stopped in her tracks. *What's that?* Did Alexandra actually say something nice for a change? Did she really give Harper the thumbs-up? It was all so cheesy and so unlike anything Alexandra normally would do.

Afterward, the girl spun around and strode to the exit, the heels of her Jimmy Choos pinging against the concrete as she walked. Before long, even that sound disappeared.

Skye whirled around again. Harper had finally stopped smiling long enough to pluck the sheet music from a stand in front of her. She didn't notice Skye until they stood only a few feet apart.

"Hey, up there." Skye deliberately kept her voice light. They weren't exactly on the best of terms right now, and she didn't want to push it.

"Hey, yourself." Harper gripped the music as she straightened. She had the whole stage to herself now, since everyone else had rushed for the exits.

"Your mom and dad come tonight?" Skye hadn't seen Harper's parents in the crowd, but, then again, she hadn't really been looking.

"They left at intermission." Harper shrugged. "At least they stayed for part of it."

"Yeah, you're right. Sometimes my dad didn't even last that long."

"So, what're you doing here?" Harper obviously wasn't in the mood for small talk.

"I dunno. I thought you would've done the same thing for me."

"Probably."

"Look, I wanted to tell you—"

Before she could finish, someone new walked onto the stage. It was the orchestra's conductor, who strode purposefully toward them, as if they'd done something wrong.

"I need to lock the place up, girls." He scowled, as if he couldn't be bothered with two lowly college sophomores. As if they weren't the reason he had a job in the first place. "Wrap it up, please."

"Yes, maestro," Harper said.

"Really?" Skye laughed, once the man left. "He still makes you call him 'maestro'?"

"Pathetic, right? Hey, if it helps my grade, I don't care. But, c'mon. What're you doing here?"

Skye paused. It was now or never. Time to come clean with Harper. "Okay. Here's the deal. I was worried about you. I thought you were being set up."

"Set up?" Harper scrunched her nose. "By who?"

Either she had no idea, or the girl was a great actress.

"By Alexandra and her friends. I thought they were going to pull a prank on you. Do something awful. I wouldn't put it past them."

"Well, I would." Harper kept the act going, even though she didn't really have to. "We're cool now. I thought I told you that. Oh, that's right. You don't care anymore."

"I care." It was hard not to sound defensive. Why couldn't Harper see she was only trying to help? "I thought they were going to do something bad to you. They messed with me last year, remember?"

"Yeah, well, that's you. They wouldn't do anything like that to me. We're good now."

"What do you mean, 'good'?"

"Look, as long as I help them out, we stay cool."

Now it was Skye's turn to wrinkle her nose. "I don't understand. How do you help them out?"

"Let's just say those girls like to party. But they don't know where to get the stuff. That's where I come in."

"Stuff? What do you mean, 'stuff'?" None of this made sense. She'd come to expect a little confusion with Harper, but this was over the top.

"Do I have to spell it out for you? Geez, for someone on the dean's list, you're not very smart, are you?"

"Excuse me?"

Harper glanced over her shoulder. "Give it up, Skye. You know what I'm talking about."

Whatever noise was left in the auditorium slowly dissipated.

"No, Harper. I have no idea what you're talking about."

"I thought for sure you'd figure it out by now. Especially when you started talking about that cute guy at your store."

"You mean Reef?" Skye struggled to understand. She heard the words, all right, but they floated around aimlessly and refused to line up in the proper order.

"Look, I'm sorry about what happened to Libby," Harper said. "I really am. But no one told her to guzzle a bottle of vodka, too. Rookie mistake. Who drinks a whole fifth, anyway?" Harper paused. "Of course, there was this guy in Russia who set a world record—"

"Don't." Skye didn't mean to raise her voice, but she couldn't help it. "Just don't."

Harper shrugged. "Suit yourself. I still can't believe you didn't figure it out. All this time I'm working with Reef and you're dating him. Kinda funny, when you stop to think about it."

She gazed at Skye as if she expected her to respond, but then she didn't wait for her to answer. "Well, I've gotta go. You heard the maestro. He wants us out of here. See you around."

Harper abandoned the music stand and headed for the nearest exit with her clarinet. All the while, her shadow bobbed along the velvet curtain behind her. Like a specter. Or, like a vapor, maybe.

Chapter Thirty-Nine

Boudreaux

Once more, Boudreaux sat in a stale cubicle at HPD headquarters, surrounded by a stack of black file folders and one colored navy-blue.

He felt like a fugitive on the lam. Everyone knew only screw-ups went to the office on a weekend. Who else would go to HPD headquarters on a Sunday night? No one, that was who. Or, if he did, it only meant he couldn't get the job done during the regular nine-to-five so he had to leave his comfy couch behind and haul himself back to a stuffy cube like this one.

He wanted to be anywhere else. Like sitting in his La-Z-Boy at home, watching Netflix and scratching the dog at his feet. Or maybe working in the kitchen, ironing five dress shirts for the workweek to come. Although, pressing scalding steam into hot cotton didn't sound so appealing at the moment, given the building's air conditioner had shut down already.

Blame his lousy mood on last night's poker game. A game that didn't end until the sun rose over the JP Morgan Chase Tower downtown. By that time, he'd kissed away five hundred bucks and seats on the thirty-yard line for the next Houston Texans game. Traded them away for the chance to sit in a sweaty cubicle with the taste of sour whiskey on his tongue.

He still felt tipsy. And for what? Round after round of crappy cards that even a pro couldn't finesse. He lost his mojo early on during the game, so he bet high when he should've folded and folded when he should've taken a chance. Not just once, but all night long.

By the time he dragged his ass home, sunlight glanced off the mirrored tower. And he had to face facts: Today was the day. D-day. The day Cap officially pulled the Sullivan case and the one that followed out from under him.

Boudreaux couldn't really blame the captain. He had weeks to get a bead—any kind of bead—on this guy called the Fireplug. When he couldn't, Cap had no choice but to yank the case out from under him and give it to the DEA. He would've done the same thing. Although, he would've waited until the detective in question admitted defeat, instead of running an end game around the guy.

Boudreaux slowly stood. Maybe a soda would help. Dull his headache with some carbonation and sugar. It couldn't hurt. So, he took out his last two dollars and left the cube, careful to scan the reception area first for signs of life before he moved to the soda machine.

All clear. He shuffled over to the vending machine. The box glowed soft blue under the fluorescent lights, like an underwater pod in a sea of gray cubicles.

Diet or regular? Ah...the age-old question. Since he didn't really deserve the good stuff tonight, he fed the dollars through the slot and stabbed a button for diet soda. Just when a metal arm inside the contraption swung wide to grab the drink, a telephone rang.

Crap. He stabbed the button anyway. Given the ringer's volume, the sound came from somewhere near his cubicle. He followed the *bbbrrriiinnnggg* back to his desk without grabbing the soda, wishing more than anything he had put the ringer on mute so he wouldn't have to deal with random phone calls at night.

Too late for that.

"Boudreaux here." Why bother with niceties at this point?

"Um, hello?"

The caller sounded young and terribly nervous. Her voice rose on the last syllable, as if she couldn't quite trust the telephone connection.

"Can I help you?"

"Yeah. I think so. I, uh, need to talk to a cop or something."

"Or something?" He parroted the words back to her, since he didn't have the energy to make a wisecrack. She was the one calling, so let *her* fill in the blanks.

"Yes. I need to speak with a police officer." She apparently made up her mind. "Are you one?"

"I like to think so."

"Excuse me?"

"It's a joke. Yeah, I'm a cop." Although the messy desk in front of him made it hard to believe. Most cops didn't spend their weekends staring at a pile of case folders. Most cops were too smart for that.

"Good. I want to report a crime."

Slowly but surely, he sat down again. "I'm listening."

A beat or two of silence on the other end. "You're not taping this, are you?"

"What? No, of course not." He calmly depressed a button on the side of the telephone to set a recording device in motion. "We don't tape our calls."

Look, if it was up to him, he'd tell her the truth. But Texas happened to be a one-party state, which meant he could record anyone's call—even the President's—without telling the caller. Rules were rules.

"Okay, then," she said. "No one can find out about this."

"Why's that?"

"Because it's not cool. If anyone ever found out…"

"Look, they won't. I get anonymous calls all the time." Which wasn't true, either, but she didn't have to know that. Let her think he took this kind of call every day. Strength in numbers and all that. "Go on."

"Okay." A quick inhale. "You know that girl who died a few weeks ago? Elizabeth Sullivan?"

"Yeah? What about her?" He didn't mention the part about another kid who was found at the same house. No need to muddy the waters.

"I know who sold her the drugs."

Boudreaux automatically squinted, which didn't help the headache any. "Interesting. And who might that be?"

"Just a second. First, tell me what's going to happen to her." The caller quickly corrected herself. "To *them*. Will they go to jail?"

Boudreaux shrugged. "I don't know. It depends. Are we talking about a one-time thing here? Some friends who went a little too far?"

"No, it's not that." At least the girl sounded sure about something. "They knew what they were doing. It wasn't the first time."

"And you know it was more than one person?" In his experience, most dealers didn't work with anyone else. Probably because they couldn't trust anyone else. Too many thieves out there. Which was ironic, but true.

"Yeah. There were two people. They both go to Immaculate Word."

Boudreaux began to chew his lip. Given the headache, he barely noticed the pain, anyway. It was important to keep the girl talking, to let her ramble on until she said what she had to say. If nothing else, the awkwardness would make her want to fill in the silence.

"Are you still there?" she asked.

"Yeah, I'm still here. Go on. I'm listening."

"Anyway...one of them is named Harper Rosenblatt. And she has a partner named Reef Abdullah. That's not his real name, though. His real name is Raynesh."

"Okay then."

He quickly jotted the names on a Post-It note. The caller had just presented him with the perfect gift: enough information to request a search warrant and enough information to convince a judge to say yes.

Once he took care of the technicality with the warrant, he could paw through the dealer's house until he found enough evidence to make an arrest. Or, in this case, the dealers' houses.

"They both live near the Galleria." For someone who didn't want to talk very much, the caller couldn't stop herself now. "The guy works at Space City Lock Shoppe, and the girl plays clarinet in the school's symphony. That's where you'll find her in the afternoons. Do you need anything else?"

To be honest, given the choice, he'd ask for cell numbers...addresses... physical descriptions...the whole enchilada. But he didn't want to push his luck. And he could find out that stuff on the internet. She'd already given him the most important things: first and last names.

CHAPTER THIRTY-NINE

"I've got what I need, unless you want to..."

The caller abruptly hung up. She must've realized she'd said enough. And it was too late to take any of it back. Much too late for that.

Boudreaux leaned back, the sweating Diet Coke all but forgotten by now. The question was whether he could believe the caller. *That* was the question of the hour. Should he take the word of a stranger and risk his reputation on it, since no judge wanted to be woken up in the middle of the night for a wild goose chase. Or, was it a crank call from someone with a grudge to settle? Someone who figured the best way to get even with her enemies was to turn them in for a crime they didn't commit?

With any luck, the caller would phone him again tomorrow. It sometimes happened that way. Sometimes, people called a day, a week, or even a month later. Whenever they decided to spill the rest of their guts because they still couldn't sleep at night.

He always tried to picture the person on the other end of the telephone. Did they sweat when they dialed the number for HPD? Did perspiration freckle their foreheads and bead against their lips? Or did they hang up from the call twenty pounds lighter, happy to be free of whatever soul-crushing secret had been eating away at them?

Either way was okay by him. Every time he took an anonymous tip, it was a win-win situation. Except for the crooks, of course.

Now he just had to convince the captain to let him stay on the case, even if it meant going halfsies with the guys from the DEA. Since he'd already faxed them the case notes, he couldn't take it back. Some stiff in Washington was going to walk into an office tomorrow and find a dozen fax pages staring at him no matter what. Nothing Boudreaux did could change that. But at least Boudreaux could ask to stay on the case, even if it meant sharing credit for the bust.

He dropped the old-fashioned telephone receiver onto its cradle. He no longer felt a headache pulsing at his temples, but he still wanted the ice-cold pop from the vending machine. It had become a celebration, of sorts.

The only thing missing was his buddy, Gene. Since he told Gene about the case from the get-go, maybe he should tell him the latest turn of events.

221

Boudreaux reached for the telephone again. It was the least he could do.

Epilogue

Skye

The tinny bell on the plate-glass door jangled as someone new entered the shop. It was a well-dressed woman in a peach pantsuit, her hair silvered with age, and she gazed timidly around the nearly empty space.

Skye spied her from her place at the counter, where she held a stack of yesterday's mail. Mostly bills, with a newsletter from the Associated Locksmiths of America thrown in to make it interesting.

"Hello." Skye set the mail aside.

The woman softly cleared her throat as she crossed the room. "Ahem. Good morning."

"May I help you with something?" Granted, Skye didn't often see elderly women in the shop, so she understood the lady's hesitation. Sometimes, a grandmother-type accompanied a grandfather into the store, but then she'd get bored after a hot second and wander away to check out the safes.

"Maybe," the stranger said. "I'm looking for someone."

Skye cocked her head. The woman didn't look like one of Albert's regulars. Usually, Albert's customers dashed through the door in a frenzy because they'd locked themselves out of their minivans. Or they called him in the middle of the night because they forgot how to turn off a security system. But not this lady. And this lady definitely didn't drive a minivan.

For one thing, she had a ginormous diamond ring on her left hand, and her flowery perfume was much too expensive for Albert's housewives. Now that Ted wasn't working at the shop anymore, and hadn't worked there for six months, he couldn't be the reason for the visit.

"That so," Skye said. "Who do you need?"

"I think he's the manager. Maybe the owner?" A little laugh to downplay her confusion. "I'm not quite sure, you see."

Slowly, recognition dawned. Of course. Skye should have thought of that first.

"You must be talking about Mr. Jacks."

The woman didn't blink. If anything, she looked even more confused.

"I guess. I didn't catch his name."

"Was it an older gentleman?" Skye ventured. "About yay tall?" She lifted her hand over her head to indicate his height. Sensing nothing, she tried one last time. "I'll bet you he was wearing a black polo and had crazy hair."

"That's him!" Finally, the woman smiled. Her teeth looked like they belonged in a toothpaste ad. "Could you please find him for me? I want to thank him personally. He told me about this wonderful padlock, you see."

Skye's own smile faltered. Now that they'd established the reason for her visit, there was no getting around the truth.

"I'm sorry, but he passed away. It happened a few weeks ago."

"Oh." The woman's smile crumbled, too. "I didn't know he was ill."

"It was all pretty quick." Although, that wasn't entirely true. To be honest, the hospital visits stretched out much too long by the end, because Skye couldn't bear to see him in pain. Thank God for morphine.

"I'm so sorry," the woman continued. "I had no idea."

"He had ALS." Although Skye didn't know the stranger in front of her, and she didn't owe her an explanation or anything, it couldn't hurt to tell her the truth. At least she came to the shop to see him. "How did you two know each other?"

"He helped me buy a lock, remember?" The woman chuckled, and out came the white teeth again. "To be honest, I couldn't figure out how to work the darn thing. I had no idea what a 'blue tooth' was, but I didn't want to tell him that. Thank goodness my grandson helped me. Anyway, that's not really the reason why I came here."

"It's not? And by the way, his name was Gene." The lady might as well know the whole story.

"Gene." The woman said the name as if trying it on for size. "He was a lovely man. So very sweet."

Little by little, Skye's apprehension faded. She could picture Mr. Jacks chatting up this pretty woman by the counter and selling her a lock she had no idea what to do with. He always did like the ladies.

Especially toward the end. Whenever Skye visited him at the hospital then, she always found a group of nurses clustered around his bedside. The women—plus a few men—wouldn't even pretend to work at that point. They pulled up whatever industrial-grade chair they could find and leaned forward while he told them stories about safecracking. He seemed to grow younger and younger whenever he started a story. While his body failed him, his brain, and his sense of humor, took up the slack.

Those final visits were the best. Once he found out about Reef and Harper, he slowly worked his way back to being her friend. The easygoing banter, the playful teasing, the silences that never got uncomfortable. It all came back, little by little.

He never talked about the future. Or about the store, and what would happen to it. About the only worry on his mind involved Knox. Finding a good home for the dog, with somewhere to run and people who wanted him.

Thank goodness Axl learned to share their house. The cat tolerated Knox, as long as the dog stayed on his side of the house and out of Skye's bedroom.

The stranger's voice snapped Skye out of her reverie. "I'm sorry. What did you say?"

"It was nothing, really. I guess I just wanted to confess to you why I'm really here. I told you a little white lie. I didn't really come here to thank him."

"You didn't?"

"No. I was hoping he'd ask me for coffee or something. Maybe a movie." Skye's gaze dropped to the woman's ring finger. "Really?"

"Now, don't get the wrong idea." The woman hurried to explain, obviously mortified by the unasked question. "I lost my husband a long time ago. Never could take off his ring, though. You know."

"Sure. Well, I'm sorry. I wish I didn't have to be the one to tell you about Mr. Jacks."

"It's not your fault." The stranger paused, as if sidetracked by a completely different train of thought. "But what on earth will happen to the store?"

Skye glanced at the pile of mail in front of her before she carefully turned the stack sideways, so the woman could read it, too. Beneath the name of the store on the newsletter's mailing label came her Skye's own name, followed by her brand-new title: Owner.

"Oh." A little gasp of surprise from the stranger. "Is that you? Well, that's marvelous, dear. Good for you. But aren't you a little young?"

"Not really." Skye softened her voice. "I had to drop out of college. But it's what we both wanted. What we all wanted." Even her dad, in the end, although he took more convincing than anyone else. Luckily, she had an ace up her sleeve: her dad felt so guilty about going behind her back and staying in touch with Skye's mom, he couldn't say no. She never wanted to blackmail her father, but it all worked out in the end.

"Best of luck to you, dear."

"Thank you. And don't worry…he taught me everything he knew. And he was a great teacher."

The woman slowly walked away, the scent of her perfume following behind. It was true. Mr. Jacks was a great teacher. The best she'd ever had.

About the Author

Sandra Bretting is the author of a bestselling cozy mystery series that ran for five years with Kensington Publishing in New York, as well as several standalone titles. A graduate of the University of Missouri School of Journalism, she began her career writing for the *Los Angeles Times, Orange Coast Magazine,* and others. From 2006 until 2016, she wrote feature stories for the award-winning business section of the *Houston Chronicle.*

The Missy DuBois Mystery Series follows milliner and bona fide Southern belle Missy DuBois. Book four in the series ranked as an Amazon bestseller. Bretting also wrote a Christian memoir, *Shameless Persistence,* which was featured on The 700 Club and Cornerstone Broadcasting Network. She invites readers to connect with her at www.sandrabretting.com.